Death Before Dawn

Jack Mallory Mysteries - Book 4

William Coleman

Death Before Dawn

This is a work of fiction. Names, characters, places, and incidents either are the product of the author's imagination or are used fictitiously. Any resemblance to actual persons, living or dead, events, or locales is entirely coincidental.

Dedicated to my lovely wife, Vicki, who has supported me every step of the way through each of my novels by allowing me the time to write, being my first beta reader as well as my main editor. By being my biggest fan and my sharpest critic, she has helped me produce final manuscripts for you to enjoy.

1

What's with the uniform?" Reginald Hutchins was on his second cup of coffee when his wife walked into the kitchen decked out in her police blues, pressed and crisp. At the office, she normally wore slacks and jacket, the more appropriate attire for her position. Their son, Brian, a seventeen-year-old junior at North High, looked up from his double stack and cellphone just long enough to see her. The boy had gone through a growth spurt the last two years that left him just shy of his father's six feet and three inches.

"I told you I had court today, Reggie." Chief Sharon Hutchins took the pot and poured a cup for herself, holding it out in an offer to refill her husband's mug.

He shook his head. "That was the Carmichael case, wasn't it?"

"The Levine case." She moved around the island that dominated the center of the room. She had insisted it was too big, but her architect husband overruled her and now they lived with the proof that she had been right. "I also have a press conference this afternoon."

"Is that about the case, too?" Reggie rinsed his mug and set it in the sink.

The chief walked back around the island, took the mug, and placed it in the dishwasher. "That and an announcement for a new initiative to get tough on crime."

"I thought the police were always tough on crime." Brian raised his head again. "Why would they need to announce it?"

"I know. Right?" Sharon ruffled her son's hair, always her little boy.

"Mom." Brian moaned and swatted her hand away.

"Don't worry. You're still handsome." She took a pancake from the platter, rolled it, and dipped the end into the syrup on Brian's plate. He rolled his eyes at her. "I think I'll tell the mayor to cancel the press conference because we don't need to announce that we're going to be tough on crime."

The lights flickered, causing them all to look up. It was six o'clock and still very dark out.

"Now what was that about?" Reggie looked up to the ceiling fixtures.

The lights flickered a second time, and everything went dark except for the glow of Brian's phone.

"Great," Sharon grumbled. "Not again. Just not what I need. I better head in. See if this is isolated or city-wide. Please let it be isolated."

"Maybe wait a few minutes," Reggie suggested. "Could come back on."

"You're right," Sharon agreed.

They stood in the dark, listening to sounds that were normally too soft to be heard over all the usual noises of a powered day. Somewhere in the house, an analog clock ticked the seconds away.

"This isn't working." Sharon was never a patient woman. "I'm going to go."

"Just be careful on the roads," Reggie warned. "Too many people don't know what to do when there aren't any traffic signals."

"Don't I know it." Sharon pulled out her phone and turned on the flashlight. It guided her to where she had left her gun belt which she wrapped around her waist, fastening it tight. She moved to the coat closet to retrieve her uniform jacket. Early February still delivered chilly weather, especially in the mornings. She opened the front door, turned off the flashlight, and called out, "Have a good day!"

As promised, the early hour delivered darkness and a cold breeze, cold enough to make her consider going back inside for a heavier coat. Knowing she would be inside most of the day, she decided against it and started for her car.

Sharon looked up and down the street to verify that it was more than just their home with no power. There was something eerie about being inside the city limits and not seeing lights. She could see a faint glow from a mile or so away, so not city-wide. That was some relief anyway.

She stopped beside her car and dug into her pocket for her keys. She clasped them with her fingers and froze. She heard the rushed steps just before something heavy slammed into her back, pinning her to the car. Her cop mind started cataloging approximate height, weight, and build.

"You don't want to do this," she growled.

She felt a hand on her torso, high on the left side. It wasn't a sexual motion. It was almost a pat down, a search. Normally she would have her shoulder holster there. Her assailant was going for her gun.

Releasing her keys, she pulled her right hand free of the pocket and placed it on top of her weapon pushing downward with all her strength. Her assailant caught on and groped at the handle yanking upward again and again. They were stronger, and Sharon worried she might lose the battle to keep her weapon out of their hands. She could only imagine what crime spree they might go on with a cop's gun.

The metal of the glide cut into the webbing between her thumb and forefinger. Slippery with blood, she felt herself losing her grip. One last yank and the gun pulled free of its place in the holster. She had lost the weapon, something she would have to report as soon as she got to the department.

To her surprise, she felt the barrel of the gun dig into her back. She heard the shot and a burning sensation before slipping into a darkness more intense than the morning.

2

Maureen Weatherby's mind became aware of the sound of a ringing phone. She allowed one eye to open a crack. The room was still dark, no light trying to penetrate the blinds. Whoever was calling, it was bad news. Her head rolled toward the nightstand where her phone lay dormant on its surface, though the ringing continued. Rolling in the opposite direction, she reached out and shook Jack Mallory's arm.

"It's yours," she muttered.

His lids were closed but he was awake, having heard the same ringing she had.

"Can't be." He did not open his eyes. "I'm off today."

"Well it's not mine." Her tone was more forceful. "So answer it."

The ringing stopped, suggesting the caller had given up. Jack grinned. "Problem solved."

They readjusted themselves and started drifting off. The ringing started again.

"You've got to be kidding!" Jack sat up and snatched his phone off the charger. "Mallory! This better be good."

"Jack." The voice was familiar but he couldn't place it. "This is Chief Grimes."

Jack stiffened. The Chief of Detectives was calling him at home. His mind raced trying to figure out what he could have possibly done. Nothing presented itself. "Chief?"

"I'm texting you an address." The Chief was straight to the point. "I want you there in five minutes."

"I'm off today, Chief." He regretted it as soon as the words came out.

"Not anymore!" The chief barked. "Five minutes!"

Even Maureen heard him.

Jack pulled the phone away from his ear and looked at the screen. "He hung up."

His phone chimed, announcing he had received the text the chief had sent.

"That didn't sound like Chief Hutchins." Maureen sat up and stretched.

"It was Grimes." Jack was typing into his phone. He stopped and studied the results. "It's a residential address at least a ten-minute drive. Won't be there in five."

"The Chief of Detectives is assigning cases now?" Maureen rose to her knees and wrapped her arms around his shoulders. "How often has that happened to you?"

"Never." He twisted his neck and kissed her. "Guess I'm working today."

"Maybe we can have lunch," she suggested. "And you can tell me all about it."

"I'll let you know." He stood and headed for the bathroom where he could run water through his unkempt hair and brush his teeth before getting dressed.

He came out to find Maureen fully clothed with a scarf wrapped around her head. "I guess I'll go to my place and get a proper shower. See you at work."

Jack leaned in and gave her a peck on the cheek as she passed by. Dressing quickly, he stepped into his shoes as he pulled on his sportscoat. He clipped his shield to his belt and slid his service pistol into its shoulder holster. Grabbing his phone he dialed his partner, Shaun Travis. It took three rings for him to answer.

"I'll be there in five," Jack said. "Be ready and out front."

"I thought we were off today."

"I did too. See you in five." The detective disconnected the call, dropped the phone into his pocket, and locked the door behind him.

3

"Seriously?" Shaun was incredulous. "The Chief of D's calls you personally and gives you a case. Then you show up late?"

"For one thing, he never mentioned a case." Jack steered into the neighborhood and started reading street signs. It was a challenge without streetlights. The sun had risen just enough to assist. "Second, getting here in five minutes was beyond unrealistic."

"Wait a minute," Shaun sat up a little straighter. "There's no case? He may have called you in to rip you a new one and you thought you would just bring me along?"

"If it's a case, you'll be expected," Jack reasoned. "If I'm getting chewed out it's probably because of something you did, so . . ."

"Something I did?" Shaun challenged. "You're the one who pisses everyone off."

"But not recently." Jack waved a hand as if to brush his partner's next response away. "So, it must be you."

Jack steered around the next turn where they were greeted by a sea of flashing lights that masked the fact there were no streetlights. "What the hell?"

"Definitely a case," Shaun searched for an epicenter. "Who do you think the victim is?"

"Someone important," Jack stated the obvious. He navigated the gaps between emergency vehicles with a focus on the ambulance parked at an angle in front of a three-story home just shy of mansion status. When he was as close as he could get, he braked and threw the car into park. "This should be fun."

The two detectives stepped out onto the street and walked toward the largest concentration of uniforms. As they made their way, they could see the sheet-covered body lying on the driveway. Jack gazed at it as if he might see the victim underneath.

Shaun spotted Chief Grimes and a couple of other department bigwigs standing in a smaller cluster close to the house and tapped his partner on the shoulder. Jack followed Shaun's pointing finger and reluctantly changed course, signaling for Shaun to hang back.

He continued forward on his own until he was standing in front of the chief where he stood silently waiting for the brass to finish their conversation. They weren't in any hurry to do so, and Jack made no attempt to interrupt.

"Glad you could join us, Jack." The chief finally turned to the detective. "Sorry to call you on your day off."

Jack was surprised by the complete attitude change from the phone call. "What is this? You've got way too many people here. Even if the victim was important, why am I here?"

"You don't know." The chief raised an eyebrow and grimaced. "Detective, the victim is Chief Hutchins."

"Hutchins?" Jack glanced toward the driveway and the sheet-covered body, surrounded by a sea of uniforms. "My Chief Hutchins?"

"Our Chief Hutchins," Chief Grimes confirmed. "Yes."

"And what? You want me to assist?"

"You have the highest clearance rate in the department." The chief looked Jack in the eyes. "I want you to take the lead. This needs to be solved quickly."

"This is my case?"

"That's what I said."

"Then I have one question." Jack returned the same stern glare.

"What is that, detective?"

"Why are all these people contaminating my crime scene?"

4

A quick order from Chief Grimes and one of the ranking uniformed officers was using his radio to direct all unnecessary personnel to the street. While Shaun assisted in making sure everyone retreated, Jack took the opportunity to insist the brass move beyond the barrier as well. There was some grumbling as they walked away.

With the perimeter cleared, Jack circled Chief Hutchins' car with a flashlight, examining every detail as he went. Several feet beyond the sheet-covered body, a blood-stained pistol lay on the edge of the driveway. Jack guessed it to be the murder weapon, although it would be up to ballistics to determine whether that was the case.

There was a run of grass about four yards wide between the chief's drive and the neighbor's. Miraculously, the trampling had been kept to a minimum and Jack hoped there might be some evidence to be found there. If the killer had dropped the weapon as he fled, he may have dropped something else as he went.

Shaun stepped up to him, standing shoulder-to-shoulder with his partner. "What are you staring at?"

"I'm wondering if that is where the gun landed," Jack pointed. "Or if our friends in uniform managed to kick it about."

"Surely they wouldn't have," Shaun moaned.

"Yesterday I would have said there was no way," Jack admitted. "But after seeing the fiasco this morning, I can't be positive about anything."

The two detectives approached the body together. Jack didn't know how many shots were fired, but he could see that one had been a through and through. Blood splatter on the car door surrounded the bullet hole just to the left of the handle. Was it the kill shot?

The coroner arrived, parked behind Jack's car, and walked toward them dragging her toolkit behind. Valerie O'Conner took confident strides as she powered up the driveway. She looked at the blood-stained sheet before turning to the detectives.

"What's with the circus?" She threw a thumb toward the crowd of officers.

"The victim is Chief Hutchins." Jack frowned. The words gave him a bitter taste in his mouth.

"Seriously?" Valerie stepped closer and kneeled at the sheet's edge. "Someone killed a chief?"

Jack joined her in a mirrored position. Shaun remained standing to one side. Valerie grasped the corner of the sheet and flipped it away, exposing the woman beneath it. Early in her career, a detective rushed her to get a time of death on a victim. At the time, she took a thermometer and jabbed it into the body to check the liver temp. To this day she can remember the woman's scream. Also to this day, the first thing Valerie did at any crime scene was check for a pulse.

The streetlights flickered before lighting up the neighborhood, competing with the slowly rising sun. Porch lights and lamps in windows showed that all power had been restored. A small cheer rose from the crowd of officers that died out just as quickly. One house's sprinkler system came to life, sending a group running for drier ground.

Jack never took his gaze off the chief, his eyes jumping from detail to detail in rapid fashion. "What do you see, Shaun?"

The younger detective was also scanning the scene. "Body position suggests she died quickly. Fell where she was."

The chief's legs were buckled beneath her and she lay on her back, knees toward the car. "She was pressed against the car when she was shot. The killer either let her fall or guided her down. What stands out to you?"

"Other than it being the chief?" Shaun shook his head. "She's in uniform. I don't think I've ever seen her in her blues."

"That's close." Jack pointed. "Look at her holster."

"Empty," Shaun observed.

"So the gun on the driveway may be hers." Jack nodded in the direction of the weapon.

"Killer must have thrown it out of her reach." Shaun studied the gun. "Disarmed her in an effort to subdue her, before ultimately killing her."

"She was shot with her own weapon." Jack stood and stepped away for a better angle.

"How do you figure?"

"I want to hear this." Valerie did not take her eyes off the body she was examining.

"We can assume the chief put up a fight." Jack positioned himself between the body and the weapon, glancing over his shoulder and gesturing. "She would have tried to turn, so he had to be holding her against the car. She would have gone for her gun. If the attacker shot her with a gun he brought, she would have dropped her weapon next to her. Being behind her, he would have kicked it away, to the side, or under the car. Not behind them. It only makes sense that he managed to disarm her and shot her with her own weapon, tossing it after."

"Maybe he shot her and then pulled her gun from her hand," Shaun offered.

"Possible."

"What if he held her at gunpoint and told her to toss her weapon?" Shaun tried again.

"She would have tossed it to the side, not behind her." Jack moved his hand to his waist and then tossed an imaginary gun to demonstrate. "And I don't think the chief would have tossed it. If she got her hand on it, she would have tried to use it."

"She may have thought throwing the gun would keep her alive," Shaun said.

"She was in uniform." Jack pointed at the chief. "He knew she was a cop. You don't stick a gun in a cop's back unless you plan to use it. She would have fought."

"Single shot," Valerie reported. "Through and through. She most likely died instantly."

Jack turned to the chief's body again. The exit wound was in the upper abdomen area. "She wasn't wearing a vest?"

"No." Valerie rolled the body to its side. "Entry just below the right shoulder blade, downward angle. Would have hit multiple vital organs. I'll have to autopsy to be sure. This guy knew what he was doing."

"Professional hit?"

"Not my purview." The coroner rolled the chief onto her back again. "I'll get her back to the morgue and do a full workup."

Jack nodded, turning to his partner. "Did you happen to find out who was first on scene?"

"Officers Owens and Estrada." Shaun turned, searched the crowd until he found the two men, and pointed.

Jack did not know Owens. From the look of him, he was a rookie fresh out of the academy. Officer Julio Estrada, on the other hand, had been on the force for nearly two decades. Their paths had crossed numerous times over the years.

"Estrada!" the detective called out. The tall, muscular officer turned his way and Jack waved them over.

The two detectives walked down the driveway and met them halfway.

"Julio," Jack greeted. "I haven't seen you in a while."

"I've been babysitting Owens here." Julio patted the young officer on the shoulder. "Mostly domestic disturbances and burglaries. Traffic stops and breaking up fights. Nothing in your world. This is his first murder."

"You picked a good one." Jack looked back at where the coroner and her team were bagging the body. "What can you tell me? Who found her?"

Julio turned to the rookie. "You're up. Give the detective a report."

"Yes, sir," Owens responded. "Detective, sir."

"Mallory."

"Detective Mallory, sir," Owens corrected. "We arrived about five minutes after the call."

"About five minutes?" Jack questioned. "Was it five minutes, or wasn't it?"

"I, uh..." Owens pulled out his notes and started searching.

"He's pulling your chain, officer," Julio smiled. "Get on with the report."

Jack grinned.

"I, uh, I mean we arrived to find a deceased female in the driveway," he reported. "She was in police uniform and appeared to have suffered a GSW. We called it in immediately."

"And who found her body?" Jack asked again. "Who called nine-one-one?"

"Uh, the body was discovered by the neighbor when he came out to go to work." Owens checked his notes. "The husband called nine-one-one."

"Which neighbor?" Jack asked.

Owens scanned his notes.

"To the east." Julio pointed at the next house over. "Mr. Randy Keyes."

The home was similar to Chief Hutchin's home, only smaller and not as well kept. Jack noticed a 'For Sale' sign in the yard. "Did you talk to him?"

"Briefly," Julio answered. "He spotted the body on the way to his truck. Ran over to offer aid. Called out for help. The chief's husband came out and called it in. She was already gone by the time paramedics arrived."

"Where is he now?" Jack noted the empty driveway.

"Who, sir?" the rookie asked.

"The neighbor," Jack clarified.

"We released him," Julio said.

"You what?" Jack turned on him. "You released my witness?"

"He's an electrician," Julio defended. "He was called to work on the power outage. I figured we needed the lights back on."

"You figured wrong," Jack grumbled. "They could have called someone else. Next time, no one leaves until I say."

"Sorry, Jack," Julio apologized. "Won't happen again."

"It better not." Jack turned to the neighbor's house. "His truck's still in the driveway. Where did he go when you released him?"

"His clothes were bloody, sir," the rookie said. "I think he went inside to change."

"To change?"

"Yes, sir."

"Julio, you and your trainee need to grab one of the techs and go over there and bag the man's clothing," Jack ordered. "And tell him he's unreleased. He doesn't leave until we talk to him."

"Yes, sir," Julio started for the neighbor's house. "Come on Owens. Let's go redeem ourselves."

"One more thing," Jack said.

Julio stopped in his tracks and turned to the detective.

"Did you talk to the husband?" Jack asked.

"No, sir," Julio said. "He's inside with their son."

"Son?" Jack turned to the house. "I didn't know she had a son."

5

An officer stood next to the front door of the Hutchins' home. Jack nodded at him as he stepped onto the porch. The detective's eyes were drawn to a red stain on the video doorbell.

"Make sure the photographer gets a shot of that." Jack pointed at the device.

"Yes, sir." The officer glanced at the door. "Is that blood?"

"Have forensics get a sample after the photo." Jack stepped past the man and opened the front door, letting himself in.

He walked a few steps into the large foyer before stopping to take in the grand stairway and chandelier. It made him wonder what a chief was paid.

"Hello?" He tried not to shout while projecting his voice enough to be heard.

"In here." The responding voice was deep and authoritative with a hint of sadness.

Jack turned in the direction he thought it had come from. Passing through an archway into a family room complete with an assortment of seating and a television, the detective saw a man sitting on a comfortable-looking sectional with his arm around the shoulder of a teenage boy. The younger had tears on his cheeks and an expression that could only be interpreted as anguish. The older sat limply, with a hollow darkness in his eyes.

"Mr. Hutchins?" Jack asked, doubting it would be anyone else. Reggie nodded and the detective continued. "I am Detective Jack Mallory. I have been assigned your wife's case. I want you to know how sorry I am for your loss. I worked for Chief Hutchins and I know what a good person she was."

The man on the sectional turned his head to Jack. "What do you need, detective?"

"I know this is a bad time," Jack responded. "Truth is there's never a good time to talk about a loss like the one you're experiencing. But for me to have the best chance of bringing the man who did this to justice, I need to ask the two of you some questions."

"Ask them."

"Separately."

"Separately?" The man's brow knotted. "Why?"

"To verify the facts, it's best to have you both tell me," Jack explained. "Sometimes people remember things differently and if one of you says something the other may go along even though they thought something else."

"You don't want us to have the chance to get our stories straight?"

"That's not what I'm saying." It was exactly what the detective was thinking. "I just need to know everything. And I don't want one of you to prevent the other from saying what they remember."

"I didn't kill my wife."

"I believe you," Jack said. "I still have to do my job."

The man stared at the detective, willing him to leave. When it didn't happen, he turned to his son. "Go to your room and pack a bag."

"We leaving?"

"We're going to get a hotel," the father said. "For a day or two. Go pack."

The boy glanced at the detective before sliding off the furniture and disappearing the way Jack had entered. He could hear the thumping of feet on the stairs leading to the second level.

"I'm sorry about this."

"Just get on with it."

"Could I get your first name?" Jack opened his notepad and poised to write.

"Reginald."

"Reginald Hutchins." Jack wrote in his pad. "What is your profession?"

"Architect."

"Did you design this house?"

"How is that relevant?"

"It's not." Jack backtracked. "Tell me about your relationship with your wife."

"I didn't."

"Pardon me?"

"I didn't design the house." Reggie looked around the room before turning back to the detective. "Our relationship?"

"How would you characterize it?"

"We were good." Reggie seemed proud when he said it.

"No problems?" Jack probed.

"Are you married, detective?"

"Not anymore."

"Then you know," Reggie nodded as if they were in a secret club. "We struggled. But at the end of the day, we were solid."

"Okay," Jack moved on. "Why don't you tell me what happened this morning."

"This morning was typical," he said. "The boy and I were having breakfast when Sharon came down. She was going to eat with us, but the power going out made her think she should go see if she was needed."

"How long after the power went out did she leave?"

"I don't know." Reggie looked up at the ceiling. "Ten, maybe fifteen minutes."

"She was in uniform," Jack said. "Not usual for her. Do you know why?"

"There was a trial that she was going to testify at."

"A trial?" Jack frowned. "She wasn't a detective anymore."

"It was from before she became chief," the man said. "I don't know the details."

"I'll look into it." Jack wrote in his pad.

"Oh, and she had a press conference scheduled." Reginald wagged a finger. "Getting tough on crime."

"Really?"

The husband nodded.

"Okay." Jack shifted his weight. "Let's go over what happened after the power went out."

"Like I said," Reggie sighed. "She thought she might be needed. So, she left."

"And then what?"

"And then we heard Randy yelling."

"Randy?"

"Our neighbor," Reggie pointed in the direction of the house with the For Sale sign in the yard. "Randy . . . Keyes."

"You heard Mr. Keyes yelling," Jack prompted. "What did you do then?"

"I didn't know it was Randy at the time," Reggie said. "I heard yelling and I went out to investigate."

"You didn't hear anything before the yelling?" Jack asked. "Like a gunshot?"

"I was listening to a podcast," Reginald said. "As soon as Sharon closed the door, I put my earbuds in and turned it on. I didn't take them out until it was over."

"How long was the podcast?" Jack saw an opportunity to help establish a timeline.

"They usually run thirty to forty-five minutes," Reginald thought. "But I had already started this one, so I'm not sure."

Jack nodded. His disappointment showed. "You heard the yelling and went to investigate. Did your son go with you?"

Reggie shook his head. "He came out a little later."

"So you went out the front door?" Jack said.

"Yes." Reggie sat up straighter. "I walked to the door and opened it." He stopped, staring in that direction. It took a moment before he continued. "It was louder when I opened the door, the yelling. Louder and clearer. He was yelling my name. Calling for help. I thought he was hurt, although I didn't know yet who he was. So I picked up the pace. To go help. And when I came around the car . . . I saw her. Randy was cradling her head, telling me to call nine-one-one."

"And you did," Jack concluded.

"No." Reggie was somewhere else, lost in his memory of the morning.

"No?"

"I didn't have my phone."

"I was told you called."

"I didn't have my phone," the man repeated.

"Then who called?"

"My son."

"Is that when he came out?" Jack asked.

"I don't know," Reggie looked at Jack like he was just seeing him for the first time. "He was just there."

"So he may have followed you."

"He was still sitting at the table when I left the room," Reggie insisted. "I don't know when he came out."

"Did you check on your wife?"

"What?"

"Did you check to see if Sharon was still alive?"

"Of course," Reggie was offended by the idea he hadn't. "As soon as I saw her, I pushed Randy away and checked for a pulse, tried chest compressions, but..."

"But what?"

"There was so much blood." For the first time, the man started crying.

"We're almost done."

Reggie closed his eyes, nodded, and tried to pull himself together.

"How long was it after Sharon left the house that you heard your neighbor yelling?" Jack leaned forward.

Reggie caught the detective's gaze and held it. "Twenty, no, thirty minutes? I don't know. Maybe less."

"Were you still in the kitchen?" Jack asked.

"Yes," he nodded. "I was standing in the dark while Brian finished his pancakes. I had my phone on flashlight mode, propped against the salt and pepper shakers so he could see. That's why I didn't have my phone."

"Okay. Good." Jack wrote in his notebook. "In retrospect, is it possible you heard the gunshot? Maybe dismissed it?"

"You know," Reggie frowned. "I think I may have. I thought I heard a car backfire. I didn't think anything of it at the time. Was that when they shot her?"

"Possibly." Jack tried to get the man focused again. "Twenty to thirty minutes passed between Sharon leaving and your neighbor yelling. At what point did you hear what you thought was a car backfiring?"

"I don't know." Reggie shook his head. "I just didn't think anything of it at the time. I'm sorry."

"It's okay," Jack dismissed. "Just one more question. And I need you to think about this. Be sure you get it right."

"What?"

"When you came back in the house," Jack narrowed his eyes. "Did you touch the front doorbell?"

"The doorbell?"

"Did you touch it?"

"No."

6

To the east was the home of the witness who found the chief, the one who had been released prematurely to go to work. Shaun glanced at the 'For Sale' sign in the man's yard then turned his attention to the house on the west side of the chief's home. He walked through a small group of officers who were still in the area. After Chief Hutchins' body had been removed the crowds thinned quickly, with the brass leading the retreat.

Shaun followed the driveway and walkway up to the massive front door of the colonial-style home. He rang the doorbell and waited. From inside, children screamed, shouted, and laughed. Small shadows passed behind the frosted glass windows set in the wood. There was a sharp yell, louder than any before it, followed by silence. Another shadow appeared behind the glass, growing larger until the door opened.

The woman standing in the doorway looked tired. It was a look Shaun remembered his mother wearing when he and his brother were young. It was a tired that children could never identify with. A tired all parents shared at some point in their children's lives.

"May I help you?" she asked.

"Detective Shaun Travis," he introduced. "I'm canvassing the neighborhood hoping maybe you saw or heard something this morning."

"I'm sorry," she said. "I don't even know what's happening."

"Who is it, dear?" A man called out.

"A detective," she called back. "He wants to talk to us."

They stood in the doorway until a man appeared from the back of the house. "I really need to go. I'm already late. I couldn't get the garage door to open before the power came back on."

"He's going to tell us what's happening," the woman announced.

"Do tell," The man said. "I don't think I've ever seen that many police cars in one place."

"Can I get your names?" Shaun opened his notepad. "For the report."

"Al and Celia French," Al answered.

"Thank you. This morning," Shaun started. "After the power went out, did you hear or see anything unusual?"

"It was too dark to see anything," Al said. "At least until the police arrived."

"Four kids aged six to fourteen," Celia said. "We didn't hear anything but them."

"What's this about?" the husband asked.

"Your neighbor was shot and killed this morning," Shaun reported.

"Which neighbor?" the man asked.

"Al, that's rude." Celia slapped her husband's arm. "It doesn't matter which neighbor. It's a tragedy just the same."

"Sharon Hutchins," Shaun answered anyway.

"Sharon?" The wife covered her mouth with both hands. "Not Sharon. She's dead?"

"Yes, ma'am," Shaun confirmed. "I was hoping you might have heard the gunshot. We're trying to establish a timeline."

"That poor boy," Celia ignored him. "He was really attached to his mother. Wait. Wasn't she a policewoman?"

"A chief," Shaun said.

"I think I heard it." Al seemed to drift off.

"Heard what?" the woman turned to her husband.

"I think I heard the shot," he said. "I just didn't know. I mean, I didn't think it was a gunshot. Not a real one anyway."

"When did you hear it?"

"I'm sorry," Al shook his head. "It was dark. All of our clocks are digital, and the power was out. I just don't know."

"Can you tell me about your relationship with the Hutchins?" Shaun asked.

"With Reggie and Sharon?" Celia said. "I mean, their boy is only a couple of years older than our oldest. When they were young, they played a lot. But lately, you know, sixteen and fourteen may as well be ten years apart."

"What she's saying is we're friendly," the husband said. "But not friends."

"And what about the Hutchins themselves?" Shaun decided not to correct the woman on the seventeen-year-old Brian's age. "What can you tell me about them and their relationship?"

"They're good people," Al said. "Always friendly. Polite."

"Reggie mowed our lawn for us a couple of times last fall after Al broke his leg." The woman patted her husband's chest. "We never even asked him to do it."

"He just didn't want to be next to a messy lawn." Al rolled his eyes.

"He was being nice," the wife said.

"If you say so, dear," he grinned unconvincingly.

"You don't think so?" Shaun asked.

"Have you seen his lawn?" The man raised his chin in their neighbor's direction. "He's very particular about appearance."

"You make it sound like he was the yard police," the woman argued.

"The man is uptight about the yard," Al's tone changed. "He practically harassed me until I trimmed the bushes last year."

"Was that before or after he mowed your lawn for you?" Shaun asked.

"Before." Al crossed his arms.

"Al fell off the ladder." She lowered her eyes and her voice. "That's how he broke his leg."

"So he pressured you into trimming your bushes," Shaun summarized. "Which led to you falling off the ladder and breaking your leg, which led to him mowing your lawn for you."

"But not out of guilt." Al was adamant.

"Not guilt?"

"No." Al wagged a finger. "He just knew I couldn't do it and didn't want my unmowed lawn next to his manicured one."

"So when you said they were friendly?"

"We meant Mrs. Hutchins," Al said.

"Stop it," the woman said. "Reginald isn't a tyrant. He's a nice man who is opinionated about his lawn."

"As best you can recollect," Shaun changed the subject. "Have either of you noticed any cars or people you didn't recognize, maybe hanging around too much? Watching the Hutchins' house?"

"I don't think so." Celia looked up at her husband. "How about you, honey?"

"No cars," Al said. "No people."

"Thank you for your time." Shaun handed them a card and turned to leave, stopping just before they could shut their door. "One more thing. Do you own any firearms?"

"No, sir," the woman grimaced. "Don't want one in my home."

"Okay." Shaun smiled. "Thanks again."

7

Jack sat in an uncomfortable desk chair in Brian Hutchins' room. The teenager was perched on the edge of his bed fidgeting with his cellphone. The detective had offered to wait in the family room while Reginald went up to get his son, but the father simply pointed at the stairs and gave Jack directions. When he arrived at the bedroom, there was clear dismay in the boy's expression. Reluctantly, he let the detective in and offered him the worn-out seat Jack was now trying very hard not to fall off of.

The walls were adorned with posters of bands Jack had never heard of. A couple more were young, popular actresses in seductive poses. The rest of the room was filled with representations of the latest video game fad. There were no personal photos. Nothing of his parents, friends, or girlfriend. Looking at the teen, Jack had a hard time seeing his mother; the strong, confident woman who led a team of hard-headed detectives.

"I need to ask you some questions about this morning," Jack said.

"I know."

"You were all together when the power went out?"

"Yes."

"Where were you?"

"Kitchen."

"How long after the power went out did your mom leave?" Jack watched the boy's face as he asked the questions. Brian in turn watched his phone.

"I don't know."

"That's okay," Jack assured him. "When did you know something was wrong?"

Brian looked up at the detective for the first time, a fierceness in his eyes. "When I saw my mom was dead."

Jack paused to give the boy a minute. The anger retreated and his facial features softened.

"I'm sorry for what you're going through." Jack wanted to kick himself for asking the question incorrectly. "And I'm sorry I have to ask these questions. I promise there won't be much more."

"Whatever." His eyes fell back to his phone.

"After your mom left," Jack backed up. "What happened next?"

"Someone shot her." He gave Jack a look that suggested he might be the dumbest detective on the planet.

"I mean you and your dad," Jack clarified. "What did the two of you do?"

"I sat in the dark eating my pancakes and watching videos."

"And your dad?"

"I don't know," Brian said. "It was dark. I assume he drank his coffee and finished getting ready for work."

"He wasn't with you?"

"I can't say," Brian shrugged. "It was dark. He must have been. He walked past me when he went outside."

"What made you go outside?"

"My dad."

"What about him?"

"I couldn't see very well," Brian admitted. "But when he walked by on his way out, the light from my phone let me see him. Something about the way he was walking made me follow."

"The way he was walking?"

"You know," Brian shifted in his seat. "He was walking fast. I mean, real fast. I followed to see what was wrong."

"You went out when he did?" Jack asked.

"Yes."

"And what did you see?" Jack put a hand up. "Besides your mother."

"I saw Mister Keyes holding mom's head." Brian closed his eyes.

"Mister Keyes?"

"Our neighbor."

"And what did your dad do?"

"He pushed Mister Keyes away and tried to give her CPR." He didn't open his eyes.

"And what did you do?"

"I called nine-one-one." His eyes opened and he looked at the detective. "Lotta good it did."

"Did you hear anything before you followed your dad out?" Jack asked. "Something that sounded like a gunshot?"

"I had headphones on, watching my videos." He pointed at the listening device draped around his neck. "Didn't hear anything."

Jack nodded. "I need to ask you some difficult questions now. But I need you to answer them as honestly as you can. Okay?"

"Harder than my mom being killed?" Brian snarled. "I think I can handle it."

"I hope so," Jack said. "I need you to tell me about your parents. How was their relationship?"

"You want to know if my dad killed my mom?" Brian challenged. "He didn't."

"That isn't what I was asking," Jack tried to dial the teen down. "I just need to have all the facts."

"Mom and Dad were good," Brian said. "Did they fight? Sure. Who doesn't? But they've been good since they got back together."

"Back together?" Jack frowned. "They were apart?"

"Last year." Brian looked like he had just forsaken his last friend. "They separated for a couple months."

"Do you know why?"

"Sure, they sat their teen-aged son down and explained just what it was that had them so mad they couldn't stand to be in the same room." Brian's sarcasm surprised the detective.

"Understood." Jack remembered his parents fighting when he was young. He never knew why. "But they worked it out."

"I guess." Brian shrugged. "They've been good since then."

"Have you noticed anything different about your mom lately?" Jack asked. "Like was she more cautious or maybe nervous?"

"Did you know my mom?"

"Yes. I worked with her."

"She was never nervous."

"True." Jack grinned. "She was quite a woman, huh? Good mom, I'm guessing?"

"She was okay," Brian's head dropped, but he wasn't looking at the phone this time. "Gone a lot, with work."

"When you were outside the past few days," Jack continued. "Did you ever notice someone lurking around who you didn't know?"

"I never went outside." The boy pointed at the large television on his wall. "I play video games."

Jack fell silent for a minute, looking around the room. "Do you know anyone who didn't like your mother?"

"Enough to kill her?" Pain shone in Brian's face. "No."

8

The next house to the west was empty. The owners must have left before the police arrived in the neighborhood or managed to clear out during the chaos. Shaun stood in their driveway checking out the houses across the street before deciding to back track and go to the home on the far side of the house that was for sale.

Walking past the crime scene, the detective's eyes were drawn to the blood stain on the concrete next to the chief's car. He had seen blood stains before, more than he cared to remember at this point. None of them had ever been people he had known.

Shaun passed the neighbor's house noting the realtor's sign was leaning slightly to one side. He considered straightening it but could hear Jack's disapproving comments in his head. He moved on to the next house and walked toward the front door.

The sun had been on the rise for only a short time and the windows of the home were still aglow from the lights within. Shaun paused to look back at the crime scene before continuing to the porch.

The moment he stepped in front of the door, he heard a dog bark inside announcing his presence. He considered whether it would be enough or if the animal barked at everything and thus ignored by its owners. He waited briefly before pushing the doorbell. The eruption of barking caused Shaun to take a step back.

Through the door, Shaun could hear yelling and intermittent sharp commands, an effort to control what the detective now knew to be two dogs that had worked themselves into a frenzy. Shaun was wondering if he would be able to speak to the residents at all.

Everything went suddenly quiet and the door opened. A man stood between Shaun and two Golden Retrievers sitting on their haunches, watching the detective with intense interest. The sight was in stark contrast to the chaos Shaun had heard only moments before. The detective must have been staring a bit too much.

"They're harmless." The man glanced back. Their tails wagged wildly. "Unless you're allergic to being licked."

"Beautiful dogs." Shaun shifted his attention to the man. "Are you the homeowner?"

"We're not buying anything."

"No," Shaun held up his shield. "I need to ask you some questions about this morning."

"Oh, the excitement," the man looked past Shaun to the street beyond. "What was that all about?"

"Are you the homeowner?"

"I am."

"Are you here alone?"

"No." The man pointed to the stairway behind him. "Wife's upstairs."

"Could you have her come down?" Shaun's eyes followed the man's finger. "I need to ask you both some questions and it would be faster if we could just do it once."

"Michelle!" the man shouted. He waited a minute and called for her a second time.

"What!" Michelle shouted back down to him. At the sound of her voice, the dogs bolted up the stairs.

"Come down!" the husband shouted again. "There's a detective who needs to ask you some questions!"

The woman appeared at the top of the stairs flanked by the two dogs. "There's a what?"

"A detective with questions." The man pointed at Shaun. "Now, come on."

The woman seemed to contemplate her next move. Decision made, she started down, taking the steps rapidly. She arrived at the door with her escorts who she gave a quick command to sit. They obeyed immediately.

"What's going on?" she asked.

"The commotion this morning," the husband answered. "He hasn't said what it was about."

"May I get your names?" Shaun opened his notepad.

"Dave and Michelle Bartlett," the husband answered.

"One of your neighbors was murdered this morning." Shaun watched the couple for a reaction. Both seemed to be appropriately shocked.

"Who?" Michelle asked.

"Sharon Hutchins." Shaun watched their faces again.

The edge of Dave's mouth curled upward ever so slightly. "The cop?"

"Did you just smile?" Shaun accused.

"Me?" Dave put a hand to his chest. "Of course not."

"You didn't." Michelle turned on him. "A woman's been killed."

"I'm sorry." The husband shrugged. "It's just not the worst news I've heard."

"How could you?"

"Am I missing something here?" Shaun interrupted.

"Dave's happy because Sharon was always getting onto him about his motorcycle." Michelle crossed her arms across her body.

"What about your motorcycle?"

"It sounds like a freight train," Michelle offered.

"It's loud," Dave admitted. "But it doesn't sound like a freight train."

"It makes the whole house shake," Michelle said.

"It does not."

"How would you know?" Michelle asked. "You aren't inside when you're riding it."

"Well, Sharon was the only one who complained," Dave defended.

"Just because she's the only one who complained," Michelle countered, "doesn't mean no one else thinks it's too loud."

"Excuse me," Shaun interrupted. The couple turned to him as if they had forgotten he was there. "How often did she complain?"

"All the time," Dave sighed. "Wait. You don't think I killed her?"

"Did you?"

"No," Dave denied. "Sure she complained. But she also helped me out when Samantha accused me of killing her cat."

"And Samantha is?"

"I guess you wouldn't know that." Dave was amused. "She's Randy's ex."

"Excuse my husband." Michelle took over. "He doesn't always think. Randy Keyes is the neighbor between us and Sharon. Samantha was his wife. She accused Dave of killing her cat because, well, he hates cats."

"And she thought you killed hers?" Shaun asked.

"Yeah," Dave shrugged. "I mean, I get it. If your cat ends up dead, it makes sense to look at the cat hater. But I didn't do it."

"Sharon used her cop skills to find out that Dave was innocent." Michelle took hold of her husband's arm.

"My noisy bike saved me on that one," Dave snarked. "They realized they heard me leave that morning while the cat was still in the house. Crazy woman."

"Dave," Michelle slapped the arm she held with her other hand. "You know she was going through some stuff."

"Going through stuff?" Shaun asked.

"She and Randy hadn't been doing too well," Michelle lowered her voice. "Apparently, it was a last straw for her," she added. "She left him shortly after that."

"Good riddance," Dave said.

"You don't mean that," Michelle said. "She was nice."

"She accused me of killing her cat."

"I think we need to get back on track." Shaun tried to regain control.

"That's right," Michelle smiled at him. "You had some questions."

"I do," the detective nodded. "This morning, the power went out. Can you tell me what you were doing?"

"I was in the garage washing the bike," Dave said.

"Of course you were," Michelle shook her head.

"And you ma'am?"

"I was doing my daily exercise routine."

For a brief moment, Shaun thought she was posing to show off her success. Dave rolled his eyes.

"And after the power went off?" Shaun asked. "What did you do then?"

"I had to stop exercising." Michelle was blunt. "I couldn't see what I was doing, so I went back to the bedroom to change."

"I came in to deal with the dogs," Dave grumbled.

"Deal with them how, exactly?" Shaun looked down at the two animals.

"The power outage must have spooked them," Dave said. "They were going nuts at the back door. I quieted them down and looked out, but there wasn't anything there."

"Maybe it was a rabbit," Michelle suggested.

"They bark at everything," Dave addressed the detective. "They used to have an absolute fit when Samantha's cat came in the yard."

"I bet." Shaun was dismissive. "Did you see or hear anything out front, in the direction of Sharon's house? A gunshot, for instance?"

"Sorry," Michelle said. "I wear headphones when I'm working out."

"I didn't hear anything," Dave said. "Any sound outside will set the dogs off. They started again a little while later. Barking and growling. You don't think that's what they were barking at?"

"I really couldn't say," Shaun sighed.

"He said the gunshot was in the front," Michelle said. "You said the dogs were barking at the back."

"Not the second time," Dave defended. "The second time they just started barking in the middle of the room."

"Have you seen any cars in the neighborhood, in the past couple of weeks, that maybe didn't belong?" Shaun tried again to gain control.

"Now that you mention it," Dave waved a finger at him. "There was one."

"Can you describe it, please?" Shaun asked.

"A black pick-up," Dave remembered. "It was in front of the house when I left for work. There was a man sitting inside."

"Are you serious?" Michelle turned to her husband.

"What?"

"That was Aaron."

"Who is Aaron?" Shaun asked.

"He's been our pool guy for five years." Michelle gave her husband a look.

"That was Aaron?" Dave's eyes grew. "He looks different without a net in his hands."

"Anyone else?"

"I saw a green sedan earlier this week," Michelle said. "It was parked across the street a few houses down, a couple days in a row."

"Did you ever see the driver?"

"No." She looked past Shaun to the street. "I never saw anyone inside."

"Green sedan?"

"Yes." Michelle grinned. "Not very helpful, huh?"

"It's okay," Shaun assured her. "Every little bit helps."

"I hope so."

"Do either of you know Sharon or Reginald well enough to know if she had any problems with anyone?" Shaun asked. "Or maybe someone that would want to hurt her to get back at him?"

Both shook their heads.

"Okay," Shaun pulled out a card. "If you think of anything, give me a call. Thank you for your time."

Shaun heard the door close behind him as he walked away.

9

Jack was standing in the center of the street when Shaun left the Bartlett's house. The two detectives converged and headed for Randy Keyes' home.

"Learn anything?" Jack asked his younger partner.

"Al and Celia French," Shaun pointed to the east. "They say they were friendly with the chief's family but grew apart after the Hutchins boy outgrew their son."

"How apart?" Jack asked. "Enough to have bad blood?"

"That's not what I sensed." Shaun slowed when they reached the driveway of their destination. "The wife, for one, was upset to know of the chief's death."

"Not the husband?"

"Harder to read." Shaun glanced back toward the French's house. "He claims he may have heard the shot but wasn't sure."

"Anything else?"

"Not with them." Shaun gestured to the west. "Dave and Michelle Bartlett. Their story is more interesting. Seems the chief complained about the noise Dave's motorcycle made. He almost smiled at the news of her death."

"Well, that doesn't sound good, does it?"

"I didn't think so either." A squad car raced away with lights and sirens blaring. Shaun waited before continuing. "But he followed that with a story of how she helped him with a dispute."

"Was he trying to overcompensate?" Jack asked.

"Maybe," Shaun shrugged. "The wife claims to have seen a green sedan a couple of houses away in recent days. She didn't know who it belonged to."

"We'll need to look into that." Jack pointed at Shaun's notepad.

"How did it go with the family?"

"Sharon's son thinks his father was in the house with him while she was being murdered," Jack said. "But he was watching a video and can't be sure. He did run out when he saw his father go. And they both corroborated what the neighbor told the officer. At least what they saw after they came out of the house."

"So we're not clearing the husband?"

"I don't see how we can," Jack confirmed. "At least, not yet. Don't want to be accused of not following every possible suspect."

"Ture."

Jack looked up at the home they were standing in front of. Officers Estrada and Owens were coming down the driveway with one of the forensics technicians close on their heels carrying evidence bags with the electrician's clothing.

"What took so long?" Jack asked the senior officer.

"When we first got to the door, we couldn't get in," Julio replied.

"Couldn't get in?" Jack frowned. "He wouldn't open the door? Do you think he was trying to hide evidence?"

"No," Julio dismissed. "The guy had blood on him. He took a shower. Said he didn't hear us until he turned the water off. He was cooperative. Gave us the clothes he had been wearing."

"Okay. Thanks." Jack turned to his partner. "Shall we?"

The detectives walked to the front door and knocked. It was opened almost immediately.

"We are detectives Mallory and Travis," Jack introduced. "We need to ask you some questions about this morning."

"Yeah," the man said, stepping to one side. "The officers told me to expect you. Come in."

Inside they were greeted with various stacks of large, packed moving boxes. The living room was void of anything personal. The walls and shelves were bare. All the furniture was shoved to one side of the room. The other side was filled with more boxes.

"I saw the sign out front," Jack said. "Have you sold?"

"There's been some interest," Randy directed the men to the only piece of furniture not blocked in one way or another, a leather sofa. "A couple of bids."

"So you'll be moving soon?" Shaun asked. He and Jack sat side by side.

In the kitchen was a small round dining table with one chair. Randy dragged the chair over, positioned it to face the detectives, and straddled the seat. "I suppose so."

"If you move before this investigation is over," Jack shifted, "we'll need you to let us know where to find you."

"Okay?"

"Just in case we have more questions," Shaun explained. "Or if we need clarification."

"Okay," Randy said. "I understand."

"They told me you are the one who found Chief Hutchins this morning," Jack said.

"You mean Sharon? That's right," Randy said. "Not that it did any good."

"What do you mean?"

"Didn't save her, did I?" Randy pursed his lips. "Maybe if I had been a few minutes earlier."

"Then you may have been another victim," Shaun pointed out.

"Oh," Randy said. "I didn't think about that."

"Can you tell us what happened?" Jack asked.

"Well, where do you want me to start?"

"The beginning would be good," Shaun said.

"Start from the time you woke up," Jack agreed. "And go from there."

"Okay," Randy nodded. He took a minute before he began. "I was sleeping and my phone woke me. Power was out and dispatch was calling to have me check it out."

"What time was that?" Shaun asked.

"I don't know," Randy said. "It was still dark out. Maybe six."

"Do they always call that fast?" Jack asked.

"I don't know what you mean," Randy said.

"The power went out," Jack clarified. "And you were called almost immediately after."

"I didn't know how long it had been out, seeing as I was sleeping," Randy wiped his brow. "But that does seem fast. Maybe someone called it in as soon as it happened."

"What happened after the call woke you?" Jack asked.

"I got up and threw some clothes on," Randy said. "Oh, out of habit I went to the kitchen to put some coffee on. Which was stupid since the power was out. Then I went back to the bedroom, got dressed, gathered my stuff, and headed out."

"How much time passed from when you got the call until you left your house?" Shaun asked.

"Let's see." Randy crossed his arms. "Maybe ten, fifteen minutes."

"So you may have just missed the killer," Shaun thought aloud.

"I think I did," Randy bobbed his head. "I came out of the house and this guy ran across my yard."

"You didn't find that odd?" Jack asked.

"Sure I thought it was odd," Randy said. "At the time I thought someone was trying to break into my truck. But then I thought it was probably just a teenager trying to get home before his parents realized he was out past curfew. It wasn't until later that I realized it may have been the killer."

"Can you describe him?" Shaun asked.

"All I saw was a pair of jeans and a hoodie."

"What about height and build?" Jack pressed.

"I don't know," Randy wavered. "Five-eight, Five-nine maybe. Average build, maybe."

"What about skin color?" Jack asked. "Or hair?"

"Sorry," Randy shook his head. "It was dark. I wasn't thinking I would need to identify them. Like I said, all I saw were jeans and hoodie."

"Okay," Jack said. "You said they ran across your yard?"

"That's right."

"Were they running toward the Hutchins' house or away?"

"Away," the electrician answered quickly. "Definitely away."

"Then what happened?"

"I went to get into my truck," Randy said. "And that's when I saw her."

"In the dark?" Shaun asked.

"Something seemed off, you know," Randy said. "Something that made me look over. Maybe she moaned or moved. I don't know. Something just made me turn in that direction. And there she was."

"Chief Hutchins?"

"Sharon. Yeah."

"And what did you do next?" Jack asked.

"Well, I thought she must have fallen," he continued. "You know, it was dark and she could have tripped over something. So I ran over to offer my assistance. I thought I would be helping her to her feet. But there was so much blood."

"What did you do when you realized she was dead?"

"She wasn't dead."

"She wasn't?" Jack cocked his head. "Did she say anything?"

"No," Randy seemed to drift. "She just looked up at me. So much fear in her eyes."

"And what did you do?"

"I shouted." The man snapped back. "I just kept calling for help until someone arrived."

"Who arrived?"

"Reggie," Randy said. "Um, Mr. Hutchins."

"He was first to arrive?" Shaun asked. "Are you sure?"

"Well, I think so," Randy looked from one face to the other. "Was he not?"

"You were there, Mr. Keyes," Jack reminded him. "You tell us. But you have to be sure."

"I understand." Randy took a deep breath and let it out. "Yes. Reggie was the first to arrive."

"What happened next?" Jack asked. "What did Reggie do?"

"What do you think he did?" Randy was incredulous. "It was his wife. He tried to save her."

"Was there any hesitation?" Shaun asked.

"Hesitation?"

"When Reginald came out of the house and saw Sharon lying on the ground," Shaun explained. "Did he hesitate before trying to help her?"

"No," Randy said. "He pushed me aside and started trying to give her CPR."

"Who called nine-one-one?" Jack asked.

"I'm not sure," Randy thought for a minute. "The kid maybe."

"Not you?"

"I know." He lowered his eyes to his feet. "I know I should have. But it went from helping her up to holding her and yelling for help so fast. I honestly just didn't think about it."

"What about their door?" Jack asked.

"Whose door?"

"Did you go to their porch to get help?" Jack remembered the blood on the doorbell at the Hutchins home. "Knock on the door? Ring the bell?"

"No." Randy shook his head. "I stayed with Sharon."

"Why didn't you do CPR?" Shaun asked.

"I told you. Reggie did it."

"But before he came out," Shaun continued. "Why didn't you give her CPR?"

"I, um," Randy lowered his voice. "I don't know how."

"You don't know how?" Jack studied the man.

"No, sir."

Jack shifted forward to sit on the edge of the couch. "Let's discuss the Hutchins."

"What about them?"

"What can you tell me about their relationship?"

"Their relationship?" Randy scoffed. "I don't know them that well."

"You were neighbors," Jack said. "You didn't know them?"

"My wife was friends with Sharon," Randy said. "But Reggie and I didn't have much in common."

"So you did know them," Jack said.

"Sure, I knew them," Randy confessed. "But not well enough to know about their relationship."

"You said your wife and Sharon were friends," Jack said. "Did something change?"

"I don't know." His face went blank. "After Sam left me . . . I don't know if they kept in touch."

"Sam was your wife?"

"Samantha. Yes," Randy sighed. "I call her Sam."

"So she's your ex?" Jack questioned.

"She will be soon." Randy closed his eyes. "Not my choice."

"Is that why you're selling the house?" Shaun asked.

"Don't really need this much house for just me," Randy explained.

"Do you mind if I ask what happened?" Jack asked. "Between you and your wife."

Randy looked at him as if deep in thought. "She says it's because of what happened with the Bartletts. But I have to believe there's more to it than that."

"The Bartletts?" Shaun interjected. "As in Dave and Michelle Bartlett?"

"You've met them?"

"I interviewed them," Shaun confirmed.

"They're part of the reason I'm moving."

"What happened with them?" Jack asked. "That had your wife so upset?"

"How is all this relevant to Sharon being killed?" Randy asked.

"Dave Bartlett didn't come across as a fan of the chief," Shaun said. "So, everything we can learn will help us with the case."

"I could see him doing something like this." Randy looked down at his hands. "Fine. If you talked to them, they probably told you about the cat."

"They did," Shaun nodded. "Your wife accused Dave of killing it."

"We were sure he had," Randy said. "And I might have convinced Sam that it was him."

"You were the reason Sam suspected Dave?" Jack asked.

"Well, I was sure he did it," Randy said. "The man hates cats. Sam's in particular. So I told her I suspected Dave and she ran with it."

"Then what?"

"Well Sam wanted Sharon to prove that he did it, you know," Randy explained. "She was a detective after all."

"How did that go?" Jack asked.

"Well, instead of proving Dave did it," Randy whined, "she proved he didn't."

"That must have been awkward," Jack raised an eyebrow.

"Any shred of friendship we may have had was gone," Randy nodded.

"How does that lead to Sam blaming you?"

"You know," Randy said. "Sam was mad at me for convincing her that Dave was guilty. Like she wasn't thinking it before I said it out loud."

"The Bartletts said your wife left you shortly after that," Shaun said.

"She said she was too embarrassed to live there anymore," Randy said. "So she moved out and filed for divorce."

"Seems harsh," Jack said.

"You're telling me." Randy narrowed his eyes. "She ruined our entire future over a stupid cat."

He sat silent for a moment; his eyes focused on a distant spot.

"You said Sam and Sharon were friends," Jack said. "Would Sam know about the Hutchins' relationship with one another?"

"Probably," Randy looked down. "You'd have to ask her."

"We'll need her contact information."

"Sure thing."

Jack looked at his notes. "So your company called you about the power outage?"

"That's right," Randy confirmed.

"The power came back on without you," Jack commented.

"They must have called someone else out when I didn't get there," Randy said. "I'll probably get reamed for that."

"Could the killer have done something to cause it?"

"The outage?" Randy smirked. "Not likely."

"But possible?"

"Maybe," Randy shrugged. "Listen. I really need to get to work."

"Okay," Jack stood. "But we may have more questions. And don't forget to let us know if you move."

"I will."

Randy showed the men out of his home, locking the door behind them, and jogging to his truck. He was making his way down the street by the time the detectives reached the road.

10

The detectives made their way across the street to the house directly across from Randy Keyes' residence. The two of them followed the driveway to the sidewalk and up to the door. Standing side by side, Shaun reached out and pressed the doorbell. Almost immediately they were greeted by a child wailing and a woman's groan.

"Well, you're in trouble," Jack grimaced.

"Me?"

"You're closest to the bell." Jack pointed.

The door opened and a very tired-looking twenty-something woman stood on the other side of the storm door with an infant cradled in her arms.

"What?" she snapped, causing the child to up its volume. The woman was startled by her own reaction. She started bouncing the baby. "I'm so sorry."

Jack wasn't sure if she was apologizing to them or her baby. "Sorry to bother you. Detectives Mallory and Travis. We are questioning neighbors about the incident this morning. We'll try to keep it brief."

"What incident?" She looked from one detective to the other, never missing a bounce. "Did you say detectives?"

"You didn't notice the activity across the street?" Shaun gestured toward the chief's house.

"Honestly?" The woman looked down at the baby and tried making faces as she spoke in a baby voice. "This one was up most of the night. My husband works second shift and I didn't want her to bother him. So we came down and fell asleep on the couch. The doorbell woke us up, didn't it?"

The baby smiled.

"Your husband is here?"

She looked up at the adults. "He's sleeping upstairs."

"Are you sure he's asleep?" Shaun's eyes raised to the second floor.

"He gets home at two in the morning." She looked down using the baby voice again. "So we know he's asleep, don't we? The man could sleep through a hurricane."

"We'll let him sleep." Jack leaned in and looked the baby in the face. "Cute kid."

"Thank you." The mother beamed. "We think she's perfect."

"You have every right to." Jack returned to his original position. "Could I have your name? And your husband's?"

"Trish Carmichael," the woman answered. "My husband is Perry."

"Thank you." Jack wrote in his notepad. "Are you familiar with the Hutchins family?"

"I'm sorry," the woman apologized. "We've only lived here a few months. Which ones are the Hutchins?"

Jack half turned and extended his arm in the direction of the chief's house. There was still a high presence of police out front.

"Oh, my." The woman looked concerned. "Is everything okay?"

"Do you know them?" Jack pressed.

"They've been so nice." Trish smiled. "The day after we moved in, she, I can't remember her name..."

"Sharon." Jack filled in the blank.

"That's right." The woman looked at her baby and made a big goofy face. It giggled in return. "She brought us a casserole. They're so nice. I hope they are alright."

"Unfortunately, Mrs. Hutchins was killed in her driveway this morning," Jack informed her. "We're hoping someone saw or heard something. It would have been ten or so minutes after the power went off."

"The power went off?" Trish was confused again.

Shaun turned away grinning. Jack gave him a stern look and the young detective composed himself.

"Okay." Jack redirected. "Let's try something else. Have you or your husband noticed anything in the past few days that wasn't the norm? Anyone out of place, or maybe cars on the street that weren't there before?"

"Now that you mention it, there was a car." The woman swung her arms and pointed with her elbow. "One day it was a couple of houses down in that direction. The next day we saw it a half a block in the other direction."

"Did you see anyone inside?" Shaun asked.

"No," she frowned. "I wasn't really looking."

"Do you know what kind of car it was?" Jack asked.

"Green."

"Green?"

"Yes," she grinned. "I don't know much about cars."

"Can you tell me if it had two doors or four?" Jack questioned.

"Four." The woman was proud. "I remember because I thought it would be nice for Andrea's car seat."

"How many times did you see it?"

"Just the two times."

"And when was that?"

"Two or three days ago," she searched her memory. "Three. I think. Sorry I'm not more help."

"You're doing fine," Jack assured her. "We'll let you go so you can try to get her back to sleep."

She grinned unconvincingly and shut the door. The detectives walked back to the street and turned to the next house.

"What did you think?" Jack asked.

"Not much information," Shaun said. "But that's the second mention of a green sedan."

11

The detectives' next stop was the house directly across the street from the chief's home. A couple of uniformed officers were searching the bushes at the front of the property, presumably looking for clues, maybe a weapon the killer discarded. The detectives exchanged greetings with them as they passed. The house was very well maintained, the yard immaculate. Jack had mowed lawns as a teen. He had never made a lawn look like this one.

To avoid waking another sleeping baby, they chose to knock on the large, ornate wooden door. They stood awkwardly on the porch waiting for someone to come to the door. After sufficient time had passed, Jack rang the doorbell, no longer caring about sleeping children.

Several more minutes passed and the men were debating whether they should move on when they heard the deadbolt slide. Another minute passed before the door swung inward in a steady motion. The man standing on the other side of the threshold was well past retirement. He stood about five and a half feet tall but was solidly built. On his right forearm was a marine corps tattoo, faded but unmistakable.

"What do you gentlemen need?" The man studied his visitors with narrowed eyes, his jaw set.

"Detectives Mallory and Travis," Jack introduced. "We need to ask you about the incident across the street this morning."

"The shooting." It wasn't a question.

"Yes, sir," Jack nodded.

"Come in." The man stepped to the side to allow them passage. He watched their every move and followed close behind after closing the door. "Take the first right."

They turned where the man directed them and entered a large family room that faced the front of the house. A woman about the same age as the man, but more frail sat in a glider next to the window. A floor lamp next to her illuminated the work she was doing with knitting needles and yarn. She looked up over her glasses when they entered the room and smiled broadly.

"Hello." She let her hands fall into her lap. "Marty, you didn't tell me we were having company."

"They aren't company, Betty," the man continued past the detectives and sat in the recliner next to her. "They're detectives."

"Detectives?" She raised her needles again and her hands went to work again. "Isn't that exciting?"

"Marty and Betty," Jack said. "Can I get your last name?"

"Martin Tripp." The man sat rigidly on the edge of the seat. "She's Betty Shuster."

"Sorry," Jack apologized. "I assumed you were married. How long have you been together?"

"Fifty-six years this spring." He sounded like he was reporting to duty.

"You can take the man out of the marines." Betty did not look up from what she was doing. "But you can't take the marine out of the man."

"Why would you want to?" Marty asked.

"I wouldn't, dear," she grinned.

"Fifty-six years?" Shaun was impressed. "Why didn't you marry?"

Marty crossed his arms, furrowed his brow, and turned to the woman sitting next to him. She pursed her lips and let her hands fall into her lap again. She gave the man a quick glance before turning back to the detectives.

"When we met," Betty began, "we were eighteen and twenty years old. Marty was a beautiful specimen of a man, dressed out in his marine uniform." She closed her eyes and smiled softly while thinking back. "And he picked me out of all the girls who were at the dance. It was wonderful. And after that we were inseparable. Until he shipped out."

"I picked her because she was the best-looking girl I had ever seen," Marty added. "And we clicked like I never dreamed I could."

"Okay." Shaun looked from one to the other. "That doesn't explain why you never married."

"Tell them why we never married, Betty." The man became rigid again.

"Like I said," she continued. "Inseparable until he shipped out."

"What did you say to me that day?"

"I said I would never marry a marine," she said.

"That's what she said," Marty said.

"When he came back," she said, "I was waiting for him. And you know what he did?"

"What?" Shaun asked.

"I took her home and told her she was living with me from that day forward." Marty smiled. "That's what I did."

"And that's what I did." Betty started knitting again. "And the man never asked me to marry him. Fifty-six years."

"Fifty-six years," Marty repeated.

"Congratulations," Jack said. "Can we ask you some questions about this morning?"

"Ask away." Marty relaxed slightly.

"Were either of you up when you lost power?"

"Sure thing." He stiffened again. "We both were."

"And what were you doing when the lights went out?"

"I was sitting on the deck," Marty responded, "drinking my coffee."

"And you, Ma'am?"

"I was right here." She held up her work. "Knitting."

"What did you do after the power went off?" Jack asked.

"I can't knit when I can't see." Betty turned her attention back to her knitting as if saying the word reminded her that it was what she was doing. "I could only sit here in the dark."

"I understand," Jack sympathized.

"I was outside and saw it was the entire neighborhood," Marty said. "I just kept drinking my coffee. That is until the gunshot."

"You heard a gunshot?"

"A good fifteen, twenty-minutes after the lights went off," Marty reported.

"You're sure it was a gunshot." Jack knew it was, but wanted to be sure the man was a good witness.

"I was in the marines, son," Marty lowered his voice. "I know a gunshot when I hear one."

"Very good," Jack said. "I had to be sure."

"I heard it too," Betty looked up. "Or at least I heard something. It made me look outside."

"Did you see anything?" Shaun asked.

She directed her gaze to him. "Young man, I'm knitting a sweater and I think it'll be just your size. Would you like to have it when I'm done?"

"Betty, stop flirting with the detective and answer his question," Marty grumbled.

"I'm a single woman," Betty grinned, mischievously. "If you didn't want me flirting, you should have married me."

"Bah."

"Did you see anything, Ms. Shuster?" Jack asked.

"I saw someone across the street." She returned to her knitting.

"You saw someone?" Jack's eyebrows raised. "What can you tell me about them?"

"Not much," she said. "It was dark. They were wearing dark clothes. I couldn't even tell if it was a man or a woman."

"Tall or short?"

"Tall," she answered quickly. "Maybe."

"Thin or heavy set?"

"I would say thin," she said. "But it was dark. I can't be sure."

"That's okay." Jack gave her a faint smile. "You've done well."

"Oh, my, where are my manners?" Betty set her knitting on the end table next to her and stood. "Would you gentleman like some coffee?"

"We're good, thank you," Jack answered for them both. "What can you tell me about the Hutchins family?"

"Reggie keeps a very nice yard." Marty sat straighter. "Their son, what's his name?"

"Brian, dear."

"That's right." Marty snapped his fingers. "Brian. He used to mow our lawn. Did a nice job. His father taught him well. Unfortunately, he has gotten too busy with school, sports, and girls."

"What about Reggie and Sharon?" Jack asked. "How was their relationship?"

"Good people," Marty offered.

"They were always so sweet on one another," Betty answered. "Always smiling. Unless they were fighting. You could always tell when they were fighting."

"How so?" Jack asked.

"When they were fighting, there were no smiles," Betty elaborated. "You could see the tension in their bodies, especially their faces."

"Did they fight often?" Shaun asked.

"No." She shook her head. "Not often."

"Anything recently?" Jack focused on the woman who obviously watched the neighborhood from her window.

"A few months ago they had a really bad one." Betty leaned forward and whispered as if someone might overhear. "Reggie moved out for a couple of months."

"That was almost a year ago, Betty," Marty corrected. "And they worked it out. Reginald came home and life went on."

"Do you have any idea what the fight was about?" Jack directed the question to Betty.

"Sex or money," Marty answered. "It's always about sex or money."

"You don't know that, dear."

"I do know that." Marty stood. "Hey. You guys have been asking a lot of questions about the Hutchins. Is everything alright over there? A gunshot can't be good."

"Sharon Hutchins was killed," Shaun informed them.

"No." Betty raised a hand to her face. "It's just not safe anywhere. Not even your own home."

"She was in her driveway."

"And you think Reggie did it." More a statement than a question, Marty looked from detective to detective. "I doubt that."

"Why is that?" Jack asked.

"Because he's a good man." The tone Marty took seemed to dare them to challenge him. "Good men don't kill their wives."

"Although the husband is always a suspect," Jack said, "we are a long way from making him our sole subject of investigation."

"I hope you catch whoever did it." Betty was working on her knitting again.

"We will."

"It won't be Reggie," Marty assured them. "I've known the man twenty years. I think I'd know if he were capable of murder."

"We should be going." Jack decided it was a good time to end the interview.

The senior detective thanked the couple for their time, gave them a card, and led the way as the detectives left the home. Marty was close on their heels, maybe to be sure they left. Once they were out the door, the homeowner shut it tight. They could hear the locks sliding into place.

Jack smiled. "Reminds me of my parents when they were that age."

"Really?" Shaun knew little about the other's private life.

"No." The senior detective turned on his partner. "How old do you think I am? My parents aren't retired, yet."

12

The detectives left the older couple's house and walked down the driveway toward the street. They reached the sidewalk just as a dark blue pickup truck drove into view, cruising down the street at a speed that was obviously over the limit. Humored by the audacity of the driver with so many police in the area, Jack watched him pull up to the curb and stop directly in front of the chief's house. The man behind the wheel opened his door, slid to the ground, and walked to the house, lifting the crime scene tape to clear his way. The two detectives exchanged a look.

"Well, isn't that interesting?" Jack raised an eyebrow. "You go on. I think I'll go see who our visitor is."

Shaun acknowledged his partner and, with a last glance at the man who was entering the Hutchins' home, continued to the next house on the street. He arrived at the door and pressed the bell. He waited long enough for someone to get to the door and rang it again. Shifting his weight from leg to leg, he tried to look through the frosted glass in the door. There was no sign of movement inside.

With a heavy sigh, he spun around to make his retreat. He had only taken a few steps when a minivan pulled into the driveway, rolling up to and inside the garage. Once inside, the door lowered back down until it was closed. The detective returned to his position on the front porch, waiting for what he felt was long enough for the driver to get inside the home and rang the bell for a third time.

This time, within a few minutes, the door opened and a woman in her early thirties greeted him. After a quick introduction, she invited him into the house where they would be more comfortable.

"What is this about?" She led the way into the kitchen where she offered him a chair at the table.

Shaun sat, noting the dirty dishes stacked neatly beside the sink. "Can I get your name?"

"Julia Pollard."

"Thank you," Shaun said. "We're canvassing the neighborhood about the incident this morning."

"Incident?" Confusion covered her face. "What happened?"

"Shortly after the power went out..."

"I didn't know the power went out," she interrupted. "When was that?"

"About six, six-fifteen," Shaun said.

"That explains it," she nodded, knowingly. "The kids spent the night with their grandparents last night. I left the house at six to go pick them up so I could make sure they got to school on time. I must have gotten out just before it happened."

"Must have," Shaun agreed. "You didn't happen to see anyone as you left?"

"No. I don't think so." She appeared to be searching her memory. "What was it that happened?"

"Your neighbor, Sharon Hutchins, was shot and killed in her driveway this morning," Shaun informed her.

"Oh, my God, not Sharon," she exclaimed. "Did you get the shooter? Should I be worried? I always thought this was a safe neighborhood."

"We haven't apprehended the killer yet," Shaun answered.

The woman sighed heavily and looked around the living room with a scattering of books, toys, and sports equipment. "I love the schools here. But should I move? I can't stand the idea of living in a violent neighborhood. I need my kids and me to be safe. It's just us. What should I do? Do you know a safe place to live?"

"This is generally a very safe neighborhood," Shaun offered. "I would consider this to be an isolated incident. But keep your eyes open and be diligent about keeping the doors locked."

"Great," she sighed again. "The kids never lock the doors."

"Are you familiar with the Hutchins family?" Shaun tried to redirect the conversation.

"It's so sad about Sharon," the woman said. "Why would anyone want to harm her? She's such a lovely person. She was so supportive when I went through my divorce. My husband was, well, not a nice person. He used to hit me and verbally abuse me and the kids. Sharon gave me the courage to get out of that situation. And when he would come by and harass me, she put a stop to it. Oh, God. You don't think he did it? Is it my fault she's dead? Will he come for me next?"

"Why don't you give me his name," Shaun suggested. "I can follow up."

"Dan," she blurted. "Dan Pollard."

"And you think he might be capable of doing something like this?" Shaun wrote in his notepad.

"Like I said, he used to hit me," she said. "He wasn't happy about the divorce, or the restraining order Sharon helped me get. He told me more than once he would kill me. So, yeah, I think he's capable."

13

J ack considered walking right into the Hutchins' home as their visitor had done but decided to show the respect Sharon deserved to her family. He knocked loudly and stepped back to wait. Seeming to take too long for someone to answer, Jack was reconsidering his decision not to barge in, when Reginald opened the door with the look of a man who had just lost his best friend, and rightfully so.

"Detective?"

"Mr. Hutchins," Jack shifted to one side. "Can you tell me who drives that truck? He crossed the perimeter without authorization."

"He did?" Reggie glanced over his shoulder. "I'm sorry about that. He's my best friend. We grew up together, so he's like family. I called to tell him what happened and he insisted on coming over."

"And his name?"

"Logan," Reggie answered. "Logan Carr."

"I'm going to need to speak to Mr. Carr." Jack stepped past the man and walked toward the voices he heard. In the family room, Brian and another man, presumably Logan Carr, were sitting on the sofa. Logan was talking to the boy who did not acknowledge him in any way.

"Logan." Reggie crossed the room to stand closer to his son and friend. "This detective would like to talk to you."

"Me?" Logan turned in his seat to face Jack. He was a thin man with curly hair and round glasses. "Why would you possibly want to talk to me?"

"Come with me, sir." Jack gestured for the man to follow.

Logan stood, brushed the wrinkles from his pants, and walked after the detective. They came to a stop next to a couple of chairs in Reggie's home office where they faced one another.

"Do I need a lawyer?"

"Have you done something wrong?" Jack asked.

"No."

"Then you shouldn't need a lawyer."

"I guess I'm going to trust you." The man glanced toward the family room. "You have some questions?"

"You got here pretty fast," Jack commented.

"That's not a question," Logan said. "But, yeah, I don't live very far away."

"How did you know to come?"

"Reggie called me."

"What time was that?"

Logan looked at his watch. "Twenty minutes ago, maybe."

The detective jotted down the time, noting that it was about the time he finished his interview with the new widower. "And you came right over?"

"I made a couple of calls first."

"Calls?"

"I called my work to let them know I was going to be taking a personal day," Logan elaborated.

"What kind of work do you do?"

"I'm a civil engineer," Logan said. "I specialize in roads and bridges."

"You design them?"

"Design, oversee their construction," Logan added. "Schedule maintenance and repairs."

Jack wrote everything down. "You said calls. Who else did you call?"

"I called my wife to let her know what happened," Logan sighed. "She and Sharon were friends."

"You called your wife?" Jack narrowed his eyes. "Where was she?"

"Work," Logan said. "Her day starts pretty early."

"What does she do?"

"She's an OR nurse," Logan answered.

"And you thought a phone call was the best way to tell her that her friend had been killed?"

"Not my finest moment, I'll admit." Logan shrugged.

"How long have you known Mr. Hutchins?" Jack knew what Reggie had told him.

"I don't know." Logan drifted into thought. "Since we were kids."

"And Mrs. Hutchins?"

"I met her when we were in college," he said. "I actually dated her first. But we didn't click. When she met Reggie, that was it. I wasn't getting in their way."

"She dumped you for him?"

"I wouldn't say dumped," Logan defended. "Like I said, we didn't click. And it was easy to see they did. So, I backed off and let them happen."

"No hard feelings?"

"Of course not."

"And how was your relationship with Sharon?" Jack asked.

"Well," Logan hesitated. "I mean ..."

"Listen," Jack leaned. "If your relationship wasn't the best, tell me. If you lie and I find out later, you could end up at the top of the suspect list."

"Okay, but understand, we used to be good," Logan explained. "Lately not so much."

"And why is that?"

"Sharon found out I was cheating on Alecia." Logan looked down at the floor.

"Alecia's your wife?"

"Yes."

"And Sharon told her you were cheating on her?"

"No." Logan glanced at the door. "But she wanted me to tell her."

"And have you?"

"Told my wife?"

"Yes." Jack nodded. "Have you told your wife?"

"Not yet."

"And did Sharon say she was going to tell Alecia if you didn't?"

"Yes, but ..."

"So you have a motive," Jack stated.

"Motive?" Logan shook his head and waved his hands. "No. No motive."

"You don't want your wife to know that you cheated on her," Jack said. "Sharon was going to tell her. Now Sharon is dead and can't tell your wife. That's what we call motive."

"I wouldn't hurt Sharon," Logan insisted. "She's my best friend's wife. I was going to tell Alecia. It's just never a good time to blow up your life, you know."

"That may be true," Jack said. "But I have no way to verify that."

"Ask Reggie." Logan snapped his fingers. "He knew about it. Sharon told him. He talked to me. He knows I'm planning to tell Alecia."

"You and Mr. Hutchins have a good relationship?"

"As well as anyone, I would say." Logan crossed his arms.

"Tell me about the relationship between him and Sharon." Jack leaned into the desk that occupied a large portion of the room.

"You can't think Reggie had something to do with this," the man scoffed. "He's not that type of man, detective."

"Tell me about their relationship," Jack insisted. "The ups and the downs. I was told they separated for a while."

"Well, yeah," Logan sighed. "That happened. But they're well past that."

"What was the issue?" Jack asked. "What did they need to get past?"

"It was a long time ago."

"About a year," Jack said.

"That's right."

"What happened?"

"That's just it," Logan whined. "It was so hypocritical."

"What do you mean?"

"She acted like I did something so awful," Logan looked at the detective with a stern expression. "But while they were separated, she cheated on him."

"And how do you know that?"

"Reggie told me."

"Do you know how he found out?"

"Apparently," he said. "While they were working through things, she admitted it to him."

"And how did Reggie take it?"

"Not well," Logan confessed. "But they still got back together, and have been stronger ever since."

14

Detective Mallory followed Logan back to the main room where Reginald and son sat side by side with almost identical expressions of woe. The man Jack had just interviewed walked into the room personifying confidence that everyone could feel.

He crossed the area rug and sat in a chair that matched the sofa and turned to his friend. He worked his jaw a couple of times, then, in what Jack felt was the wisest thing the man had done, he closed his mouth, inhaled deeply through his nose, sat back in the soft inviting cushions, and let them hug him.

"Mr. Hutchins," Jack spoke just loud enough to be heard.

The father shifted his chin in the detective's direction.

"We need to talk."

"We already talked." His voice was drained.

"I have a few more questions."

"Then ask them." Reggie sat back into the cushion of the sofa trying to vanish.

"I would rather not ask in front of the kid." Jack looked at the boy who was suddenly looking at him, a silent protest to being called a kid.

Reggie stared up at the detective. With a glance at his son, he pulled himself to his feet and followed Jack to the next room.

"What could you possibly ask that you couldn't say in front of Brian?" Reggie started in as soon as they cleared the doorway.

"Why didn't you tell me you and your wife were separated recently?" Jack asked.

"That was almost a year ago," Reggie argued. "Not recently."

"And the fact that Sharon cheated on you?"

"Also, almost a year ago." Reggie shifted uncomfortably. "It honestly didn't cross my mind."

"When I asked about the relationship between the two of you," Jack crossed his arms. "Infidelity and separation didn't cross your mind?"

"We had moved on," Reggie explained. "We got back together, worked through our problems, and forgave."

"Did she have reason to forgive you?" Jack pressed. "Were you unfaithful as well?"

Reggie's shoulders sagged. "My indiscretions were not with women. They were financial. I had gambled away our savings. Brian's college fund. All gone. So, yes, she had reason to forgive me."

"That slip your mind as well?"

"Detective," Reggie became direct. "We weren't perfect people. We didn't have the perfect marriage. But we loved one another. And we loved our son. We wouldn't do anything to damage that."

"Is there anything else that slipped your mind?" Jack asked. "Anything that I might dig up that will make you look even more guilty? Secret bank accounts? Large insurance policies that you took out last week?"

"No." Reggie's face stiffened. "Nothing."

"What can you tell me about the man your wife had the affair with?"

"The man?" Reggie frowned. "I don't know anything about him."

"Nothing?"

"I never asked for his name," Reggie said. "You think I told her to invite him over for dinner? I didn't know who it was and I don't want to. Why does it matter anyway?"

"If he thought Sharon was the one for him and she suddenly called it off," Jack tilted his head. "Maybe he held a 'If I can't have her nobody can' kind of grudge."

"You think this guy waited a year to get revenge?"

"Unless they were still seeing each other," Jack suggested. "Is it possible they kept things going behind your back?"

"No."

"You were awfully quick to answer," Jack said. "Take a minute to think. Was she working late more than normal? Did she have late meetings she couldn't get out of?"

"No," Reggie was adamant. "Now, if you'll excuse me, my son and I are trying to grieve."

15

etectives Mallory and Travis arrived at the department and Jack headed straight for the breakroom looking for a fresh cup of coffee. He was disappointed to find an empty pot sitting on the hot warming plate. With a few choice words for his co-workers, though they were not in the room, he brewed a new pot and leaned against the counter waiting for it to finish. As he was pouring the liquid caffeine into his mug, Shaun appeared in the doorway.

"They rushed the crime scene photos." He held up a manilla folder.

"Really?" Jack pushed off the counter, cup in hand. "I can't tell you how many times they've told me they can't do rush jobs."

The two men walked through the maze of desks until they reached their own. The detective who sat across from Jack for fifteen years had retired and Jack commandeered the location for his young partner. They settled in and Jack spread the photos out across his desk so he could study them for anything the camera might have captured that he hadn't seen.

"What did you learn at that last house?" Jack didn't look up.

"Single mother," Shaun reported. "Sharon helped her with the restraining order against the ex-husband. The man had threatened the wife's life. She believes he might be capable of doing this."

"Should we be worried about the woman?" Jack frowned.

"I suggested she take the kids somewhere safe for a while."

"Good." Jack took a drink of coffee. "Be sure we know where she is. I assume you got a name."

"Dan Pollard."

"Dan Pollard," Jack repeated. "Why do I know that name?"

"Friend of yours?"

"Are you saying I can't remember my friends' names?" Jack turned to him. "That's the second time you suggested I was getting old."

"No." Shaun put up his hands as a shield. "I said no such thing."

Jack set his computer's keyboard on top of the photos and started typing. He logged into the system and did a search for the man's name. It only took a moment to provide a result. "I remember him."

"So, you do know him?"

"I don't know him," Jack corrected. "We met when I arrested him."

"He killed someone?"

"I was off duty at a bar with Maureen." He sat back in his chair. "This guy was drunk and belligerent. Then he starts trying to hit on this woman who was there with her husband. Needless to say, the husband wasn't too happy. So Dan here started poking him in the chest, while loudly pointing out his shortcomings. The wife was trying to calm her husband down when the bouncer showed up. Dan took a swing at the bouncer, which would have been funny, but when the bouncer ducked, the punch landed in the woman's face. I thought the husband was going to kill him, but the woman punched him back hard enough to stun him. That's when I stepped in and put him in cuffs."

"When was that?" Shaun pulled his keyboard closer.

"Three months ago, maybe."

Shaun typed for a minute. "That's about the time Chief Hutchins helped her get a restraining order."

"So, either he got upset after the arrest and took it out on his ex," Jack said. "Or the restraining order sent him to the bar, where he hit on the woman who ultimately decked him."

"Rejected by his wife, the woman in the bar, and the chief." Shaun rocked back in his chair. "Sounds like he could be our man."

"He's definitely at the top of our suspect list." Jack nodded. "Let's get a conference room and a whiteboard."

"How do we do that, now?" Shaun gestured toward Sharon's empty office. "She always signed off on rooms."

"You think someone's going to stop us?"

"Well . . ., no."

"Go get a whiteboard and meet me in room B." Jack stood and started gathering all the photos and files into a single pile. "And be sure you get markers."

"One time," Shaun shook his head. "I forgot them one time."

"That's because I have reminded you every time since."

"Whatever." Shaun moved off in the direction of the storeroom.

Jack carried his bounty to the conference room and began spreading everything out on the large table in its center. He was just finishing when his partner wheeled in the whiteboard and parked it against the wall of windows that separated the room from the common area.

Jack took a headshot of Dan Pollard that he had printed from the man's DMV record and taped it at the top of the board. Underneath he wrote the man's name. He repeated the process with a photo of Reginald Hutchins. And again for Dave Bartlett, the neighbor with the motorcycle. Last, he added a photo of Randy Keyes.

"We have four suspects and we haven't even left the neighborhood," Shaun commented.

Jack turned his attention to the crime scene photos. "If I'm right, he shot her in the back with her own gun."

"I hope you're not right." Shaun grimaced.

"She would never turn her back on someone she didn't trust." Jack scanned each photo. "So she either trusted him, or he came at her from behind."

"Makes sense."

"There aren't a lot of places for someone to hide." Jack pointed at pictures of the surrounding area. "The bushes on the side of the house. The trees in each yard, although none are really big enough to hide behind."

"But it was dark," Shaun interjected. "Power was out, so no lights. If she wasn't looking for trouble, she might not have noticed someone sticking out around a tree."

"Randy Keyes' truck was parked at the end of his driveway," Jack remembered.

"It would be a good place to hide." Shaun pointed to a photo of the neighbor's house.

Jack pulled the shot of the electrician's house to the front and tapped on the truck. "So our killer may have been hiding behind it, waiting for Sharon to come out."

"That'd be risky, wouldn't it?" Shaun asked. "I mean, the power went out. Wouldn't you expect an electrician to respond?"

"True." Jack nodded. "Unless he didn't know the guy was an electrician."

"Wouldn't it be on the side of the truck?"

"It was dark. And some companies have their name without 'electrician' standing out," Jack said. "We should check that."

"If Randy had come out first," Shaun sighed. "The killer may have run away and we wouldn't be here right now."

"Or we might have two homicides instead of one," Jack countered. "Unless the electrician did it. Then he would know he was safe to hide there."

They stood silent for a few minutes.

"Premeditated or opportunity?" Jack pondered.

"At that hour of the morning?" Shaun said. "Premeditated for sure."

"Then why didn't he bring a weapon of his own?" Jack challenged. "Seems pretty presumptuous to think you can disarm a decorated, veteran cop and use their weapon on them."

"Assuming she was killed with her own weapon," Shaun said. "Maybe the original plan wasn't to kill her."

"So, you show up early in the morning to what?" Jack crossed his arms. "Talk?"

"To confront her," Shaun thought aloud. "Maybe to intimidate her and it didn't go as planned."

Jack shook his head. "Then you're suggesting she turned her back on an aggressor, which we know she wouldn't do. Unless it was someone she knew."

"Someone she trusted," Shaun said.

"If it was someone she trusted," Jack started. "That would be her husband, her son, friends, some neighbors."

"Cops," Shaun added.

Jack gave his partner a side glance. "Cops?"

"A cop would know not to use his assigned weapon or ballistics would come back to him."

"A cop bad enough to kill their chief is going to have a throwaway gun," Jack dismissed the idea. "Something they pulled off a suspect and never reported. Or maybe taken from the evidence room."

"True." Shaun took a long. "The husband is the most obvious choice."

"She cheated on him," Jack thought aloud. "According to Reginald, they reconciled and moved on. What if the man she was cheating with wasn't ready to move on?"

"Hasn't it been a year?"

"The husband thinks so," Jack confirmed. "But what if she didn't quite end it until more recently?"

"You think she confessed she had an affair?" Shaun asked. "Then kept having it?"

"I don't know," Jack admitted. "But if she did and then finally broke it off, the man may not have taken it well."

"And he may have been there to try to win her back," Shaun concluded.

"But would she turn her back on him?" Jack asked.

"If he's trying to win her back, she might not consider him a physical threat." Shaun snapped his fingers. "Maybe the green sedan some of the residents have been seeing was him stalking her."

"Good thinking." Jack moved to the whiteboard and drew a question mark in the space next to Dan Pollard's photo, writing the word 'affair' below it. "We need to find out who he is and what he drives."

"The husband didn't tell you?"

"Claims he doesn't know who it was." Jack could not hide the skepticism in his voice.

"You're not buying it?" Shaun asked.

"Your wife sleeps with another man and you don't want to know who it was?" Jack shook his head. "If he told me it was no one he knew, I might buy it. But he said he never asked."

"That is hard to believe," Shaun agreed. "Human nature would be to want to know."

"Would you want to know?" Jack looked at his partner.

"Me?" Shaun hesitated. "I don't know that I would want to know. But I think I would ask."

"And if you knew him?"

"I don't know," Shaun shrugged. "I suppose I would want to kill him."

"Exactly." Jack's eyebrow rose. "When we find out who this guy is, we need to see if he's married. We may have to add the wife to the list of suspects."

Shaun pulled out his notepad and made a note to check it out. As he slid the book back into his pocket, he took a deep breath and let it out slowly, turning his head to the chief's office. "I can't believe she's gone."

"She was a good chief," Jack said. "And it's our job to find who did this and bring them to justice."

"What if it was just a random act?" Shaun faced his partner. "What if we never figure out who did it?"

"We'll worry about that when we run out of suspects." Jack pointed to the whiteboard. "Right now we have five and the list will grow. Now who else would she turn her back on?"

"Besides her son?" Shaun pursed his lips. "People she would think of as friends. What about Reginald's friend? The one in the truck."

"Logan Carr." Jack turned to the board and wrote the name. "He's Reginald's best friend, the friend he called when this happened. And Sharon did threaten to expose his affair."

"Or maybe he did it for Reginald," Shaun suggested.

"If he did," Jack crossed his arms. "Did he act alone, to kill his best friend's cheating wife? Or did Reginald ask him to do it?"

"Can't rule out either one."

"Anyone else?"

"A neighbor maybe," Shaun offered. "But besides Dave Bartlett, they all seemed to like her."

"Which brings us to other possibilities." Jack shifted gears. "She was supposed to testify in court today and she had a press conference scheduled to announce a new initiative to get tough on violent crime. We need to talk to whomever she was testifying against and also find out who had the most to lose with the new initiative."

"You mean criminals?"

"I mean, was this new plan targeting anyone in particular?" Jack said. "She was Homicide. Most of our cases are individuals. Was she going after a violent gang, or criminal organization, using this initiative as a broad approach to a single objective?"

"You think she was targeting a specific group," Shaun said, "who found out and took her out before she could unveil her plan?"

"I think it's a possibility," Jack confirmed. "So we look into it."

"Understood."

"I will look into the court testimony angle." Jack moved across the room. "I need you to find out who she may have spoken to about this initiative. Make an appointment to talk to the Chief of Ds. Find out what he knows about it."

"Me?" Shaun put a hand to his chest. "Shouldn't you be the one to talk to him?"

"Just because he assigned me to the case doesn't mean he likes me." Jack stood in the doorway. "He'll talk to you. But remember he's a politician. He'll only tell you what he thinks you need to know. So pay as much attention to what he doesn't say as you do to what he says."

"I still think you would be the better choice," Shaun protested.

"Noted." Jack dismissed the thought. "But I have faith in you. Besides, I'm not asking."

16

Because Chief Hutchins wanted to keep her office in the department she commanded, her assistant was on another floor. As Detective Travis stood in front of the young woman's desk, watching her field phone call after phone call while tears rolled down her cheeks, he struggled to remember her name.

"I can't confirm anything." She spoke into the phone with adamancy, her eyes focused on the detective standing before her. "All inquiries should be directed to public relations. No. I can't transfer you."

The assistant hung up and answered the next call, giving almost the exact same response. After the fourth or fifth time, she hung up the phone and stared at the row of glowing lights indicating incoming calls.

"Ignore them for a while," Shaun suggested.

She gave a half grin, forsaken by the sadness in her eyes. "Why would they kill her? She was such a good boss."

"We're going to find out," Shaun assured her. "That's why I'm here, actually."

"You think I ..."

"No." Shaun raised his hands to wave off any suggestion of her involvement. "I just need some information."

The woman's shoulders dropped in relief, her attention drawn briefly to the blinking lights on the phone.

"Chief Hutchins was going to hold a press conference today." Shaun distracted her.

"Yes," she confirmed. "At three."

"Can you," Shaun stopped himself. "I'm sorry, I've forgotten your name."

"Sheila," she said.

"Okay, Sheila," Shaun smiled. "Can you tell me what she was going to say at the conference?"

"She was going to announce a new initiative to crack down on violent crime," Sheila told him what he already knew.

"Do you know any details about the initiative?" Shaun asked.

"Sorry." She shook her head. "She typed her own speech."

"She didn't give you any indication as to what she might be planning to say?"

"Not at all."

"Was that normal?"

"It wasn't the first time," Sheila said. "But it wasn't the norm. Especially on something like this."

"A press conference?"

"Yes," Sheila said. "Usually, she would have me type it up and proofread it."

"So if you didn't proofread it," Shaun asked. "Is there someone else she might have asked to do it?"

"Not that I know of," she said. "Sorry I'm not more help."

"That's okay." Shaun straightened. "Do you know how I would go about getting a meeting with the Chief of Ds?"

"That I can help you with." Sheila picked up her phone and with quick hand movements hung up on whoever was calling in and immediately pressed the button on that line to establish a connection. She entered the four-digit number for whom she was calling. It connected and was answered in fast succession. "Bonnie. It's Sheila. Thank you. I will miss her. She was so great. But anyway, I have one of the detectives here who is investigating her murder. No. The other one. Yeah. He needs to talk to Chief Grimes. I would think as soon as possible."

Sheila put her hand over the receiver. "She's checking."

"Thanks." Shaun nodded.

"Oh, she says he'll see you now," Sheila said. "Thanks, Bonnie."

She set down the phone.

"Thanks again."

"No problem," Sheila replied. "Do you know the way?"

"Fifth floor?"

"Well, yes," she said. "But do you know where to go once you get there?"

"I figured I'd just ask." Shaun shrugged.

Sheila looked down at the row of blinking lights, then stood. "Come on. I'll take you. I want to see Bonnie anyway."

Shaun fell in behind the woman who had more pep in her step than her demeanor suggested she would. She reached the elevator a good four to five strides ahead of the detective. Having pushed the button upon arrival, the doors were opening by the time Shaun joined her. Together they entered the car and Sheila pushed the five. When the doors closed, isolating them, the woman turned to him.

"How long have you been a detective?"

"A couple of years."

"You've been on some pretty important cases though, haven't you?"

"A benefit of being Jack Mallory's partner, I guess." Shaun watched the numbers above as they changed. They arrived at the fifth floor rather quickly. The car stopped and the doors started to open. "This is us."

She gave him a brief smile and faced the opening, taking the lead again when they exited. It became apparent to Shaun that having Sheila guide him was a good idea. The maze of halls would have been difficult to navigate without knowing where he was going.

Sheila came to a stop at a desk behind which a woman, about the same age, sat. Bonnie rose to her feet and moved to give Shaun's chaperone a hug. The two of them embraced long enough that the detective felt uncomfortable.

"You need anything," Bonnie said. "You call."

"Thank you," Sheila stepped back and composed herself. "This is him."

"Detective Travis," Bonnie looked him in the eyes. "It'll be just a minute. He's finishing up something."

"No problem." Shaun stepped to a nearby wall where he stood at attention, with his hands locked behind his back.

The two women chatted for a few minutes. At one point, Bonnie glanced at her phone and then to the detective. "He's ready for you."

Shaun nodded and stepped to the door leading to the Chief of Detectives' office. He knocked and waited for permission to enter before continuing. The office was massive, larger than Shaun's first apartment, a studio downtown. The detective couldn't help but scan the room.

"Quite something isn't it?" Chief Grimes said.

"Sorry, sir." Shaun's face flushed red.

"Don't be." The chief pointed at one of the chairs across from him. "Personally, I think it's too much. But those who came before me were concerned about appearing important."

"Thank you, sir." Shaun settled into the chair, which was one of the more comfortable seats he had ever been in.

"You have any updates?"

"We have a few leads we're following," Shaun reported. "Nothing definitive, but we're just getting started."

"I understand you have some questions for me."

"I do." Shaun pulled out his notebook. "About the press conference Chief Hutchins was going to have today."

"What about it?"

"We understand that she was going to announce a new plan to reduce violent crime," Shaun said. "Primarily murders, I would assume, since she was homicide."

"She was," he confirmed.

"Can you give me the details of the plan?" Shaun asked. "We want to see if we can identify anyone who might not want the plan to go into effect. Someone who might kill to keep it from happening."

"First of all," Chief Grimes frowned. "The only people who would not want the plan to go into effect would be the killers in our city. And second, they would be very mistaken if they believed the death of Chief Hutchins would stop such a plan from rolling out."

"Any specific information would be helpful," Shaun said.

"Son, these announcements happen regularly in our business," Chief Grimes said. "There's no magical plan. There is just the threat of coming down harder on offenders and the promise to be more diligent. Nothing she was going to say was enough for someone to want to kill her. If it was, many more of us would have been targeted over the years."

"Understood."

"Do you have anything else?" The chief moved some papers on his desk making it clear to Shaun what answer he wanted. "Or are we finished here?"

"I guess that's it." Shaun stood. "Thank you for seeing me so fast."

"This case is important," the chief reasoned. "We need results and we need them quickly."

"Yes, sir."

"Make sure Detective Mallory understands," Chief Grimes said.

"He does, sir," Shaun assured him.

"Very well." The chief turned away. "Keep me updated."

Shaun was being dismissed. He showed himself out, where he found Sheila and Bonnie still deep in conversation. He nodded to them and retraced the route back to the elevators.

17

In the District Attorney's office, the assistant told Jack it would be a few minutes before the prosecutor would be available and directed him to a chair where he could wait. He was there to find out in what case Chief Hutchins was supposed to testify so he could determine if it had any bearing on the woman's death. The detective checked his watch regularly for nearly an hour before the DA appeared from nowhere, barked some orders to his staff, and vanished into his office.

Jack gave the assistant a look and the woman shrugged an apology. "He's not having a good day. I'll let him know you're here."

"I'll let him know." Jack stood and was through the door before the protesting woman could stop him.

The DA was on the phone when Jack barged into his office. "I said to cancel my meetings. Mallory? What do you think you're doing? Where's Bonnie?"

"Here, sir," the assistant called over the detective's shoulder. "I told him to wait, sir."

"I've waited an hour," Jack snapped. "I don't have time to wait any longer."

"I'll have to call you back," the DA said into the phone, dropping the receiver into its cradle. "Not everything is about you, detective. We are in a bit of a crisis, right now."

"Frankly, I don't care." Jack was direct.

"Excuse me?"

"Whatever your crisis is," Jack said. "My case takes priority."

"What case is that?"

"Are you serious?" Jack was dumbfounded.

The DA simply stared at him.

"Chief Hutchins?" Jack said.

"Hutchins?" The DA repeated. "Where is she? She didn't show up for court. I had to request an extension, so I could find her."

"She won't be testifying."

"Why not?" The DA raised his voice. "She knows how important this case is."

"She's dead." Jack was blunt.

"What?" The DA was stunned. "When?"

"This morning." Jack put his hands on his hips. "How is it you don't know this?"

"Well," the DA went on the defensive. "I was running late this morning and went straight from home to court, where I spent a good part of the morning arguing why I needed an extension to find my witness. So, I haven't heard much of anything. What happened anyway? Car accident?"

"Are you serious?" Jack looked at him as if he were crazy.

"What?"

"I'm a homicide detective," Jack said. "The chief was murdered."

"Murdered?" The DA made eye contact with his assistant, who nodded and stepped out of the office. "Someone killed her?"

"That's usually what it means when someone is murdered."

"I'm not in the mood for your attitude, detective." The DA's demeanor changed.

"And I don't have time for stupid questions," Jack matched his tone. "The chief was to testify this morning. I need to know what case it was."

"You think her murder is related to the trial?"

"The timing is too much of a coincidence not to look into the possibility," Jack said. "What case was it?"

"It's the Trey Levine case," the DA responded.

"Trey Levine?" Jack tried to recall the name. "I'm not familiar with that one."

"I don't doubt it." The DA sat back in his chair. "She was working narcotics at the time."

"So this is a drug case?"

"Drugs and murder," the DA clarified. "Trey Levine was an up-and-coming dealer who was managing to build a small empire. He was on an upward trajectory and getting himself on a lot of radars. And he was assigned to Hutchins and her partner."

The DA paused a moment before continuing. "They were collecting evidence and details, making a case against him."

"So, they were doing their jobs," Jack grumbled.

"They were." The DA nodded. "Problem was, they were talking to people in Levine's circle, visiting places he was known to frequent. Soon, they were on his radar as well. It became a classic game of cat and mouse between them. A lot of contention. Levine filed a complaint against them for harassment, if you can believe it. But Hutchins was relentless."

"I could see that in her personality." Jack remembered numerous occasions when the chief would hound him; for results, for answers, for paperwork. She did not let up until she got what she wanted.

"Anyway." The DA's voice became grave. "One night the detectives arranged a meeting with a possible witness, someone from Levine's crew. But when they arrived at the meeting spot, it was a setup. Hutchins was put in the hospital, shot three times. Her partner wasn't as lucky. He was hit twice, and both were fatal. He never had a chance."

"I had no idea." Jack was surprised to hear how close the chief had come to death before he had ever met her.

"It took her a month to recover and get out of the hospital," the DA continued. "The first thing she wanted to do once she was back on the job was to go after Levine. She saw him pull the trigger."

"So she became the witness in her partner's murder case," Jack summarized. "And if he tried to kill her once, what's to prevent him from trying again."

"Except he wasn't the triggerman this time," the DA said.

"How can you be sure?"

"He's still in lock-up." He grimaced. "He killed a cop. The judge ordered him held without bail."

"But he could still have arranged to have someone stop her from testifying," Jack argued.

"Without a doubt."

"I'm going to have to talk to him."

"I'll let them know you're coming," the DA offered. "I'm sure he'll want his lawyer there."

18

Detective Travis came out of his meeting with the Chief of Detectives feeling he had just wasted time he could have been using to investigate. Jack was out of the office, so Shaun decided to go through the threatening letters and phone messages Chief Hutchins had received over the past year. Having requested the records, at Jack's insistence, early that morning, the three boxes were already at the detective's desk. Shaun wondered how so many people could hate a woman they most likely had never met. He took the top off the first box.

Stacking the other two boxes on the floor next to him and placing the open box on top, he reached inside and pulled out a stack of letters with the envelopes they arrived in, paper-clipped to them. Taking the first letter, Shaun read its contents. Though the gist of the letter was aggressive, the threat was more to the tune of 'you should lose your job' than anything physical. The detective deemed it harmless and set it aside. The harmless pile grew as fast as the original stack shrank until one letter forced Shaun to create a second pile.

It was written as a rant of almost incoherent thought with no punctuation and multiple misspellings. The contents seemed to accuse the chief of taking part in the accident that killed the writer's wife, not because she was there, but because the man driving the other car was out on bail shortly after being arrested. The author was convinced that the chief had been the reason for his release. There was no evidence presented to support the accusation, but Shaun decided the second pile would be for those just crazy enough to be dangerous.

Shortly after that, Shaun found the first letter to create a third pile. The letter was written by an Ian Fielding, an inmate at a nearby prison. The detective read the pages that had no direct threat but contained several references that could be taken as threatening. There were mentions of her family and home. Shaun did a quick search and found that the man had served a five-year sentence for second-degree murder and was just recently released. The letter became the base of those Shaun deemed a high threat.

By the time Shaun had gotten to the bottom of the second box, nearly two hours had passed. The harmless pile towered over the others, with the crazy pile having only three and the certified threat pile still having just the one. Reading all of the comments from those who wished the chief harm was draining. Shaun rubbed his eyes and removed the top of the third box. This one did not contain letters, but transcripts of phone messages. Shaun pulled the entire stack out of the box and set it on one side of his desk. He stared at the papers for a second before standing and heading for the breakroom for a cup of coffee. His phone rang as he walked and he pulled it from his pocket and pressed it to his ear.

"Detective Travis." He entered the breakroom and grabbed a mug.

"Oh, detective, is it?" The familiar voice sang in his ear.

"Liza?" He smiled for the first time in hours. "It's so nice to hear your voice."

"Bad day?"

"You have no idea." He wasn't allowed to discuss the case. The news of the chief's killing had not yet been released.

"Well, I hope I can make it better." The enthusiasm in her voice was uplifting. "Do you know when you'll be off?"

Shaun filled the mug with coffee and added two spoons of sugar. Looking across the room to the stack of phone messages and knowing the chief's phone records waited as well, he had no idea how long it would take to finish. Adding to that the time needed to interview possible suspects and witnesses, he sighed a little louder than he intended.

"That doesn't sound good."

"It's not," he confessed. "The case I'm on is big. I don't know when I'll be getting home."

"I understand." Her positivity wasn't gone, but it was diminished. "I'll be happy to see you when I can."

"Same here." Shaun closed his eyes. "I can't wait."

He returned to his desk with a little more pep in his stride. Settling in, he started reading and was returned to the despair he felt before Liza's call.

19

The warden stood next to Jack as the detective checked his weapon with the guard who stood on the other side of bullet-proof glass. The uninterested man handed Jack a claim ticket like he had just dropped off dry cleaning. A buzz followed, indicating that the door next to him was unlocked for his entry. He pulled it open and stepped through with the warden close on his heels.

Jack had requested a list of the visitors that Trey Levine had for the past year and the warden was happy to provide it. The round man held out a printed document and Jack took it from him without losing stride. He scanned the document and stopped.

"His only visitor has been his lawyer?" Jack questioned the accuracy of what he was seeing.

"What can I say?" The warden spread his hands and shrugged. "He's not a likable guy."

"No family at all?"

"If they aren't on the list," the warden pointed at the paper in the detective's hand, "they didn't come see him."

According to what Jack had read, Trey Levine had his parents, three siblings, a wife, two children, and a mistress, all living within a ten-mile radius. The detective had a hard time believing that none of them came to see the man.

"Tell me about Levine." Jack fell into step next to the warden, who breathed hard as he made his way down the corridor to the next door.

The warden looked at the camera above them and waited for the familiar buzz so he could pull the door open. "What do you want to know? I mean, most everything is in his folder."

"I want to know what's not in the file." Jack had no trouble keeping pace with his guide. "What is he like? How does he get along with other prisoners? Where is he in the hierarchy?"

"Trey Levine is a nasty piece of work," the warden huffed. "As for how he gets along and his place in the prison. That's easy. No one likes him. Most of them are afraid of him. The rest just leave him alone because, well, like I said. They don't like him."

"Afraid of him?" Jack asked. "Why is that?"

"His cellmates always have problems." The warden said. "Two of them demanded they be reassigned within days of being placed with him. One in particular, was accident-prone. He kept ending up in the infirmary for injuries that he claimed were the result of falling. Once we moved him, the accidents stopped. Two died."

"So," Jack opened the folder. "You have him for two counts of murder?"

"Oh, no." The warden shook his head. "Neither happened in the cell. One was found in the showers. The other, in the laundry room."

"So you can't prove he was involved." Jack skimmed the pages.

"Exactly." The warden inhaled deeply as they came to the next door. "Witnesses placed him in nearly every block in the prison at the time of the killings."

"If they don't like him," Jack asked, "why cover for him?"

"They don't want to be next," the warden suggested.

"So you don't have proof he did anything," Jack mumbled.

"Everyone in the prison knows he did it." The warden raised his voice above the buzzer. "If he didn't do it. He arranged for it to be done. But as a detective, you know, knowing and proving are two different things."

"Very true."

"What's this about, anyway?" The warden stopped in front of a door and produced a key. The lock gave an audible click and the door swung inward smoothly.

"A case I'm working on." Inside the room was a metal table with a ring welded on top where prisoners could be handcuffed. There were two chairs on either side, facing the table. All of the chairs were bolted to the floor. "Where is he?"

"On his way." The warden leaned against the wall.

"And where is his attorney?" Jack's easy demeanor changed.

"He was notified," the warden shrugged. "Said he would be here."

Jack checked his watch. "Well, he's late."

"It's not like you gave much notice," the warden argued. "People have lives."

"I happen to know they were supposed to have court today." Jack leaned against the wall to the warden's right. "The man had nothing else scheduled, I'm sure."

The door they entered opened again and a briefcase entered the room followed by the suited, middle-aged man carrying it. Jack had seen the lawyer before but had never interacted with him. He also hadn't heard much about him, although what he had heard was not kind.

"Warden." The man nodded his greeting before turning to Jack. "You must be Detective Mallory."

"I am." Jack did not move. "And you are?"

"Christopher Sinclair, Trey's attorney." The man held out a hand.

Jack looked at the hand and then up to Christopher's eyes. "You're late."

Christopher pulled back and frowned. "First my client is falsely accused. Then he is denied his day in court. And now you show up to interrogate him without warning or explanation. You're lucky I'm here at all."

"Feel free to leave." Jack hooked his thumb to the door. "But I'm talking to your client either way."

The attorney lay his briefcase on the prisoner's side of the table. "What's this about anyway?"

"Murder."

"Murder?" Christopher's head snapped up. "Not the one he's in here for?"

"That's right."

"What?" The warden turned to him.

"Why is this the first I'm hearing of this?" the attorney demanded.

"It just happened this morning," Jack said.

Christopher chuckled. "You do know my client was behind bars this morning, right?"

Jack stared at the man without responding.

The door behind the attorney opened and Trey Levine was led into the room by a guard, his hands cuffed in front of him. The guard sat the prisoner down and proceeded to link his cuffs to the ring on the table.

"Is that really necessary?" Christopher asked.

The guard looked at the warden who, in turn, looked at the detective.

"Doesn't matter to me," Jack said.

The warden nodded to the guard who removed the handcuffs and left the room with them. Trey made a show of rubbing his wrists. Jack rolled his eyes and sat in the seat across from him.

"Who are you?" Trey asked.

"Detective Jack Mallory," he introduced.

"You here to explain how you found evidence of my innocence?" Trey grinned in a way that made Jack want to slap it off his face.

"I'm here to ask you how you did it." Jack leaned back.

Trey looked at each of the men in turn. "How I did it?"

"Yes."

"Did what?"

"You arranged a hit on Sharon Hutchins," Jack explained. "But your only visitor has been Mr. Sinclair here, which means he must have helped you."

"Wait just a minute, detective." Christopher nearly came out of his seat.

"That crooked cop is dead?" Trey's lips curled into an ugly smile. "That's why she didn't show up in court this morning."

"Detective," Christopher interjected. "Do you have any evidence to support your accusation? Or are you just looking for someone to take the fall? Because my client obviously didn't kill anyone this morning and, as you said, I have been his only visitor. And I promise you, I had no hand in helping arrange a hit."

It was Jack's turn to chuckle. "And if you did, I'm sure you would come out and tell me straight away."

Christopher did not reply.

"Pardon me for not taking your word for it," Jack added.

"Let me get this straight." Trey put his arms on the table and leaned on them. "You think I used nim-rod here to arrange a hit on a cop?"

"Why am I a nim-rod?"

"I'm still in jail aren't I?" Trey kept his eyes on the detective. "And I did this to keep her from testifying against me?"

"That's right," Jack confirmed.

"And how did I convince this guy," Trey tilted his head in Christopher's direction, "to kill a cop?"

"Money," Jack said. "Threats against him or his family. I can think of lots of ways to get him to do what you want."

"Check his bank account," Trey suggested. "The only money he's gotten from me is what he charged me when he failed to get me out on bail."

"You were charged with killing a cop," Christopher argued. "No one could have convinced the judge to set a bail."

Trey muttered under his breath and shook his head. "Can you believe this guy? And you think I would ask him to help me put a hit on someone?"

"Hutchins' testimony was going to guarantee you would be going away for a long time." Jack leaned on the table. "You were desperate. So, yes. I think you would have asked this guy to do just about anything that would help you."

"Her testimony was nothing," Trey snarled. "She planted those guns and drugs on me. And I didn't kill her partner. It wouldn't surprise me if she did it herself. She's as crooked as they come. So, yeah. I would have loved to be the one to put her down. But it wasn't me. And now that she's dead, and their whole case against me goes away, I'm going to sue the city for keeping me locked up for a year waiting for a trial that isn't even going to happen."

"I reviewed your file." Jack stood and loomed over the prisoner. "Hutchins' testimony was only part of the evidence against you. So, don't worry, Mr.Levine. You will get your trial."

20

Shaun rubbed his eyes. He had been reading through copies of Chief Hutchins' internal phone messages that could be taken as a threat. Most were minor, suggesting where she could go and what she could do when she got there. Some suggested she go back to where she came from and even offered to escort her out of town. The fact that she was born and raised just a few miles from where she was killed made those threats almost humorous.

Shaun was amazed at how many people seemed to have an issue with the chief, although it did occur to him that these same people may have had an issue with whoever was in charge. Of all the dozens of threatening callers, there were two names that stood out.

The first, Vince Abrams, called several times claiming that the chief had targeted him and lied in order to ruin him and his business. He never stated the name of his business, leaving Shaun the task of following up to find out what actually happened.

At the top of each dictated message, it was noted which of her phones received the call. Shaun noticed that Vince Abrams had left messages on her work phone, home phone, and her cell. The detective wondered how he had gotten the latter two numbers. He wrote down the man's phone number and, after a quick search, added his address.

Second was Edward Simmons. The young detective was very familiar with the man. One of many cases of Detective Bret Peterson that Shaun had been tasked with reviewing, Mr. Simmons' daughter had been murdered a few years ago, at the age of sixteen. Bret had arrested a man for the crime. He was tried and sentenced to life. The problem was, Bret had been a bad cop. He had manufactured evidence to get a conviction. Upon review, the man convicted of the killing was released. Shaun was pretty sure the man had been guilty, but the fake evidence against him was dismissed. So a killer walked free. The father was furious. He got it in his head that the chief was responsible for the man's release and called her repeatedly demanding to know why.

Although he did not remember Edward Simmons' address, he did know where the man lived. Shaun had accompanied the chief to tell him his daughter's killer was to be released. The agony in the man's face was a moment the detective would like to forget, but probably never would. Edward had pleaded with them to do something to stop it. As much as they would have liked to, they simply couldn't.

Shaun opened his desk drawer, retrieved his weapon, and was in the process of clipping it to his belt when he got the feeling he was being watched. His eyes rose. Standing across from him on the far side of Jack's desk was Chief Grimes. The chief of detectives was staring at him.

"Chief?"

"Where's Mallory?"

"At the prison, sir." Shaun was very uncomfortable.

"The prison?" The chief scrunched his brow. "What is he doing there?"

"Interviewing a possible suspect," Shaun said.

"At the prison?" The chief frowned. "He does understand she was killed this morning? No one in prison could have done it."

"Our theory is he may have arranged it though," Shaun explained. "We're just covering all the bases."

"And you?" The chief pointed. "Where are you off to?"

"I'm going to talk to some people who left threatening messages for the chief."

"Good. Good." Grimes nodded his approval. "Have you learned anything yet?"

Shaun hesitated. He could see that the chief wanted something that showed positive progress. "Not yet, sir. We do have a list of suspects. But none of them stand out."

"Very well." The chief turned away. "Keep me updated."

"Yes, sir." Shaun addressed the man's back as he walked out of the department.

The detective shook his head, gathered his things, and jogged to the elevator bank. He arrived just as the doors were closing. Shaun caught a glimpse of the chief's pinstriped suit in the thin gap before they sealed. He waited a second to be sure the car had moved off and pressed the down button.

A half hour later Shaun stood on the front porch of a large home in an older neighborhood where houses were called estates. He waited after pressing the doorbell wondering if it would be answered by the owner or a butler.

The door opened and a woman just past middle-aged greeted him with a pleasant, although wary smile. "May I help you?"

Shaun held up his badge, triggering a questioning look from the woman. "Detective Shaun Travis. Is Vince Abrams available?"

"Come inside." She waved him in and shut the door behind him. "I'll let him know you're here."

"Thank you, ma'am," Shaun said.

She exited the foyer through one of the three openings, leaving the detective alone, staring up at the giant chandelier overhanging the massive stairway that dominated the entry. In the many messages left by Vince Abrams, he had said the chief had ruined him and his business. It was hard to believe anyone living in this home was ruined.

On the second floor, Shaun saw a child's face looking down at him through the banister. He waved at them and they ran away giggling.

"Detective?"

The deep voice startled Shaun who spun toward the source. The man standing before him was easily six-four, maybe taller. He had broad shoulders and a barrel chest. His hair was graying and his skin was tracked with signs of years in the sun. On his arm, a fading tattoo suggested he had been in the Navy in his younger days.

"Shaun Travis," he introduced himself.

"Why are you here?" Vince asked.

"I need to ask you some questions about Chief Shannon Hutchins," Shaun said.

The man's face hardened and his stance tensed. "Why?"

"Can you tell me where you were this morning?" Shaun asked. "Just before sun up."

"I was here." Vince shifted.

"Can anyone confirm that?"

"My wife," he dismissed. "What's this about?"

"You made a number of calls to the chief," Shaun reported. "You displayed a lot of anger in those messages."

"I would guess so," Vince said. "I was angry."

"And now?"

"Now?" Vince said. "I'm still angry. She made up a bunch of crap about my company and crippled my business. If you're here to pressure me to drop the lawsuit, you are wasting your breath. You can tell her that."

"Lawsuit?"

"You're not here about the lawsuit?"

"No." Shaun's eyes were drawn to the child who had returned to the second-floor banister. "Some of your calls were almost threatening in nature."

"I threatened to sue her," Vince grumbled. "And I did. Is there a law against that?"

"No, sir," Shaun said. "But there is a law against murder."

"Murder?" Vince's eyes widened. "Who was murdered? The chief? Am I a suspect? Is that why you asked where I was this morning? Do I need a lawyer?"

"The chief was murdered," Shaun confirmed, knowing the news would announce it soon enough. "You're not a suspect, but we are questioning anyone who threatened her recently."

"Well, I didn't kill her," Vince assured him. "If you want to talk to someone who wanted her dead, talk to Carl Delacruz."

"The politician?"

"Yes."

"Why do you think Delacruz wanted her dead?" Shaun asked.

"I don't know," Vince answered. "Word is, the man hated her guts. But I never heard any more than that."

Shaun wasn't sure if the businessman really didn't know or was just reluctant to say. His gaze shifted to the man's arm. "You were in the navy?"

"If you're asking if I know how to kill someone," the man sighed. "The answer is yes. But it's been a long time. I haven't used those skills since I left that life."

"I wasn't suggesting . . ."

"You were." Vince clenched his jaw. "I think you should leave. If you want to speak again, it'll be with my attorney present."

Shaun closed his notebook. "Thank you for your time."

The man said nothing in return.

The detective gave a quick wave to the child above before leaving the residence.

21

After his conversation with Trey Levine, Detective Mallory was left with a bitter taste in his mouth. He was ready to have the warden lead him out of the prison when he received a call from Shaun informing him that there was another inmate they needed to talk to. Ian Fielding was serving a fifteen-year sentence for aggravated murder. He had also written two letters that were flagged as threatening.

Jack asked the warden about the prisoner and the man rolled his eyes.

"Not a fan?"

"Well, no." The warden waved at the guard who quickly pressed the buzzer to let them pass through the next door. "But you can't talk to him."

"Why?" Jack asked. "Don't tell me we have to get his lawyer."

"No," the warden said. "Ian Fielding was released just over a week ago."

Jack stopped in his tracks. "A week ago? What can you tell me about him?"

"Fielding was one of those guys who was always trying to play an angle," the warden said. "Always trying to exchange information for favors. But never anything major. He didn't want to be on the bad side of any of our dangerous prisoners, so he only reported minor violations by our small-timers. We fed him a bone from time to time just in case he ever brought us something useful."

"Was he ever violent?"

"Ian?" The warden laughed. "I think he was beat up a couple of times. Otherwise, he was never involved in violence."

"Wasn't he in for murder?"

"According to him," the warden said. "It was completely justified."

"I'm sure it was." Jack nodded. "You run a hotel for the innocent, after all."

"Don't you know it." The warden started walking again. "If we took all the 'innocent'," making quotes with his fingers, "out of here, we could probably house the rest in a single cell."

The rest of the journey was made in silence. They reached the exit in short order and Jack thanked the warden for his time as the guard passed him his weapon. Outside, he stood next to his car and made a few calls. The second was fruitful, providing him with the name of Ian Fielding's parole officer. A quick call to him, in turn, and the detective acquired the ex-con's address and place of employment.

A half-hour later, Jack parked in front of a family restaurant that offered a varied menu and breakfast all day. It was just past the lunch rush, so the parking lot was beginning to thin out. The detective walked in and scanned the dining room. A dozen or so patrons were lingering, and most of the staff seemed to have fallen into casual mode.

A waitress, seated on a stool at a low counter in front of the kitchen, jumped up when he entered and grabbed a menu. "Just one today?"

"Is the manager available?"

Her smile collapsed. "Hold on."

She walked away to a swinging door where she shouted the manager's name. She waited for the woman to reach her before pointing to Jack and explaining that her presence was requested. The manager frowned and approached, shifting to a smile just before she reached him.

"I'm the manager." She was wary of what was about to come her way, obviously experienced at receiving complaints. "Is there a problem?"

Jack held up his badge. "You have an Ian Fielding working here?"

"Yes?" She was hesitant. "Is there a problem?"

"Probably not." Jack had no idea. "Is there somewhere private I could talk to him?"

The woman crossed her arms and shifted her weight from leg to leg. "The dining area on the other side of that partition is empty. Would that do?"

"That would be fine." Jack started in that direction. "Could you send him out?"

He found a booth in the back corner of the separated dining room and sat facing the doorway to the back. He watched the manager make her way through the open kitchen, speaking to employees as she passed them. Most of them glanced the detective's way before quickly looking away again.

The manager disappeared from view leaving Jack to stare at a door. A short time later, a thin, pale face appeared in the window of the door looking his way. The man frowned and ducked out of sight. Jack hoped he wasn't going to have to chase him down.

The door swung open and the owner of the face walked out removing his apron as he walked. He lay the garment on a counter and made his way to where the detective waited for him. He stopped about two tables away.

"Ian Fielding?"

"Who's asking?" The man's eyes darted around nervously.

"Detective Jack Mallory," Jack introduced. "Mind having a seat?"

"I haven't done nothing."

"Then this won't take long." Jack narrowed his eyes. "But if you don't sit, I'll run you in and report you to your P.O."

"You can't do that."

"I can," Jack said. "Now sit."

"Man," Ian whined. He moved closer and fell into the booth across from the detective. "What do you want with me?"

"Does the name Sharon Hutchins mean anything to you?" Jack asked.

"No." Ian shook his head, but his eyes shifted to recognition. "Wait. Do you mean Detective Hutchins?"

"Yes."

"Yeah, I know her." His shoulders fell. "It's her fault I was in prison."

"Her fault?" Jack's eyebrows raised. "How is that?"

"I was her C.I." The man jabbed the table with his index finger. "Helped her with cases. Helped her put a lot of guys away. But when I needed help, where was she? Putting me in cuffs. That's where."

"You needed help and she arrested you?"

"That's what I said." Ian crossed his arms and slouched in the booth.

"What exactly happened?" Jack asked. "Didn't you kill someone?"

"You see," Ian jabbed the table again, "you all only focus on that. But there was more to it."

"Tell me," Jack encouraged him.

"My sister," Ian said. "She was dating this dude. I kept telling her the dude was no good, but she kept dating him anyways."

"Okay."

"Anyway, one day she comes home with a shiner," Ian continued. "So I asked her what happened. She tells me it was nothing. She said something she shouldn't have and upset this creep. So he hit her."

"That doesn't sound right."

"Exactly." Ian nodded. "I told her he shouldn't be hitting her. But she told me to let it go, cause it was her fault."

"You didn't agree?"

"No, but I let it go."

"You did?"

"That's what I said," Ian said.

"How does that get you arrested?"

"Because I shouldn't have let it go," Ian explained. "A couple weeks later my mom calls me and tells me the guy put my sister in the hospital. I knew if I didn't do something, next time he'd probably kill her."

"So you killed him instead?"

"I was protecting my sister." Ian jabbed the table with each syllable.

"That's why you needed help," Jack concluded.

"I told Hutchins what happened," Ian scowled. "I was a loyal C.I. and I figured she would understand. But she arrested me."

"So you're not a fan?"

"She can rot in hell for all I care."

Jack considered his choice of words. "Is that why you killed her?"

"Wait?" Ian sat up. "What?"

"You killed Hutchins for revenge," Jack said. "After all, she cost you years of your life. So, taking hers was only fair. Right?"

"No." Ian tried to disappear into the back cushion of the booth. "Not right. Not right at all. I didn't touch her. I haven't even seen her since I went in."

"Where were you this morning?" Jack asked. "Before sunup?"

"I was at the halfway house," Ian said. "The staff can tell you."

"You're in a halfway house?" Jack sighed.

"Yes."

"I'll have to verify," Jack said.

"Go ahead."

Jack pursed his lips then said, "How is she?"

"Who?"

"Your sister," Jack said. "How is she doing?"

"She won't speak to me." Ian shrank into the booth. "I killed her precious boyfriend. But she's alive. So there's that."

22

D etective Jack Mallory entered the department with a power stride he usually reserved for exercise. His young partner, Shaun was sitting with his head bowed to a short stack of papers on his desk, allowing Jack to be almost upon him before he looked up.

"Did you get anywhere?" Jack sat heavily in his chair.

"Chief Grimes was here." Shaun leaned forward and whispered as if the walls were listening.

"I thought you went to see him." Jack turned to his computer and logged in.

"I did." Shaun looked from side to side. "That's what's so odd. I was there and he came down about an hour later looking for you."

"Of course he did." Jack rolled his eyes. "How did your meeting go with him?"

"He didn't tell me much," Shaun admitted. "Other than to express how important this case is. As if we didn't know."

"And her press conference?"

"He told me they were routine and there was nothing new about it," Shaun said.

"Routine?" Jack scowled. "I don't remember the last time a chief of homicide held a tough-on-crime press conference. They usually do updates on current cases."

"Do you think she had an ulterior motive?"

"Like what?" Jack sat back. "Political ambition? She didn't seem the type."

"What about you?" Shaun asked. "Learn anything from the bottom feeders?"

"Learned that she was to testify against Trey Levine, who killed her partner when she was in narcotics," Jack said. "He was very happy to hear of her death, but the only person he's had contact with is his lawyer. And it would be quite a leap from hard-working attorney to setting up a hit on a cop."

"That does seem like a stretch."

"We'll check him out," Jack informed him. "But I don't see it going anywhere."

"What about the one I called you about?" Shaun asked. "Ian Fielding?"

"He's an interesting case." Jack grimaced. "He was Sharon's C.I. and he blames her for the time he spent in prison. Plus he was released recently."

"Released?" Shaun frowned. "Our records don't show that."

"A glitch," Jack suggested. "Someone got lazy and didn't click the update button. Unusual, but not unheard of."

"Do you think he's good for it?"

"Could be." Jack nodded. "We should dig deeper into his movements since he got out. You talked to a businessman, didn't you?"

"Vince Abrams. He claims the chief fabricated evidence to ruin him," Shaun reported. "He ended up telling me to call his lawyer, but not before pointing a finger at Carl Delacruz."

"The Carl Delacruz?"

"Yes." Shaun nodded. "He said Delacruz hated the chief and wanted her dead."

"Did he say why?"

"Didn't know," Shaun said. "It was all hearsay."

"Still worth checking out." Jack typed the politician's name into the computer. The search results filled the screen and the detective started scanning them. "Seems he's an outspoken opponent of the entire department. Doesn't think we're doing our jobs. When we are, we aren't doing it well. Piece of work, this one."

"Any mention of Chief Hutchins?"

Jack skimmed through more articles. "Not that I, oh wait, here's something. There's an article, or rather a blog. The author writes that they noticed a pattern in Delacruz's speeches. The man takes a jab at the chief at least once every time he has an audience."

"Every time?"

"According to the author," Jack skimmed ahead, "he gives examples, and there are several. One or two are serious accusations. Most are just negative comments that serve little more purpose than to be negative."

"That brings up political ambition again," Shaun pointed out. "Maybe she was thinking of running for some office and he knew it. He might have been trying to give her some negative press without being too obvious."

"It's worth looking into." Jack closed the article. "We can talk to Reginald. If she was thinking about running for office, he would know. We should also look into the relationship between Delacruz and the chief. See if there's some bad blood there. Maybe the jabs were personal."

"Okay." Shaun jotted down some notes.

"Who else was on your list?"

"There was Edward Simmons."

"Who is Edward Simmons?"

"His daughter was killed," Shaun said. "We put her killer away, but Brett Peterson manufactured some of the evidence used to convict him, so he was released."

"Great." Jack rolled his eyes at the mention of the ex-detective.

"He made numerous calls to the chief blaming her for the whole mess."

"She wasn't even in the department when Brett was," Jack grumbled. "How could he think it was her fault?"

"She was in charge when the killer was released, I guess."

"Okay." Jack let his mind race. "Let's stick together. We'll talk to the father first. Then let's track down Randy Keyes and talk to him again. I have more questions. And maybe he remembers something more. Have we made any progress finding out who the chief had the affair with?"

"Not yet."

"We need to talk to these people so we can rule some of them out." Jack looked at his notes. "What about this neighbor with the abusive ex?"

"I haven't tracked him down yet."

"We need to find him." Jack grimaced. "If for no other reason than to be sure he doesn't feel empowered to go after the wife now that the chief isn't there to protect her."

"He's not at his last address anymore," Shaun said. "But I have an employer. I'll try to find him there."

"We have a lot to do." Jack stood and stretched. "And Chief Grimes is going to want an update. So, let's get out of here before he catches us and hinders us from doing our job."

23

Edward Simmons lived in an upper-class neighborhood, in the same colonial-style home where he had raised his daughter. His wife of thirty years had succumbed to her grief two years after the death of their only child. There was a sadness in his eyes that came from experiencing great loss.

Detectives Mallory and Travis sat side by side where they were directed and waited for the homeowner to get settled in a plush leather recliner.

"Are you here to tell me you locked that devil back up?" He was looking directly at Shaun. "Because I honestly can't think of any other reason for you to be here, in my home."

"I'm afraid not, sir." Shaun clasped his hands in front of him.

"You're afraid not?" Edward would not look away from the young detective. "You know, some mornings when I wake, before my mind catches up, I think they're alive. And for that fleeting moment, I don't feel like my heart has been ripped out of me. And then I feel it all over again. Do you know what that is like, detective?"

"No, sir."

"What about you?" The man turned to Jack expectantly.

"What about me?"

"Do you understand what I'm saying?"

"I do," Jack said. "And I am sorry for your loss. But that is not why we're here."

"And why are you here?"

"We need to know your whereabouts this morning," Jack said.

"This morning?" Edward stared the detective in the eyes. "If he's dead, there's no one going to be happier than me. But I didn't do it."

"This morning," Jack repeated. "Where were you?"

"So, we're doing this?" The man sat back in his chair. "Okay. I had breakfast at Molly's Diner. After that, I went to the park to walk and watch the ducks. After that . . ."

"What time did you arrive at the diner?" Jack interrupted.

Edward looked at Shaun. "What is this about?"

"We need you to answer," Shaun said. "What time?"

"Six."

"Can anyone verify that?" Jack asked.

"The hostess." Edward turned back to Jack. "The waitress. Probably the cook."

"And you're sure it was six?"

"Every morning," Edward said. "For five years. Same time every day. Same meal every time. They know me by name. The cook starts my order when I walk through the door. Now, are you going to tell me what this is about? Is he dead?"

Shaun looked at Jack, who nodded. The young detective said, "Not him."

"Not him?" Edward furrowed his brow. "But someone. Who?"

With another glance toward his partner, Shaun continued, "Chief Sharon Hutchins."

"Chief Hutchins?" It was Edward's turn to look at Jack. "And you think I did it?"

"You were on a list of people who have left angry or threatening messages for her," Shaun explained.

"Sure I was angry," Edward said. "But not enough to kill her."

"We're talking to everyone on the list," Jack clarified. "Don't plan on leaving town until this is resolved."

"I'm not going anywhere."

"Alright." Jack rose to his feet. "We'll show ourselves out."

Shaun stood and the two detectives left the man's home. In the privacy of their car, Shaun asked, "You don't think it was him, do you?"

"I don't think he would have had time to kill the chief, clean up, and get to the diner by six," Jack confirmed. "We'll need to confirm with the staff, but no, I don't think he was involved."

Jack started the car and pulled away from the curb.

"Did you get a location on that electrician?"

"I got a phone number for the company he works for," Shaun answered. "I'll give them a call right now."

24

Chief Hutchins' neighbor, Randy Keyes, was employed by Halstead Electric, a large company that did work for both residential and corporate clients. They were contracted by the city for installations and repairs for the local government.

Shaun was transferred twice before being connected to a pleasant-sounding woman who was more than happy to help the detective. She muttered to herself as she worked her computer. "Ah, here he is."

"He's there?"

"No." She laughed. "I found him on the computer. He's doing an installation on a new build. An office building downtown."

Shaun relayed the address to his partner, who turned at the next intersection and maneuvered traffic until he reached their destination. Jack rolled to a stop at the curb and the two of them leaned forward and looked up through the windshield.

"That's eight floors," Shaun reported.

"I can see that." Jack sat back and opened his door. "Let's locate the foreman. He can probably direct us to where they're working on electrical."

The two of them walked through the open gate in the chain-link fence that surrounded the construction area without anyone asking why they were there. Jack's posture and motions projected confidence, signifying he was supposed to be exactly where he was. Shaun followed close behind, watching those who should be watching them.

"Where's the foreman?" Jack stopped a short stocky man with sun-baked skin as he passed by.

"Third." The man twisted and pointed to that floor. "You need hardhats to go up. Blue trailer."

Someone yelled and the stocky man waved an arm, then scurried away to finish the task he had set upon. The detectives scanned the site. There were two blue trailers on opposite sides of the area. Jack weighed his options and started for the closer one. Shaun fell in step and followed. The door opened just as they reached the steps. A tall, muscular man looked down at them from under the rim of his hardhat.

"You need something?" he asked.

Jack pointed to his head. "Hardhats."

The man looked over them toward the other blue trailer. He sighed. "Just a minute."

He went back inside. A moment later he returned with two hats in his hands. He descended the steps, holding them out to the men. "Be sure these get returned to this trailer."

"Brad?" Jack read the name printed on the back of the hardhat he was given.

"He's off today." The man shrugged. "Or you can walk to the other trailer to get one."

"I'm good with Brad." Jack fit the hat on his head and helped Shaun with his. "We won't be long."

"Just leave them on the table inside."

Jack nodded and the man walked toward the skeleton of the office building. The concrete structure had very few walls at this point. But more important to the detective was the lack of a working elevator. The two of them quickly found the stairs and made their way up, still amazed that no one had asked who they were or why they were there.

The third floor was abuzz with activity. One group was framing walls while another worked on fitting pipes. A third group was running electrical wiring. Jack watched the last group with interest, wishing he knew what their witness looked like.

Centrally, a table made of scrap materials was surrounded by a fourth group who looked like they at least thought they were important. The detectives veered in that direction. As they approached, one of the men looked up at them.

"Who are you?"

Jack held up his badge. "Detective Mallory and my partner Detective Travis."

"Detectives?" The man glanced around the makeshift table. "What are you here for?"

"Are you the foreman?"

The man visibly relaxed.

"No." A man who had been standing with his back to them turned. "I'm the foreman. Darren Watts. What do you need with me?"

"We need to find a contractor on your site," Jack put his badge away. "His name is Randy Keyes and he works for Halstead Electric."

"Halstead?" The man frowned.

"Yes."

"This building is eight floors," Darren informed them. "We have Halstead on every floor today. What was his name again?"

"Randy Keyes."

"Any of you know him?" He looked around the table.

"I do." The lone woman in the group sighed. "And I think I know where he is today."

"Would you mind taking the detectives to him?" Darren asked. "Don't need them wandering around and getting hurt."

She stepped away from the table and eyed the two men. "You picked me to babysit because I'm a woman, didn't you?"

"No," the foreman looked stricken. "It's because you know where this Randy guy is."

"Relax, Darren." She smiled broadly. "I'm yankin' your chain. You two, with me."

She raised her muscular arms and adjusted her hardhat. With a tilt of her head, she started toward the stairs the detectives had just come from. Jack and Shaun followed, which proved more difficult than expected. She was tall and thick and remarkably fast for her size.

She reached the stairs, stopped, and waited for them to catch up. "Mind if I ask what Keyes did?"

"We aren't at liberty to discuss our case," Jack rambled off his go-to dismissal phrase.

"I understand." She started up the stairs. "But if you need to shoot him, feel free."

Shaun chuckled.

"I take it you're not a fan?" Jack asked her back.

"Ever since his wife left him," she said, "he's been lonely and hits on everything female. Which is funny when you know that he tells all the guys how wonderful his ex is and how he wants to get back together. He's up on seven."

The detectives exchanged a glance as they started to climb the four flights. When they reached their destination, their guide was standing in the opening, waiting for them.

"He's over there." She pointed. "The taller one."

The two detectives followed her finger and saw two men working at an electrical panel. Jack turned to thank her but she was already on her way down.

25

The electricians were easy to spot, in matching coveralls with the brightly colored Halstead Electric logo across their backs. The two men moved with practiced motions standing side by side yet never getting in the other's way. Between their singular concentration and the constant noises of the construction site, they did not know Jack and Shaun were approaching until the detectives were directly behind them.

"Excuse me, gentlemen," Jack announced their arrival.

The shorter man jumped, "My God, don't do that. Who are you?"

Jack ignored the man and turned to Randy. "Mr. Keyes, is there someplace we could talk?" Jack asked.

"I'll be back in a minute," Randy said to his co-worker.

"What happened this morning?"

"Give it up," Randy said. "There's a place on the east side no one's working on."

The three men relocated to a space that was blocked from view by concrete supports, metal framing, and stacks of supplies. On the other side was a seven-story drop. Shaun eyed to opening with hesitation.

"They're starting to close it up today," Randy offered. "Of course, they start on the ground floor."

"Great." The young detective took a few steps away from the edge.

Randy turned to Jack. "You have more questions?"

"Some of your neighbors reported seeing a green sedan in the neighborhood over the past few days," Jack said. "Did you see it? Or anything else that may have seemed insignificant at the time, but may be suspicious looking back on it?"

"Green sedan?" Randy's head bobbed at the thought. "Now that you mention it, I think I did see that car. Thought they were visiting someone, but it kept showing up in different places. Not in front of the same house every time."

"Do you know cars?" Jack asked. "Do you know what the make and model was?"

"Afraid not," Randy said. "It was just a generic-looking car. A little older maybe."

"Did you ever see anyone in the car?"

"Yes," the man said. "I saw someone in it. They were short. You know. Barely seeing over the steering wheel short."

"Or maybe they were slouching down so they can't be seen?" Jack suggested.

"I suppose."

"Could the man in the car be the same man you saw running across your lawn this morning?" Jack asked.

"I don't know," Randy said. "Maybe."

"Think about it, Randy," Jack said. "You were the only one to see this guy. Five-eight or five-nine. Medium build. What else did you notice?"

"I, uh, well I," Randy stammered. "I think I did see his arm."

"Are you sure?" Shaun asked.

"I've been thinking about it," Randy nodded. "I remembered seeing his forearm when he ran by."

"And?" Jack pressed.

"His skin was kind of dark," Randy said. "You know, like a Hispanic, or a light-skinned black. But he could have been a white guy with a dark tan. It's hard to say. It was so dark out."

"But you're sure it was someone with darker skin?" Jack said.

"Yes," Randy nodded. "I'm pretty sure."

"Pretty sure?" Jack repeated. "So you aren't sure?"

"I guess not," Randy tilted his head slightly and raised a shoulder. "Sorry."

"It's okay," Jack said. "We just need to be sure."

"I'm not very helpful am I?"

"You're doing fine," Shaun assured him. "I was curious about something though."

"What's that?" Randy asked.

"You said you didn't perform CPR because you don't know how," Shaun said.

"That's right."

"It seems that working on a job site like this one, there might be a lot of accidents," Shaun said. "Or at least a lot of opportunities to be hurt."

"Yeah," Randy said. "So?"

"It just seems to me that a company like yours," Shaun said, "one that's in construction, might require its employees to learn CPR."

"Well, yeah," Randy said. "They do."

"Then you do know how," Jack said.

"No," Randy defended. "The day I was supposed to train, I was sick. After that, it just fell through the tracks. I never learned."

"Okay," Shaun said. "I guess that explains it."

They stood silent for a minute.

"Keyes!"

The three men turned toward the voice. A bearded man with thick arms stood about thirty feet away with his hands on his hips. His eyes were in shadow underneath his hardhat visor, but they could all see anger on his face.

"What do you want, Theo?" Randy shouted back.

"Get back to work!" the man bellowed. "You're not being paid to talk."

"You know they're cops, right?"

"Don't care," the man huffed. "They can arrest you or let you get back to it."

He stormed off without another glance their way.

"Sorry about that," Randy said to the detectives.

"That's okay," Jack assured him. "We'll wrap this up. You said your wife, Samantha, might know something about the Hutchins' relationship. We still need her contact information."

"Oh," Randy pulled out his phone. "I'm sorry. I forgot."

He scrolled through his contacts until he found what he was looking for. He read the phone number and address that he had for his estranged wife. Both Jack and Shaun wrote down the details in their respective notepads.

"Did you ever hear what caused the power outage?" Jack asked.

"The power...?" Randy turned. "Oh, right. It was just one of those things. Power surge or something blew a transformer."

Jack made a note. "Okay. Thanks. We'll let you get back to work."

"Sorry I wasn't more help." Randy started back to where his co-worker was laboring away.

"You were fine," Jack said.

The two detectives made their way back to the stairway and descended to the ground floor.

"Hispanic," Shaun said. "Could be Delacruz."

"We'll need to see if anyone has a dark tan," Jack said. "We haven't exactly narrowed the suspect pool."

They returned their hardhats to the proper trailer and were on the road in a matter of minutes.

26

J ack and Shaun returned to the department and compiled the notes they had taken. Side by side they stood in front of the whiteboard and studied it with the new information and photos.

"What do you think of Edward Simmons?" Jack asked. "You know him. Is he capable of doing this?"

"Capable?" Shaun shrugged. "If the victim had been his daughter's killer, I would put him at the top of the list. But would he kill the chief just because she was in charge when the guy was released? I have a hard time wrapping my head around that. Especially, given that it was the review I did on Brent's cases that set his release in motion. If Ed was going to kill a cop, I suspect it would be me."

"Good to know." Jack patted his shoulder. "If you turn up dead, he'll be my first stop."

"I appreciate that," Shaun said.

"No problem," Jack said. "Anything for my partner."

Jack stepped forward and moved Edward's photo to the persons of interest column.

"We have the unknown subject that Randy Keyes saw running from the scene." Shaun took a sheet of paper, drew a question mark on it placed it in the suspect column. "The maybe Hispanic, maybe black, maybe tanned white man."

"His statement confirms Reginald's story of what happened when he came out of the house," Jack said.

"He said he saw the green sedan," Shaun added. "Parking in various places, just like Trish Carmichael mentioned."

"We need to know who owns that car." Jack sat in one of the chairs surrounding the conference room table.

"What about Randy?" Shaun asked.

"He had opportunity," Jack said. "But why stay at the scene? He tried to help her. We'll keep him on the maybe list."

Shaun followed his partner's example and sat as well. "What next?"

"Next we talk to Randy's ex." Jack flipped through his notes. "Samantha Keyes. And that other neighbor's ex. The one Sharon helped get a restraining order. What was her name?"

"Julia Pollard," Shaun said. "Ex-husband's name is Dan."

"We have the contact information for Randy's wife," Jack said. "Let's track down Mr. Pollard and get them off our list."

"You don't think it was him?"

"Don't know without talking to him," Jack said. "I just want him off the to-do list."

"I'll get his address." Shaun pulled his keyboard closer and started typing.

Jack's phone rang and the detective held up a finger while pulling his phone out. "Mallory."

He listened for a short time before saying, "We'll be right there."

"I've got Pollard's last known." Shaun waited for his partner to put his phone away. "Where are we going?"

"Morgue." Jack stood and stretched his frame. "Valerie says she's almost done with Sharon's autopsy."

"Almost?" Shaun grimaced. "I would rather wait until she was done."

"I'm sure you would." Jack pulled his weapon and keys from his desk drawer. "Let's go."

Shaun rose to his feet and the detectives made their way out. A short time later they were facing the coroner, separated by the stainless-steel table where Sharon Hutchins' body lay. Shaun could not take his eyes off the chief's face.

"What's wrong with you?" Jack asked him.

"I think this is the first time I've seen the body of someone I actually knew." The young detective took a step back. "Sorry. Go ahead."

"As expected," Valerie started, "cause of death was a single gunshot wound. It entered the right side of her back above her vest at a downward trajectory. The bullet traveled through her lung and stomach into the intestines. She died quickly, but not instantly. She suffered before she passed."

"And the bullet?"

"I sent it to ballistics on a rush." Valerie walked to her computer and typed. "The results should be back soon."

"Okay," Jack sighed.

"They're going to run the fingerprints they found on the gun as well," she said.

"Let's hope they identify our shooter," Jack said.

"I did find skin, blood, and hair under her nails," the coroner announced. "She got a piece of her killer."

"Good for her." Jack looked up at Valerie expectantly.

"Not yet," she seemed to read his mind. "I put a rush on the DNA test as well, but they still take time. As soon as I know, you will."

"Very good."

"There's one more thing." Valerie became more somber. "Sharon had cancer."

"I wasn't aware." Jack looked down again. "She never said anything. How bad was it?"

"Bad." The coroner turned to a viewer, attached an x-ray of a torso, and pointed. "All of this cloudy area is cancer. It's in several of her organs. She had to have been in pain."

"Any chance she was in pain without knowing what the cause was?" Jack examined the image.

"There's a chance." Valerie walked back to the table and pulled the sheet up to expose the chief's side. "But with this bruising, she had to know something was wrong. And if she went to a doctor, well, if they ran any tests at all, they would have sent her to a specialist."

"If they found it," Jack asked. "Could they have treated it?"

"I don't specialize in oncology," Valerie explained, "but from what I saw inside her, I don't think there was anything that could have been done."

"So, if we assume she knew," Jack studied the dead woman's face. "And we assume she had been told it was terminal, we have to consider that she may have had someone do this to her."

"You think she hired a hit on herself?" Shaun asked.

"I don't think she did," Jack argued, "but it's something we have to consider."

"But she's the chief." Shaun moved closer.

"Pain can make people do strange things in the name of stopping the hurt," Jack said. "Plus, if she's killed in the line of duty, the family gets a big payout."

"But the chief...?" Shaun questioned.

"It depends on how much pain she was in." Jack crossed his arms and frowned. "Or if she wanted to save her family from having to take care of her."

"Are we really entertaining this as a possibility?" Shaun asked.

"Possibility or not, someone else pulled the trigger," Jack said. "That's who we're after. We need to talk to Reginald and see if he knew her diagnosis. If not, we talk to her doctor to see if she even knew."

27

S amantha Keyes was a solidly built middle-aged woman who tried to look younger than she was by bleaching her hair and wearing clothing a couple of sizes smaller than she should. When she opened the door of her apartment for the two detectives, disappointment covered her face, which only intensified when they explained why they were there.

"Sharon's dead?"

"Yes, ma'am." Shaun tried to sound as somber as possible. "Sorry for your loss."

"My loss?" Samantha narrowed her eyes to the young detective. "We weren't related."

"We understood that the two of you were friends," Jack explained. "Is that not true?"

"I wouldn't say friends," Samantha said. "Friendly. But not really friends."

"Your husband . . ."

"Ex-husband."

"Ex-husband?" Jack frowned. "Randy told us your divorce wasn't final, yet."

"Technically," Samanta confirmed. "But almost. I prefer to think of him as my ex."

"Well, your ex told us that you spoke to Sharon often."

"On occasion, we chatted." Samantha strolled toward the kitchen. "I wouldn't say often. Although we did have lunch once or twice."

"Do you know why Randy would suggest otherwise?"

"Other than being self-centered and unobservant," she smirked, "I can't think of any reason."

"Is that why you're divorcing him?" Shaun asked.

"One of them," Samantha confirmed. "Well, I guess that's two of them."

"How many are there?"

"How many what?"

"How many reasons?" Shaun said.

"Too many to count," Samantha declared. "You don't think he was involved, do you? Would either of you like some water?"

"No thank you," Jack answered for both of them. "Is there a reason you asked about Randy? Do you think we should be considering him?"

"Listen." Samantha took a glass from the cabinet and filled it with ice and water from the refrigerator door. "Randy has his faults, and he can be an idiot at times. But I really can't see him killing anyone."

"What about Reginald?" Jack asked.

"What about him?"

"In the times that you and Sharon spoke," Jack said. "Did she ever give you any indication that she might be afraid of him?"

"She was a cop," Samantha said. "Did you ever meet her?"

"Yes." Jack glanced at Shaun. "We worked together."

"Then you know. If anyone was afraid in that relationship," Samantha sipped her water, "it was Reggie. That woman was intense."

"She was," Jack agreed. "Did she ever confide in you? Maybe she told you when she had troubles in her marriage?"

"Sure, we had 'trash talk the husbands' sessions," Samantha grinned. "But they didn't have problems with their marriage."

"What about last year when they split up for a while?" Shaun asked.

"Well, yeah," Samantha nodded. "They had trouble then. But they've been pretty solid since she moved back. Or at least they were before I moved into this dump."

"Did you know she had an affair while they were split?" Jack asked.

"I did."

"She told you quite a bit for someone who wasn't a friend," Jack suggested.

"I got the impression she didn't have a lot of friends," Samantha said. "I think she just wanted someone to talk to."

"Did she tell you who he was? The man she was sleeping with?"

"She never gave me a name." Samantha drank more of her water.

"Did she tell you something other than his name?"

Samantha scrunched her face. "She told me it was someone she had known for a while."

"Someone she knew?" Jack repeated. "Like a co-worker? A family friend, maybe?"

"I don't know," she shook her head.

"Do you know if she ended it when she went back to Reginald?"

"I assume so," Samantha answered. "Do you think she didn't?"

"We're just covering all the bases." Jack dismissed the question. "How about enemies? Did she ever mention any issues she had with anyone?"

"We didn't really have a 'talk about our enemies' kind of relationship." The woman took a long drink of water.

"Just husbands?"

"Just husbands." Samantha put her glass down and smiled. "And children. She loved to talk about her son. She was so proud of him."

"Do you have children?" Jack asked.

"No." Disappointment returned to her face. "Randy and I were never blessed with kids. Probably for the best, given the circumstances."

"What about health?" Shaun asked. "Did the two of you ever compare aches and pains?"

"No." She shook her head.

"So, she never mentioned her condition?" Jack asked.

"Her condition?" Her disappointment shifted to confusion. "What condition?"

"Cancer," Jack answered. "She was dying."

"Oh, my God," Samantha straightened. "She never said anything. That's so sad. Not that being shot in your own driveway isn't sad."

"Do you, by chance, happen to know who else she would have confided in?" Jack asked. "Who she might have talked to about more than husbands and children?"

"Um." Samantha thought a moment. "Maybe her sister."

28

The detectives pulled into the neighborhood where Dan Pollard's current address was listed. It was an older part of town where the homes were small and mostly run down. The house where Julia Pollard's ex lived was no exception. Jack pulled into the short driveway and studied what he guessed to be one of the more run down on the block.

"Are you sure this is the right place?" Shaun looked up at the peeling paint, cracked windowpanes, and deteriorating shingles.

"I'm positive." Jack was not looking at the home. His gaze was focused on the car parked in front of them, a late-model Chevy. What had Jack's attention was that the car was a sedan, a pale green sedan.

The two men exited their car and walked up the driveway on either side of the vehicle, scanning the interior as they went.

"Do you think this is it?" Shaun asked. "The green car everyone saw? Do you think he violated the restraining order?"

"If I were a gambling man," Jack looked toward the front door. "I would say yes. But we need proof. Just because he drives a green car, doesn't automatically put him in that neighborhood. And if he was there, I'm guessing he knew exactly how close he could get without violating the order."

They reached the front porch and Shaun pulled the screen open. The door swung out and promptly fell forward. The detective reacted and caught the door by its frame and worked it into an upright lean next to the doorframe it had come out of.

"Are you done breaking things?" Jack asked.

"Very funny," Shaun said.

The front door opened and an angry man stood in the doorway. "What do you want?"

"Dan Pollard?"

The man raised a cigarette to his lips and inhaled, filling his lungs with smoke. He held it for a minute while he assessed the situation. He let the stream of smoke out through his lips slowly. "Who wants to know?"

"Detectives Jack Mallory and Shaun Travis," Jack introduced. "We need to ask you a few questions."

"Do I need my attorney?"

"Are you guilty of something?" Jack inquired, focusing intently on the man's eyes.

"Nope." The man stared back, squinting. "Do I know you?"

"I wondered if you would remember," Jack said. "A couple of months ago you got drunk and started a fight in a restaurant. I was having dinner at the time. So I arrested you."

"I didn't start that fight." The man sneered.

"I'm sure you didn't," Jack said. "But from what I saw, that's exactly what happened."

"Is that why you're here?" the man grumbled. "I served three days for that already."

"No. Nothing like that." Jack softened his voice. "We're here because you've been spotted in your ex's neighborhood, despite a restraining order."

"Is that what she said?" He became defensive. "She's a liar. She lied to get that restraining order. Now she's lying to get me in more trouble."

"Wasn't her who saw you there," Jack corrected him.

"Was it that stupid cop lady?" Dan asked. "Cause she has it out for me. You can't trust her."

"So you know Sharon Hutchins?" Shaun asked.

"Yeah, I know her." Dan spat on the porch. "She's the one who ruined my marriage. Turned Julia against me with her lies."

"So they're both liars?" Shaun asked.

"That's right."

"But neither of them turned you in," Jack assured him. "It was a couple of the other residents on that street. We know you were there."

The man paused, his mind racing. "Yeah. I was there. But I didn't, whatever. What's the word?"

"Violate?"

"Yeah." The man's head bobbed. "I didn't vi-o-late the restraining order. I was at least a hundred feet away from the house."

"You were there multiple times," Jack said. "Which is clearly stalking behavior and most likely a violation as well."

"What?" Dan frowned. "No. That wasn't part of it."

"And how can you say you were a hundred feet away when you were killing the stupid lady cop in her driveway this morning?" Jack asked.

"Wait? What?" Dan's mind raced again. "Someone killed her?"

"Don't get any ideas," Shaun said. "The restraining order is still in effect. Just because the chief isn't there to watch over Julia, doesn't mean we won't."

Dan grinned. "Got what she deserved, you ask me."

"We didn't ask you," Jack said. "We do need to know where you were this morning."

"Yeah?" Dan's anger returned. "Well that's too bad. You can talk to my lawyer."

The man slammed his door and the screen fell away from the wall where Shaun had leaned it. The detective made no attempt to catch it, nor did he pick it up once it had fallen.

"I guess we have an answer to who was in the green sedan," Jack said as the two of them returned to their car. "Do you think he could have done it?"

Shaun buckled his seatbelt. "He beat his wife, which means he's a cowardly piece of garbage. The kind of coward who might attack a woman from behind in the dark. Maybe he was sitting in his car when the power went out and he seized the opportunity."

Jack turned the key and the engine roared to life. "If he did, we need to put a patrol car on Julia Pollard's house. Killing a cop would make killing your ex seem easy."

29

The sun was settling down for the night when Jack and Shaun stood on Julia Pollard's dark front porch knocking on the door. The small panes of glass rattled with each strike of knuckle to wood. Through the windows the detectives watched the homeowner make her way to the front where she turned on the exterior light before opening the door.

"Detective?" She looked at Shaun.

"Mrs. Pollard, sorry to bother you so late," Shaun said. "This is my partner, Detective Mallory."

"Ms."

"Pardon?"

"It's Ms. Pollard," she clarified. "I'm divorced."

"So sorry," Shaun apologized.

"That's okay," she said. "Nice to meet you, Detective … Mallory, is it?"

"It is." Jack held out his hand which, after a slight hesitation, she shook. "As my partner said, we apologize for the late hour."

"No worries." She gave them a half-hearted smile. "I probably won't be sleeping tonight anyway."

"Worried there's a killer on the loose?" Jack asked.

"That, and my ex," she said. "And wondering if he had anything to do with it."

"He's why we're here," Shaun offered.

"Did he do it?" Her eyes showed a mix of hope and despair. "Did you catch him?"

"We spoke to him," Shaun said.

"You spoke to him?" She spun her head to the man. "That's it? He's not in jail?"

"Though he is still a person of interest," Jack explained. "We don't have any real evidence that he had any involvement in Chief Hutchins' death. We have nothing to hold him on."

"What about after he kills me?" Her voice sharpened. "Will you have something to hold him on then?"

"Regardless if he killed her or not," Jack ignored her anger, "he knows she isn't here to watch out for you. To that end, we have arranged to have a patrol car sit out front for a few days while we sort everything out."

Julia looked past them to the street. There was no patrol car, only theirs.

"We'll wait until they arrive," Shaun assured her.

"And despite what you may have seen in the movies," Jack said. "It would be very unlikely that an abusive husband would try to sneak past police or kill them to get to the woman. Most are cowards. They don't risk challenging someone who might fight back."

"So, you're saying I should have fought back?"

"Not unless you could take him," Jack shook his head. "Fighting back only works if you can win."

She closed her eyes, fending off memories of the years of being hit and kicked, the carefully chosen words to tear down her self-esteem. Therapy showed her what happened and she recognized it now. But at the time, she believed every word, believed she deserved what she was getting.

"We'll let you go," Jack said. "And we will be here until the car arrives."

"Thank you." She gave them an unconvincing grin before shutting the door.

The two detectives made their way back to the street just as the promised patrol car rolled to a stop directly behind their car. Jack altered his course and stepped up to the driver's window. The officer inside lowered the glass.

"Officer Mendez," Jack greeted. "I wasn't expecting you here."

"You know me," the officer smiled. "Any chance I get to sit back and drink coffee all night? Besides, Wilson here has never been on an all-night protection detail. Couldn't let her miss out."

Jack bent over until he could see the younger officer's face. "Keep an eye on him. When he says he's resting his eyes, he's actually sleeping."

"I'll keep that in mind, sir," Wilson responded.

"Ashley Wilson?" Shaun bent down next to his partner. "I thought that sounded like you."

"Shaun?" She smiled. "I haven't seen you since I was a rookie. I heard you made detective."

"Shows you what hard work will do," Officer Mendez said.

"Is that why you're not a detective, yet?" she joked.

"Mendez was a detective," Jack said. "He asked to go back to patrol. And once you do that, it's hard to go back up."

"You asked to go back to patrol after becoming a detective?" Wilson crossed her arms. "Why?"

"Things were different then, weren't they, Jack?" Mendez did not wait for the detective to answer. "Anyway, it was the best decision I could make at the time."

There was a silence that was becoming uncomfortable.

"What can you tell me about this one?" Mendez pointed toward Julia Pollard's home.

"Her ex, Dan Pollard," Jack said. "There's a restraining order against him, initiated by Chief Hutchins."

"She lived across the street, right?"

"That's right." Jack glanced toward the house in question. "Now that she isn't there to keep an eye on the woman, we thought we should make sure the ex doesn't take advantage of the situation and pay her a visit."

"Are we worried he might be violent?"

"He has a temper," Jack confirmed. "We picked him up for assault at least once."

"Should we walk the perimeter from time to time?" Mendez asked.

"Couldn't hurt." Jack straightened and stretched his back. "We're going to pop in and talk to Mister Hutchins. If you have any questions, grab us when we come out."

"Will do," Mendez said. "Oh, and Jack?"

"Yes?"

"Take it easy on him," the officer said. "He just lost his wife."

Jack didn't respond, turning and walking toward the house across the street. Shaun cut off the conversation he was having with Wilson and jogged to catch up with his partner. They stepped onto the porch and Jack pressed the doorbell.

"Did we ever get anything on the blood that was on here?"

"Not that I've heard," Shaun answered.

"We need to follow up with that." Jack barely finished the sentence before the door opened.

When Jack interviewed Sharon and Reginald Hutchins' son, he was sitting with his knees pulled up to his chest as you might expect to find a teenager after learning his mother had just been killed. Now, standing in the doorway, Brian Hutchins looked to be a near photocopy of his father. Only in the boy's eyes did Jack see signs of his mother.

"Brian," Jack kept his voice low and non-threatening. "Is your father home?"

Spinning on his heels, Brian called, "Dad! Cops at the door!"

"What?" Reginald's voice was distant.

Jack considered the layout of the house and tried to ascertain where the man might be. His best guess was in one of the bedrooms or possibly the garage.

"Cops!" Brian shouted. The teenager then turned to the detectives and waved an arm. "Come on in."

Brian led the men down the hall and into the family room. He stood awkwardly with them until his father finally appeared through a door adjacent to the kitchen. Seeing the detectives, he did not try to hide his disappointment.

"Oh." His shoulders fell and he glanced at a clock on the nearby wall. "You have news?"

"Questions."

"Of course you do," Reggie said. "They can't wait until the morning?"

"Afraid not," Jack shook his head. "But we don't need too much of your time."

"Let's get it over with."

"Do you want to talk here?" Jack asked. "Or in the office?"

Reginald looked at his son. "There's nothing you can't say in front of him."

The homeowner settled onto the couch where he had been sitting the first time Jack had seen him that morning. Brian chose a seat at the kitchen island, close enough to overhear, far enough not to participate. The detectives sat across from Reginald and opened their respective notepads.

"So, what do you want?" Reggie's disappointment lingered.

"We need to ask some questions about Sharon." Jack held the man's gaze with his own.

"What about her?"

"First," Jack said, "we are following up on several leads and possible motives. One question that came up was, given that she was going to have a press conference, did Sharon have any political aspirations?"

"Political ...? Sharon?" Reggie almost laughed. "I thought you guys knew her."

The detectives did not respond.

"Listen." The man's hands, which had been resting on his knees, raised. He held them apart and shook them up and down as he spoke driving his words home. "The woman hated politics. The little bit she dealt with just to become a chief made her uncomfortable. There was no way she was thinking of running for an office of any kind. I don't know where you would have come up with that idea, but it's wrong."

"We just have to follow up on everything," Jack explained. "No matter how insignificant or unlikely."

"Okay." Reggie let his hands drop to his knees once more. "It's just so far off course."

"Let's move on," Jack suggested.

"Sure."

"During the autopsy, we learned something." Jack glanced at Brian, who was pretending to not be listening. "Did you know your wife had cancer?"

"Cancer?"

"Did you know?"

"No." Reggie struggled to process what he was hearing. "What? When did she find out? Was it serious?"

"We don't know when she found out," Jack said. "We don't even know that she knew. From what we were told, with treatment, she might have beaten it. Undiagnosed, she probably had a year tops."

"A year?"

Brian slipped off his perch at the kitchen island and walked past them toward the stairs. He climbed, taking two steps at a time. Upstairs the sound of his bedroom door closing was just shy of a slam.

"That's what they said," Shaun answered. "Do you know who her doctor was?"

"Her doctor?" Reggie closed his eyes. "Uh, yeah. She saw Doctor, uh, God, what is her name?"

"Do you have records," Shaun suggested. "Or medical bills?"

"Osborn." Reggie snapped his fingers and opened his eyes. "Silvia Osborn. She's gone to her for years."

Both detectives wrote the name in their notepads.

"Why does it matter?" Reggie asked. "She didn't die of cancer, now did she?"

"It matters because, if she knew," Jack put his hands together in front of him. "If she knew, and wasn't up for what came next ..."

"You think she asked someone to do this to her?" Reggie sat forward. "Are you serious?"

"Any detail," Jack said. "No matter how insignificant or unlikely."

"Well, you're wrong. Again," Reggie said. "She wouldn't do that to us."

"I'm sure you're right," Jack said. "Just one last thing. Did Sharon have any family? Aside from you and your son, of course. There was a mention that she had a sister."

"A sister, yes." Reggie nodded. "Marcia Winthrop. She lost her husband about three years ago, so the two of them have been spending a lot of time together lately."

"Thank you," Jack said. "That's all we need. We'll show ourselves out."

Jack stood, followed by Shaun. They left the man sitting on the couch, stunned and lost.

30

J ack and Shaun stood side by side examining the whiteboard with fresh eyes. The start of a new day would hopefully give them a new perspective to help them identify their killer. They added the details they learned from their first day of the investigation and were tasked with trying to find the hidden links between the facts that might point at a single suspect. Neither heard Detective Weatherby walk through the door of the conference room.

"How's it going?" She announced herself.

Startled, Shaun tossed the folder he was holding into the air and watched its pages scatter. "Geez, Maureen!"

"Me?" Maureen put a hand to her chest. "You're blaming me for that?"

"You …"

"I what?"

Shaun looked at Jack for support and saw that none was coming. "Forget it."

The young detective dropped to his knee and started picking up documents and placing them back into the folder, setting the folder on the table with the others.

"What brings you to our little corner?" Jack sat on the edge of the table and crossed his arms.

Maureen sat next to him and mimicked his body language. "Chief Grimes said anyone not currently on a case should report here to see what they could do to help."

"He did, did he?" Jack frowned.

"What?" Maureen turned to him. "You don't want my help?"

"Sure I do," Jack said. "I'm just just considering who else might show up."

"Are you saying there are those in this building with whom you wouldn't want to work?"

Jack grinned.

"You really think they would volunteer for more work?"Maureen curled one side of her lips. "With you?"

"True." Jack let his grin fade. "Wait. I thought you had a case. The Applegate kid?"

"Found him." Maureen beamed with pride.

"When?"

"Early this morning." She leaned closer. "After you left this morning, I got the call on a warrant I had requested. Scumbag had him locked in a windowless room with no lights."

"How was he?"

"Physically, he was okay," she sighed. "At least no obvious injuries. The doctors will determine the rest. Mentally...the kid's going to need therapy. A lot of therapy."

"But you found him."

"I did."

"That's great," Jack smiled. "Congratulations."

"Are you two done?" Shaun grumbled. "Or should I call Liza so we can double date?"

"Excuse me?" Jack turned to his partner.

"Uh," Shaun winced. "Sorry."

"How about we review the case for Maureen?" Jack suggested. "Maybe she'll see something we've missed."

Maureen studied the photos and notes on the whiteboard. "That is a lot of suspects."

Jack moved to the board. "First, because the husband always did it, we have Reginald Hutchins. We know he had motive, because Sharon cheated on him, albeit a year ago. But we still haven't learned who the affair was with, or if it actually ever ended. We learned yesterday that Sharon has a sister. We're going to talk to her, to see if she knows anything."

"I can do that," Maureen offered. "She might be more receptive talking to a woman."

"Thank you," Jack made a note. "The thing with Reggie is that according to the son, he didn't have opportunity. He said his father was in the house with him. We also know that the power was out, and the son was playing a video game on his phone with headphones. So, that makes him a less reliable witness."

"Do you really think he was involved?" Shaun asked. "I mean, he seemed sincerely torn up about the whole thing."

"I hope not," Jack said. "But we consider him a suspect until we can rule him out."

"What about the son?" Maureen asked. "It wouldn't be the first time a kid killed his parent."

"If Reggie wasn't involved, then he's Brian's alibi," Jack said. "And since the boy was playing a game on his phone, the glowing screen would make it hard to sneak out of the house unnoticed."

"So we're ruling him out?" Shaun raised his eyebrows.

"For now."

"One down." The young detective gave a thumbs up.

"Next up, we have Trey Levine." Jack pointed at the drug dealer's photo. "Sharon was supposed to testify against him at his trial this morning. Her death benefitted him the most. However, he's been in solitary for the past year. The only visitor he has had was his attorney. So unless we believe his attorney or one of the guards helped him plan a hit on a police chief, we can probably rule him out."

"The timing just seems too much of a coincidence," Shaun commented.

"I agree," Jack said. "We can look into the lawyer and the guards. But, what would be their motive to help? If they get caught, they're looking at life. The attorney, especially, would know that. I think we should focus our efforts on more plausible suspects."

"Okay." Shaun nodded in agreement.

"Which brings us to Ian Fielding." Jack pointed. "He was a C.I. of Sharon's when she was still a detective. He was imprisoned for killing his sister's boyfriend after he put her in the hospital. Sharon obviously didn't hand him a get-out-of-jail-free card, so he may have held a grudge. He was released from prison recently and we need to track his movements since then."

Maureen held up her hand.

Jack looked at her. "Really?"

She lowered her hand. "Sorry. Habit. I was just going to say that I could track his movements. That falls into my purview."

Jack turned to Shaun. "You going to let her do everything?"

"If she wants to, I won't stop her," Shaun grinned. "Besides, there's still plenty to do."

"Okay then," Jack wrote Maureen's name down again. He thumbed through his notes. "We need to know where he was for the past week or so. He says he was at his halfway house the morning she was killed. So we need to verify that if we can."

"Will do." She pulled the man's file from the stack and set it next to her.

"Next we have Randy Keyes, the good Samaritan, who found Sharon and called for help," Jack said. "We haven't found a motive for him, and we know that the killer wore gloves and none were recovered in his possession or his home."

"He could have ditched the gloves," Maureen suggested.

"True," Jack agreed. "Have we heard back from the lab on his clothing? Any traces of gunshot residue?"

"We haven't heard, yet," Shaun said.

"Okay." Jack made a note to follow up. "He stays as a possible."

"Agreed," Shaun said.

"Dan Pollard is high on our list." Jack poked the man's image with his index finger repeatedly. "He's known to have a temper. Sharon helped his wife get a protection order against him. And he owns a green sedan, a vehicle more than one resident in the neighborhood mentioned seeing in the days leading up to the killing."

"I can talk to his neighbors," Shaun volunteered. "Maybe one of them saw him leave in the morning. Seeing as it was dark out when he would have had to leave, it's probably a long shot."

"You never know what people are up to in the early hours," Jack said. "Someone may have been leaving for work or coming home from an all-nighter."

"Coming home from an all-nighter might not be too helpful," Maureen said. "They might not even remember how they got home, let alone who they saw."

"True," Jack agreed. "Maybe someone saw him coming home later, covered in blood."

"I'll head over when we're finished here," Shaun reiterated.

"What do we think of Dave Bartlett?" Jack asked. "Sharon complained about the noise his motorcycles were making at all hours."

"He almost smiled when I mentioned the chief was dead," Shaun added. "Rubbed me the wrong way."

"If he did it though," Maureen said. "Wouldn't he know not to smile? Because he would have already known she was dead."

"Unless he wasn't sure," Shaun said. "I could have just confirmed what he was hoping to be true."

"Didn't you say she had helped him in another situation?" Jack asked.

"Another neighbor accused him of killing her cat," Shaun nodded. "The chief proved he didn't do it."

"So, we'll leave him on the board," Jack concluded. "But follow up on other suspects first."

"Who is Vince Abrams?" Maureen gestured toward the man's portrait. "He looks familiar."

"He owned a construction company," Shaun answered. "A few years ago two people died when one of his buildings collapsed. The chief investigated and had his company blacklisted from bidding on city jobs. Damaged his business and his reputation."

"That sounds like motive," Maureen raised an eyebrow.

"It is," Jack agreed.

"If the chief was Narcotics and Vice before taking over Homicide," Maureen said. "Do we know why she was investigating a collapsed building?"

"No idea," Shaun said. He looked at Jack who simply shook his head.

"Is it something we should look into?" Maureen asked. "Could have been personal. Maybe she had history with Abrams and was trying to destroy him. It would make his motive even stronger."

"I can ask around," Jack said. "But if she was investigating him on her own time, which is most likely since it wasn't her jurisdiction, I'm not sure who to ask."

"But it's the strongest motive we have," Maureen argued. "If it's true."

"However Mister Abrams was attacking with legal means," Shaun added. "He filed a lawsuit against the city and Sharon. Someone going to that trouble doesn't sound like someone planning a murder."

"Unless he wants you to think that," Maureen said. "Look at what I'm doing over here and ignore what I'm doing over there."

"Possibly," Jack said. "We aren't eliminating him yet. And to add to your theory that he is just smoke screening us, he's the one who put Carl Delacruz's name up here."

"The Carl Delacruz?"

"The one and only," Jack nodded. "If Abrams is to be believed, Delacruz had a strong disliking of the chief."

"What does Delacruz say?" Maureen asked.

"We haven't talked to him," Jack said. "I guess he's on my list. Which leaves us with Edward Simmons."

"Oh, Edward," Maureen sighed. "How did you get on this list?"

"You know him?"

"Before his daughter's body was found, she was a missing person." Maureen crossed her arms. "I worked the case. Turns out she was killed the first night, long before we got involved. I really wanted to bring her home to him."

"He wasn't too happy when the guy arrested for her murder ended up walking," Jack said. "Made a few calls to the chief even though she wasn't involved. Now he's a suspect. What can you tell us about him?"

"Keep in mind, when I met Mister Simmons, he and his wife were desperate to find their daughter," Maureen thought back. "She had been missing for two days before the case was handed to me. I have no sense of the man before that time."

"But?"

"He was relentless," she said. "He organized the search parties and was with them constantly. I don't remember him taking any breaks. I would almost say he didn't sleep from the time we started looking for her until her body was found."

"And how long was that?"

"Just shy of seventy-two hours."

"And he didn't sleep?"

"I don't know for sure," she said. "But every time I was out there, so was he. When I left for the nights, he was there with a flashlight. When I came back in the mornings, he was already at it. I suppose he may have gone home at some point, but not for very long."

"You say he planned the searches?"'

"Yes," she nodded. "And led some of the groups."

"So he was good at organizing, planning?" Jack asked.

"Meticulous," she said. "He was such a man of habit."

"What do you mean?"

"The search patterns were always the same," she said. "The water breaks were at the same time, in the same intervals. Every minute was scheduled. He did everything the same way every day."

Jack paused. He searched his mind for a memory of his conversation with Edward Simmons. Then it came to him. "Breakfast."

"What?" Maureen scrunched her brow. "There was no breakfast."

"Not then," Jack shook his head. He pulled out his notepad and flipped back through the pages. "He has the same breakfast at the same diner, at the same time, every day."

"Molly's Diner," Shaun snapped his fingers.

"Did we ever follow up on that?"

"Not yet."

"Assuming he isn't lying," Jack said. "He has an alibi for the murder."

31

Detective Maureen Weatherby parked on the street in front of a two-story Victorian that was probably a work of art in its day. Now it was just a run-down building with broken shutters and peeling paint. The corner lot it sat on was in serious need of mowing, not to mention a weed treatment.

Stepping out of her car, Maureen glanced up to the second floor. A man stood behind a window there, staring down at her. Without shifting her gaze, she pulled her jacket back to expose her weapon and shield. The man backed away from the glass and disappeared into the shadows of the room.

Taking confident strides, she climbed the steps, that had a little more give than expected, to the porch. The boards beneath her feet were cracked and rotted with age and neglect. Maureen almost felt bad for the residents, living in such a dump.

The door swung open just as she was reaching up to knock. A man rushed out, stopped dead in his tracks, and stared at her. His eyes had no gleam, appearing lifeless, soulless. Instinctively, she raised her hand to her weapon. The man lowered his eyes to the ground and rushed on.

The door was still standing open, so Maureen stepped inside and pulled it closed behind her. To her left was an abandoned living space, complete with fireplace. The furniture was outdated and worn from use. To the right was originally a dining room. A glass chandelier with a number of missing pieces hung in its center. Instead of a dining table, there was a desk below the light fixture. The large man sitting behind the desk did not look up when Maureen entered the room. He held a phone to his ear.

"Like I've already told you." The man's deep voice dominated the room. "I can't give out that kind of information. So, quit calling."

Pete Meadows hung up the phone and only then looked up at his visitor. There were deep crevices in his skin, scars he had received during an undercover assignment gone wrong. After successfully infiltrating a gang, he had gathered enough evidence to put most of them away for years. Days from the completion of his assignment, a large drug deal had been set up and he was part of the protection detail. By the time he realized one of the gang members on the other side of the deal was a man he had personally arrested, it was too late. Luckily, he had little memory of the next few hours, when he was tortured and beaten. He was found the next morning after being left for dead with three gunshot wounds.

"And you are?"

Maureen showed her shield. "Detective Weatherby. I'm here about Ian Fielding."

"Fielding?" Pete bobbed his head. "That doesn't surprise me."

"Why is that?"

"I'm usually a good judge of who's going to end up back inside," Pete said. "What's he done?"

"He's a person of interest in a homicide," Maureen said. "Can you tell me when he left and returned yesterday morning?"

Pete pulled a ledger to him and opened it. "Says here he was working a third shift and returned at eight that morning."

Maureen made a note of the time. "Do you know when his work shift ended?"

"No idea," Pete said. "We just log their comings and goings."

"What about transportation?" she asked. "How does he get to and from work?"

"Gary!" Pete leaned back in his chair as he called out. "Office!"

He leaned forward again and grinned at the female detective. The scars on the side of his face seemed to mock his friendly gesture.

A moment later a uniformed officer appeared in the doorway to Maureen's left. "What's up, boss?"

"Ian Fielding," Pete said. "Does he take the van to work?"

"Sometimes," Gary said.

"Did he get picked up yesterday morning?" Maureen asked. "He would have worked a third shift the night before."

"Yesterday?" Gary grimaced. "Sure. I picked him up at seven-thirty, I think."

"You think or you know?" Pete asked.

"Seven-thirty," Gary said. "I know it was seven-thirty."

"Where did you pick him up?" Maureen asked. "Anywhere near Arlington Estates?"

"Arlington Estates?" Gary shook his head. "Where is that?"

"Sixty-fifth and Elm area," Maureen answered.

"No." Gary shook his head again. "Nowhere near that."

"Okay. When does Fielding get off work?"

"I think seven," he answered. "But I'm not sure."

"That would have only given him half an hour," Maureen thought aloud.

"What's this about?" Gary asked.

"Homicide," Pete chimed in.

"Ian?"

"Don't be surprised," Pete said. "He did his time for murder."

"Just doesn't sound like the Ian I know."

"How can you be sure he went to work?" Maureen asked. "Or know he didn't leave early?"

"We don't," Pete answered. "We drop them off. We pick them up. It's their responsibility to keep the job if they want out of the system."

"What does he do?" Maureen asked. "Where does he work?"

"He works at a warehouse, packing boxes for shipping," Gary said. "I can get you the address if you want it."

"That would be great," Maureen smiled. "I may pay them a visit."

Gary disappeared through the doorway he had first come through, leaving Maureen and Pete alone with an awkward silence between them until his return. The man held out a piece of paper which Maureen accepted.

"Thank you." She read the address on the paper and slipped it into her pocket.

32

Shaun parked on the street about three houses down from Dan Pollard's small home. The detective had checked and found the place was a month-to-month rental, leaving Mister Pollard with the ability to uproot and move on anytime he liked. The green sedan was parked in the driveway suggesting the owner had not fled yet.

Shaun stepped out onto the street and surveyed the neighborhood. Two of the houses were boarded up. One had a large dumpster in front and looked to be gutted inside. Someone was trying to update a home in a neighborhood of dilapidated houses. It seemed to Shaun to be a good way to lose money unless they planned to do every house on the street.

The detective chose the home with the nicest landscaping, reasoning that someone who took care of their yard had to spend time in it. He walked up the steps to the porch and knocked on the door. While he waited for someone to answer, he looked around in search of his next stop. The creak of hinges brought him back around.

"What?" The man only opened the door a small amount, exposing the security chain.

"Detective Travis." Shaun held up his shield. "I need to ask you some questions about one of your neighbors."

"Just one?"

Shaun would have thought the man was making a joke, but there was no hint of humor in his expression. "Dan Pollard. Do you know him?"

"No."

"He lives across the street there." Shaun pointed.

"Oh. Him." There was a look of disgust on the man's face.

"You don't care for him?"

"What's to like?" The man scowled. "Comes and goes at all hours. Never mows his lawn. And rude. Always so rude."

"You mentioned he comes and goes at all hours," Shaun said. "How do you know? Do you watch him?"

"No, I don't watch him," he seemed offended by the accusation. "It's his car. He needs to replace the muffler. Sounds like a freight train."

"I don't suppose you remember hearing him come and go yesterday morning?"

"Yesterday?" The man thought a moment. "Night before last he left late. Real late. Woke me up. Didn't come back until yesterday, maybe noonish."

"And you're sure about that?" Shaun asked.

"You think I'm lying?"

"No," he said. "I just need you to be positive."

"I'm positive," he snapped and shut the door.

"Okay," Shaun said to himself.

The detective retreated to the street and selected another house; the one directly to the right of Dan Pollard's. He knocked and waited. Knocked again. He was just about to give up when the door opened slowly, but all the way. For a second, Shaun thought there was no one there. Then he spotted a small boy behind the door, his head about the height of the knob.

"Hi there." Shaun smiled, keeping his voice soft and non-threatening. "Is your mom or dad home?"

The boy, wearing nothing but a diaper, spun on his heels and ran deeper into the house, giggling as he went. Shaun stood just outside the open door waiting for a parent to arrive. None did.

"Hello!" He called out. After another moment he tried again. "Hello! Is anyone home?"

The detective debated searching the house, to conduct a wellness check for parent and child. It was about that time a woman appeared at the end of the short hall. Her hair was a mess, her clothing wrinkled. When she saw Shaun, her eyes went wide and she charged at him like a bull. "What do you think you're doing? You can't just let yourself in."

Shaun looked down to assure himself that no part of him had crossed the threshold.

"Did you open this door?" she demanded.

"No, ma'am," he said.

"You want me to call the police?" she asked.

Shaun was humored by the question. No one would answer with a yes. And if he meant her harm, there was no way she could make a call before he got to her. Shaun held up his shield for her to see. "A young boy in diapers answered the door."

"Calvin?" The woman looked around frantically, the pitch of her voice rising. "Calvin? Where is he? What did you do with him? You can't just take my son."

"I didn't take your son," Shaun assured her. He pointed down the hall. "He ran that way."

The woman started to walk away, stopped in her tracks, and turned to the detective. "Wait here."

With that, she continued after the boy.

Shaun found himself abandoned in front of the open door once again. He turned an ear to the opening and tried to listen for sounds of what might be happening. A few minutes later the woman walked back to the front door with the young boy in tow. When they reached the door, she kneeled down and lifted the boy to rest on her hip.

"So, you're a cop," she said. "What are you doing here?"

"Can I get your name?" Shaun asked.

"Missy." There was reluctance in her voice. "Missy Faulkner."

"I need to ask you about your neighbor, Dan Pollard," Shaun explained.

"Dan?" she asked. "What about him?"

"How well do you know him?"

"Not well," Missy said. "He's lived here a few months. Hit on me once, 'til he saw Calvin. Then he couldn't get away fast enough."

"Do you ever notice when Mister Pollard leaves or comes home?" Shaun asked.

"Sometimes." Missy bounced the young boy. "When I'm up, I sit on the porch. So, I see people come and go."

"Were you up yesterday morning?" Shaun asked, then added, "before sunup."

"I can tell you he wasn't home yesterday morning," she said. "If that's what you're wanting to know."

"He wasn't?"

"No."

"And, you're sure?"

"The night before," she said, "my show ended at eleven. I came outside for some air and Dan was backing out of his driveway."

"At eleven."

"I went to bed around midnight," Missy continued. "And when Calvin woke me at five, Dan still wasn't home. Figured he got lucky."

"Do you know when he returned home?" Shaun wrote in his notes.

"Sorry," Missy shrugged. "I had to go to work. He still wasn't home when I left at eight, but he was there when I got home at six."

"Okay." Shaun looked toward Dan's house. "Is there anything else you can tell me about him?"

"Remember." Missy bounced the boy. "Once he saw Calvin, I never got the chance to get to know him."

"Here's my card." Shaun handed it to her. "If anything comes to mind, give me a call."

Missy took the card and held it down to her side.

Shaun turned to leave, then back again. "For what it's worth, you're lucky you didn't get to know him."

The woman stood with her son sitting on her hip, watching the detective until he drove away. When he was out of sight, she shut the door, set the boy down, and walked to her room. Dan Pollard lay stretched out on her bed.

"Who was that?" he asked.

"Nobody." Missy kept her eyes on the floor.

"That was a long conversation for nobody," he said.

"He was selling a pest control service," she said. "Didn't see the harm in hearing him out."

"You're not lying to me, are you?" Dan sat up, narrowing his eyes.

"Geez, Dan," Missy said. "Why would I lie? Why don't you go home?"

He nodded. "I'm going. That kid running around like that makes me sick."

Missy narrowed her eyes at his back as he left. Calvin walked up beside her and took her hand. She smiled down at him. "Don't worry, baby. We might just get rid of him yet."

33

Jack Mallory sat in a folding chair against the wall of the campaign headquarters for Carl Delacruz. He had called the man's office and was told the politician would be here. So far, he had been kept waiting for nearly half an hour. He watched the staff moving around the room, stopping for brief conversations, before returning to their desks to man phones. Nearly all of them glanced his way every few minutes.

A door in the back of the room opened and a man in a suit, who Jack recognized immediately, walked out and made a quick escape without saying a word to anyone. The woman who had told Jack to sit where he was, stood and passed through the door. A few minutes later she and Carl Delacruz came out together. She pointed at Jack and the politician walked straight to him.

"Detective Mallory, is it?" He held his hand out.

Jack considered a moment before accepting the gesture. "It is."

"And what brings you here, detective?" the man asked. "How can we help you today?"

"Almost sounds like a campaign slogan," Jack commented, releasing the handshake.

"It does, doesn't it," Carl smiled. "Must be the politician in me."

"I have some questions," Jack asked. "Is there somewhere we could talk?"

"Wait a minute," Carl snapped his fingers. "Detective Mallory. I've heard that name before. Aren't you some kind of super detective? John, or something."

"Jack," the detective corrected. "And no. I'm just a normal detective."

"That's not the word around the water cooler," Carl said.

"You shouldn't listen to rumors," Jack advised. "As a politician, I think you would know that."

"And right you are," Carl laughed aloud, leaving Jack to wonder why. "Let's go to my office. Emma, hold my calls please."

"Yes, sir."

The two men walked into the office and sat across from each other.

"Now," Carl said. "What brings you here?"

"How much time do I have?"

"Pardon?"

"How long before Emma does as you asked and interrupts us with an important call or meeting?" Jack watched the man's face. There was only a slight twitch in the corner of his eye. Jack smiled. "I'm right."

"Ten minutes," Carl admitted.

"This shouldn't take long," Jack said. "I just need to know about your relationship with Chief Sharon Hutchins."

"I heard about her," Carl's voice lowered. "Damn shame. She was a good cop."

"I'm surprised to hear that from you," Jack said. "The two of you didn't exactly see eye to eye on things."

"We didn't always," Carl said. "But that didn't make her a bad cop."

"So," Jack said. "Tell me about your relationship."

"There was no relationship," Carl said. "We butted heads in meetings and the media sometimes. The rest of the time we were cordial. We didn't have dinner or seek each other out at functions. We just existed in the same world."

"There's one thing I don't understand." Jack sat back in his chair. "There were other politicians she didn't see eye to eye with. But she never publically attacked them the way she did you. Can you explain that?"

"I never noticed." Carl crossed his arms. "I just assumed she attacked us all the same. I even thought she might be running for office. Maybe she was running for my seat."

"I thought of that," Jack nodded. "But I checked. She had no interest in running."

"Well, Jack," Carl grinned. "You're the detective. If you figure it out, let me know. I'd love to know why she had it out for me."

"So she did have it out for you?"

"Well, you just told me she attacked me more than others," Carl said. "So, it sounds like she did. But this is the first I'm hearing of it. It's not like we talked about it."

"Just one more question," Jack sat up again. "Where were you yesterday morning, just before sunrise?"

"You think I killed her?" Carl put a hand to his chest. "Are you crazy?"

"Just answer the question," Jack said.

"Should I have a lawyer?"

"Did you kill her?"

"No."

"Then tell me where you were," Jack said. "And I'll be on my way."

"I can't," Carl said.

"You can't, or won't?" Jack pressed.

"Semantics," Carl said. "I'm not telling you where I was."

Realization came to Jack and he smiled. "You were either killing Sharon Hutchins, or you were with a woman, not your wife."

"I'm not answering."

The door opened and Emma stepped part way in. "Sorry Mister Delacruz. You have that meeting you need to leave for."

Jack smiled and stood. "It was her, wasn't it?"

"Excuse me?" Emma looked up at him.

"Are you his alibi for yesterday morning, or not?" Jack asked her.

She looked at the politician for guidance. Carl just shrugged.

"We were working yesterday morning," she said.

"Working?" Jack laughed and put a hand on her shoulder. "Emma, if you think of it as work, he's not doing it right."

The woman blushed.

"There's my confirmation."

"Are we done here?" Carl asked sternly.

"We are," Jack said. "Unless you hired someone to kill her."

"What would be my motive?"

"You said you thought she was running for office," Jack suggested. "Or maybe she found out about Emma."

"I don't kill my opponents, detective," Carl chuckled. "If I did, there would be a lot more dead than one woman. And Sharon didn't know about Emma. Yesterday was the first time we, uh, transgressed."

Jack looked at Emma who nodded and lowered her eyes.

"Emma what?" Jack asked.

"Pardon?" She looked up again.

"Your last name?"

"Oh," she said. "Acosta. Emma Acosta."

"Thank you." Jack wrote the name in his notepad. He looked back at the politician and nodded before walking out.

34

Jackrabbit Shipping claimed to be able to ship anything. Catering mostly to a higher-class clientele, they picked up the item, packed it, shipped it almost anywhere, unpacked it, and delivered it. The shipper and receiver never had to deal with shipping materials inside their home. It was a premium service that came at an equally premium price. Housed in a warehouse on the edge of the retail district, the entry looked more like a furniture showroom than a shipping company.

Maureen felt underdressed when she walked through the front door. The employees must have had the same feeling as they gave her time to retreat before acknowledging her presence.

"Can I help you?" The man, in a fitted suit, sounded skeptical.

"Are you the manager?" Maureen looked past the man to the similarly dressed man and woman standing behind the counter.

"No, ma'am," he answered. "But ..."

"You can help me by telling your manager I need to see him."

"I assure you, I can help you with..."

Maureen pulled the shield from her belt and held it in front of his face. "Manager. Now."

The man took a couple of steps back before rushing through a door. Maureen looked again at the two employees behind the counter, who lowered their eyes. She smirked and turned back to the door just as it opened again. The employee stepped into the room, followed by a tall, thick woman in a blouse, pencil skirt, and sneakers.

The woman looked at Maureen from head to toe as she approached. "You're the cop?"

"Detective Weatherby." She showed her shield and clipped it back on her belt.

"Detective?" The woman frowned. "What's this about?"

"I need some information about one of your employees," Maureen said. "An Ian Fielding."

"Ian?" The woman shifted her weight from one leg to the other. "What do you need to know?"

"Our understanding is that he was working a shift that ended at seven yesterday morning," Maureen said. "Is that what your records show?"

"Yesterday morning?" The woman repeated. "I don't need to check the records, I was here. Ian left early."

"He did?" Maureen pulled out her notepad. "Do you remember what time?"

"Six," she said. "He said he needed to run an errand."

"At six in the morning?" Maureen said. "Did he mention what the errand was?"

"I thought it was strange too, but I didn't ask," she said. "We were almost done for the day, so I let him leave."

"Is Ian here now?" Maureen asked. "I'd like to speak to him."

"Today is his day off," the woman said.

"Is Ian close to any of his co-workers?" Maureen asked. "Anyone he would talk to? Confide in?"

"I don't think so," she answered. "Unless, maybe Jo."

"Jo?" Maureen wrote in her pad. "Is he here?"

"She is," the woman said. "It's short for Joanne."

"I'm going to need to speak to her."

The woman turned to the employee who was still standing next to her. "Go tell Jo we need her on the floor."

"Yes, ma'am," he ran through the door to the back.

Detective and manager stood side by side in silence while they waited. A few minutes passed and Maureen was beginning to think Jo had made a run for it when the young woman appeared. Her eyes shifted from her boss to Maureen and back again.

"Is there a problem, ma'am?" she asked.

"This detective wants to ask you about Ian."

Jo turned to Maureen. "Detective?"

"And your name is?" Maureen asked.

"Jo," she said. "Well, Joanne. Joanne Pinehurst."

"How do you know Ian?"

"We work together," Jo said. "Here."

"And how well do you know him?" Maureen asked. "Do the two of you talk?"

"Sometimes," she said. "We share some similar interests."

"Such as?"

"Music," Jo said. "We listen to the same bands."

"Did he talk to you yesterday morning?" Maureen asked. "Before he left?"

"I suppose."

"Did he happen to tell you why he was leaving early?" Maureen asked. "Where he was going?"

"He said he was going to meet a woman," Jo said.

"A woman?"

"Yes."

"Did he mention a name?"

"No," Jo said. "He just said it was someone he hadn't seen in a while."

"Did he say anything else about the woman?" Maureen asked. "Anything that might help me identify her?"

"No," she said. "Just that he hadn't seen her in a long time. And he had something to give her."

"What was that?"

"I don't know," Jo said. "What's this about?"

"Does the name Sharon Hutchins mean anything to you?" Maureen ignored her.

"No."

"Are you sure?"

"I don't know anyone by that name," Jo said. "Is Ian okay?"

Maureen ignored her again and handed her a card. "If you think of anything, give me a call."

The detective walked out to the sound of whispering behind her.

35

Maureen spotted Shaun as soon as she entered the department. He sat at his desk leaning toward his computer as he typed. She scanned the room for Jack but did not see the senior detective. She looked toward the chief's office knowing Hutchins wasn't there and Jack had no reason to be. Walking toward Shaun, she checked the breakroom, expecting to find Jack caffeinating. He was not there.

Maureen passed by the conference room they were using before sitting at Jack's desk across from his partner. "Where's Jack?"

"Maureen." Shaun stretched his neck. "I didn't hear you come in."

"Where's Jack?" she repeated.

"Hasn't come back yet." He looked at the clock on the wall above the breakroom. "It's been a while."

"Should we be worried?"

"I'll give him a call," Shaun said.

"I'll do it." Maureen pulled her phone out.

The elevator doors opened and she looked up to see Jack walking into the department. Slipping the phone back into her pocket, she stood and waited for him to arrive.

As he walked by, Jack waved his hand. "Let's see what we've learned."

The three of them moved to the conference room where Shaun and Maureen sat facing the whiteboard and Jack stood before them.

"What did Dan Pollard's neighbors have to say?" Jack picked up a marker.

"Dan left his home the night before Sharon was killed," Shaun said. "He didn't return until close to noon after her death."

"So, no alibi."

"Appears not," Shaun agreed.

"No wonder he didn't want to talk to us." Jack wrote 'no alibi' under Dan's name. "Any luck tracking Ian Fielding's movements?"

"He was working that morning." Maureen sat forward in her chair. "He was scheduled to be off at seven that morning but left about an hour early claiming to need to run some errands. A co-worker said he mentioned a meeting with a woman."

"Do we know who he was meeting?" Jack faced her. "Could it be Sharon?"

"I don't know where he went, yet," she answered. "But if he was meeting Sharon, the statements from the son and husband would suggest she wasn't aware of it."

Under Ian's name, Jack wrote 'gap in timeline'. He then turned to the others. "I spoke to Delacruz. It appears he was with a mistress at the time of the murder, unless she's lying for him. But one thing did come up that has me wondering. She wasn't attacking Delacruz because she wanted to run for office. It seems clear she had no such ambitions. But what made her attack him? Delacruz pointed out that he wasn't the only one she was at odds with, but he was the only one she went after publicly. Why?"

"What if he was the one she had the affair with?" Shaun suggested. "Maybe she tried to end things and he didn't take the hint, so she started to attack him to make him back off."

"Do you really see her having a relationship with a sleaze like Delacruz?" Maureen asked. "Besides, the attacks went both ways. If he was trying to hang on to her, he wouldn't have said the things he said. It sounded more like a mutual disliking of one another."

"You've never been married," Jack said. "I've heard married couples say worse things to one another at the end of their relationship. It could be he finally got the hint and retaliated. We don't rule him out until we can confirm his alibi."

"And who is this mistress?" Maureen asked.

"Her name is Emma Acosta. She is his assistant at his campaign headquarters," Jack said. "We verify. But in case they are in the clear, I agreed to leave her name out of it unless it's necessary."

"I can get her information," Shaun said. "Follow up."

"You do that," Jack nodded. "What about Sharon's sister? Have you had a chance to talk to her yet?"

"No, I've been chasing Ian's trail," Maureen said. "But I am planning to talk to her next."

Jack's phone rang and he answered it quickly. "Mallory."

The detective listened for a short time then slid the pocket back into his pocket. "Okay. Maureen's talking to Sharon's sister. Shaun is following up with Delacruz's alibi. And it appears I am going to the lab for an update on the evidence collected from the scene."

36

Where Sharon Hutchins became a police chief and married an architect. Her sister, Wendi Noble, had become a lawyer and married a doctor. The Hutchins' home was a large house in a gated community. The Noble's home was huge, on several acres, with its own gates.

Maureen sat in her car trying to figure out which of the buttons on the intercom system she needed to press to get someone's attention when a tinny voice erupted from the speaker.

"This is private property," the voice announced. "We aren't buying anything, donating anything, or speaking to anyone."

Maureen held her shield in front of the small camera at the top of the box. "Police business. I need to speak to Wendi Noble."

"This is not a good time."

"Tell her it's about her sister." Maureen put her shield away. "It is imperative that we talk."

There was no response and the detective decided that they had chosen to ignore her. She was weighing her options when she heard a loud buzzer and the gate started rolling open slowly. Maureen mused that if they ever needed an ambulance, the wait would literally kill them.

As soon as the gate cleared her bumper, Maureen stepped on the accelerator and raced down the driveway to a circle in front of the main house. The detective parked and climbed the dozen or more steps to the front entrance; double doors, each four feet wide and nine feet tall. She couldn't imagine why anyone would need an opening that large into one's home.

One of the doors opened as she reached the top step and a man in a suit and tie greeted her. "Officer."

"Detective," she corrected.

"Forgive me," he bowed his head. "If you will follow me."

Expecting to be taken to a library or sitting room, Maureen was surprised when they passed those types of rooms and emerged in a utility room in the back of the home. A woman was standing in the room's center at a worktable. She was easily identifiable as Sharon's sister. Same green eyes, high cheekbones, narrow nose, and jet-black hair. If Maureen had caught a glimpse of this woman on the street, she would have thought the chief was still alive. That is until she spoke.

"Welcome to my home," the woman smiled. Her soft, soothing voice was far from the strong, sharp note of Sharon's.

Maureen could not remember a single time the chief had smiled. She had always been stern and unemotional.

"Thank you," Maureen said. "I would like to offer my deepest sympathies. Chief Hutch...Sharon was well-liked in the department and will be missed."

"Miss...?"

"Weatherby," Maureen said. "Detective Weatherby."

"Well, detective." Wendi jabbed a gardening shovel into the soil of a potted plant she was working on and left it there, picking up a towel to clean her hands. "I am a lawyer. You don't need to handle me. I am well aware of what kind of woman my sister was. And though I loved her dearly, I know she was anything but well-liked."

"I liked her, ma'am," Maureen defended.

Wendi looked at the detective with sincere eyes. "I stand corrected. Now, what is it I can help you with? Do you need a DNA swab to rule me out?"

"Actually, I need to ask you some questions, if you don't mind," Maureen said.

"Do you think it will help you catch my sister's killer?"

"It might," Maureen nodded. "At the least, it might help eliminate a suspect."

"Then let's move to the sunroom," Wendi smiled again. "It's much more comfortable there."

They walked back the way Maureen had come, turning down a different hall to a kitchen. As they passed through, the staff stopped working and stood at attention. "Bea. Please bring us some of that lemonade you made. It really is divine."

"Yes, ma'am," one of the women said.

From the kitchen, they stepped into a room the size of Maureen's apartment. Two walls were nothing but windows floor to ceiling. It was furnished with plush seats and a baby grand piano. Wendi waved a hand, "The sunroom."

"It is definitely bright," Maureen agreed.

"Hideously so." Wendi walked to one of the chairs and sat, directing Maureen to the one next to her.

"If you don't mind my saying so," Maureen said. "I know doctors and lawyers make good money, but this seems excessive."

"It is," Wendi smiled. "My husband comes from a family of old money. He is richer than any one man should ever be. I met him at a fundraiser. He was charming, so we talked. I bid on something I wanted, don't even remember what is was anymore. Someone else outbid me. I pouted, but that was it for me. Harrington doubled the other man's bid and gifted it to me. The rest is history."

Bea appeared carrying a tray with a pitcher of lemonade and two tall glasses of ice. She set the tray on a small table, poured the drinks, and handed them to the women. "May I get you anything else?"

"No, Bea," Wendi said. "Thank you."

The two of them watched the woman retreat to the kitchen.

"You must think me pretentious." Wendi lifted her glass.

"It's not my place to judge you, ma'am."

"Please call me Wendi." The woman sipped her drink. "I get enough ma'ams from the staff. And we both know, your place or not, you're judging me."

Maureen's mouth opened as if she were going to speak, but no words came.

"Don't worry, dear." Wendi patted her knee. "My sister and I grew up in a middle-class home. We had what we needed, but no extras. Our parents put us through college with the help of scholarships. This," she waved a hand, "was never in my expectations."

"Some would call you lucky." Maureen drank some lemonade.

"Some would," Wendi agreed. "Me among them. But I do remember my roots."

"Were you and your sister close?"

"We were," Wendi said. "Not as close as we used to be."

"Why is that, may I ask?"

"Our schedules, for one," Wendi answered. "We didn't have a lot of time to see one another. And then there was the whole conflicting career thing. Sharon spent her life putting bad guys behind bars. I make my money trying to keep them out."

"But you still spoke?" Maureen said.

"Yes," Wendi nodded. "Just not about work."

"How about men?"

"Men?" Wendi got a sly smile. "You know we did."

"Did Sharon discuss Reginald with you?"

"Of course."

"How would you characterize their relationship?" Maureen asked.

"Well," Wendi thought for a minute. "The lawyer in me wants to be careful how I answer that question."

"I understand," Maureen said. "We're just trying to be thorough and look at every possibility. So, if you could give me an honest assessment, I would appreciate it."

"You think of Reginald as a suspect?"

"The husband is always a suspect," Maureen admitted. "As a defense attorney, you know that."

"Well, I don't think he would be capable," Wendi offered. "But I will give you my honest opinion. Reginald and my sister had a typical marriage. They had ups and downs. But both of them were loyal to the other."

"They fought sometimes?"

Wendi grinned. "Yes. They fought sometimes. All couples do."

"Did they ever become violent?"

"No, dear," Wendi said. "Neither one was violent in nature. Their fights were just raised voices and comments they later regretted."

"Were you aware that Sharon had cancer?" Maureen asked.

"No." Wendi frowned. "She never told me."

"We're not sure she knew," Maureen said.

"You should talk to Doctor Silvia Osborn," Wendi suggested. "We've both gone to her most of our adult lives."

"That's the name Reginald gave us."

"He didn't know either?"

"No," Maureen said.

"She must not have known then," Wendi said. "She would have told him."

"You said they were both loyal."

"I did."

"What about when Sharon cheated on him?" Maureen asked. "Sometime last year?"

Wendi pursed her lips. "You know about that?"

"We do."

"They were separated at the time," Wendi said. "It's not like Sharon was sneaking around on him."

"Is that how Reginald looked at it?"

"You know he didn't."

"So, he didn't take it well?"

"No. He didn't," Wendi said. "It almost ended their chance of getting back together."

"But they worked it out."

"Of course," Wendi said. "Sharon promised it didn't mean anything and that it was over."

"Was it?" Maureen asked. "Over?"

"It was," Wendi said. "Sharon was a woman of her word. If she said it was over, it was over."

"What about the man?" Maureen said. "How did he take it when Sharon ended things?"

"What choice did he have?"

"Do you know who she had the affair with?" Maureen asked.

Wendi tilted her head. "I do."

"We need his name."

"Reginald's best friend, Logan," Wendi said. "Logan Carr."

37

Jack arrived at the lab at the same time as another detective. The man had been on the force for almost as long as Jack but had only been a detective for a couple of years. He worked robbery, though he was usually assigned the less prominent cases.

They made small talk as they approached the building, an activity that Jack did not enjoy. But to be polite he followed the other and made the occasional comment.

Inside, Jack took the lead and picked up the pace to distance himself from his co-worker. To his dismay, the man's destination was the same.

Jack opened the door and stepped inside, scanning the room for the technician that the detective knew only as Tony. If he had ever been given the man's last name, he had forgotten it long ago.

He spotted the man, waving him over, just as the other detective entered the room. Jack gave a quick nod and moved on to where the lab tech was bending over a worktable.

"You have something for me?" Jack asked.

"Sure do." Tony stood straight. He thumbed through a small stack of folders. "First, the ballistics on the bullet that killed the chief came back as a match to her service weapon. No prints on the weapon other than hers."

"So the killer wore gloves." Jack took the folder being offered to him.

"Then there's the DNA under her nails."

"You can't possibly have the results already." Jack stared the man in the eyes.

Tony swallowed. "We were told to bump her to the front of a very long line. Apparently, a murdered police chief is a big deal."

Jack shook his head, thinking of all the DNA test results he had waited days to get. "What did you learn?"

"Your suspect is definitely a man." Tony handed the detective the appropriate folder. "Blood type is O. Which narrows it down to about a third of the city."

"Great." Jack put the folder with the other. "I assume you ran it."

"No hit," Tony said. "He's not in the system."

"You're just full of good news," Jack smirked. "Anything else?"

"The bloody clothing that was collected," Tony pulled a bag to him and pulled the items out. "We tested for GSR and only found trace amounts on the shirt. Could have easily been transferred while the man was applying pressure to her wound. Plus the pattern of the blood stains on both the slacks and the shirt were consistent with the scenario I was given. There's no high-velocity blood splatter. The shooter did not wear these clothes."

"So our good samaritan appears to be just that," Jack muttered.

"That's what the evidence suggests," Tony said.

"Is that it?"

"The bloody fingerprint on the chief's doorbell."

"Almost forgot about that," Jack sighed.

"Well, the blood came back as being the chief's." Tony picked up a third folder.

"The question is," Jack thought aloud, "how did it get from her to the front door?"

"We were able to get a fairly good partial print," Tony said.

"Tell me it came back with a match," Jack said.

"No such luck."

"Of course not."

"Bring me the killer's prints and I can match it," Tony said. "I can't do all the work for you."

"You have anything else?"

"That's it."

Jack grumbled and left the lab, being careful not to be seen by the other detective, who had his head bowed into a report. Reaching the safety of the parking lot, the detective drove back to the department and returned to his desk. On top of the stacks of papers was a sealed manilla envelope.

He picked it up and tore the flap open. Inside were the phone records for the chief's home phone, cell phone, and work cell. He pulled the three documents out and laid them side by side. The home phone was rarely used, but the two cell phones had extensive lists of calls. Jack tried to remember a single time he had seen his boss on a cell phone and could not recall any. The pages he was looking at suggested she was on one or the other almost constantly.

In the interest of time, he started with the most recent calls and started highlighting numbers that showed up repeatedly. He opened his notepad and found Reginald and Brian Hutchins' numbers so he could eliminate them. He also knew the department's generic number and ignored calls from that number as well.

The day before she was killed there were several calls from a single number. Jack quickly scanned pages with older calls and found the same number was a regular caller. The detective wrote the number down and moved on to another with a similar call history. That number went below the other.

Jack picked up his desk phone and dialed the first number. It rang several times before going to voicemail. The recording was a man with a generic message who did not give his name. He hung up and dialed the second number. It was answered after a single ring.

"This is Carl Delacruz," he said. "How can I help you?"

Jack dropped the phone onto its cradle.

38

To verify Carl Delacruz's alibi, Shaun had to first determine where he and his mistress claimed to be. In the interest of discretion, the detective looked up and called the number for the politician's campaign headquarters. It was answered on the first ring by a cheerful volunteer who started regurgitating a practiced message.

"Carl Delacruz, please," Shaun cut them off mid-stream.

"Uh." The man paused. "I don't think he's taking calls right now."

"Tell him Detective Travis is calling," Shaun said. "If he doesn't take my call, I will be coming down there."

"Just a moment."

There was a long silence, where a political message should be, and Shaun was grateful for being spared.

"Detective Travis?" Carl Delacruz came on the line. "What can I help you with?"

"I need to verify your alibi." Shaun was direct. "I understand you were with your mistress."

"I thought Detective Mallory was keeping that on the down low," the politician's voice lowered.

"I'm his partner, and right now only he and I know," Shaun assured him. "We'll keep it that way if we can eliminate you as a suspect."

"I can't believe you think I'm a suspect," Carl moaned. "Why would I kill Chief Hutchins?"

"All I need to know is where you were at the time she was killed," Shaun said. "As soon as I verify the information, we can take you off the list and move on."

"I've already told Detective Mallory," Carl insisted.

"You told him who you were with," Shaun corrected. "I need to know where you were."

"I can have her talk to you," the politician said. "She'll tell you."

"I will need to speak to her," Shaun said. "However, I still need to know where you were."

There was a rustling like the receiver was being covered. Shaun had the impression he was dismissing someone from his office. After a brief silence, Carl returned. "We were at her apartment."

"The address?"

Carl sighed and gave him the address.

"We can wrap this up faster if you have her meet me there," Shaun suggested.

"What?"

"Have her meet me at the apartment," Shaun said. "I can question her there. That way we can keep things low-key. And we can finish quickly."

"I don't think that's necessary," Carl said.

"I told you I would have to speak to her," Shaun said. "I'm offering to do so where no one will see us. No one will ask questions as to why she's being questioned. And we can get you off the suspect list."

"I don't know," Carl hesitated.

"Or I can get a warrant," Shaun said. "And everything is public record."

"Are you threatening me?"

"I'm telling you that we are investigating the murder of a police chief," Shaun said. "And we will get our answers however we have to."

Carl sighed again. "Fine. She'll be there in half an hour."

The line went dead, and Shaun stared at the phone for a moment before hanging it up.

Thirty minutes later, Shaun was standing on the steps leading up to the assistant's townhome in a gated community of rentals. The electronic gates at each entrance were locked from six in the evening until eight in the morning, remaining open during the day. As promised, Emma pulled up and parked in front of the single-car garage for her unit.

The expression on her face, as she climbed out of the vehicle, was a mixture of concern and frustration. Shaun leaned against the wall next to her door until the woman ascended the stairs and joined him.

"I don't know why you're harassing Carl." Emma fumbled with the keys as she worked to unlock the door.

"Because a woman was murdered," Shaun explained. "And until I can verify without question that your boyfriend has an alibi, he is on the suspect list."

"Ridiculous." She almost lost her footing as the door gave way and swung inward.

"Do you have any kind of security?" Shaun asked. His eyes scanned the room for anything that might help him. "Particularly, cameras?"

"No."

Shaun sighed. "I need something to place him here."

"I told you he was here," she insisted.

"Believe it or not," Shaun looked her in the eyes. "But people have been known to lie for their significant others."

"I'm not lying."

"I'm sure you're not," Shaun said. "But without proof, it doesn't matter."

"Well, it should," she huffed.

"Leave it to one lying murderer to ruin it for everyone who wants to use a hearsay alibi," Shaun muttered.

"What?"

"Nothing." Shaun stepped into the kitchen. "Listen. What about coffee shops? Could Carl have stopped nearby for coffee or donuts?"

"Do I look like I eat donuts?"

"I thought everyone ate donuts," Shaun said.

The woman gave him a look that reminded him of his mother when he was young. He would do something that she was displeased with, and she would look at him in the same manner that Emma was looking at him now.

"I would think you would be trying harder to help establish his alibi," Shaun said.

"It's not like we knew he would need one," she countered. "I still don't understand why I can't be his alibi."

"As his assistant, you could have been," Shaun said. "But since you're in an intimate relationship, there's a question of whether you're covering for him."

"So, you think I'm lying?"

"I didn't say that."

"Yes, you did," Emma argued. "You said exactly that."

"Why don't we sit," Shaun gestured toward the table and chairs in the kitchen. "I'll ask you some questions and then we can be on our way."

"Fine." Emma sat, crossing her legs and arms in one fluid motion.

Shaun pulled out the chair next to her and positioned himself to face her. "Carl said he came here the night before the murder."

"That's right."

"What time did he arrive?"

"About eleven," she said.

"Was that normal?" Shaun wrote the time down.

"Normal?"

"Well, he was married," Shaun reminded her. "And he lives in town. Did he spend the night here often?"

"I don't see how that's relevant," she muttered. "But if you must know, it was the first time we, uh…"

"I see," Shaun nodded. "So, he arrived at eleven. When did he leave?"

She thought for a moment. "Eight, maybe."

"Is it eight? Or isn't it?" Shaun asked. "It makes a difference."

"Yes." She puffed up her chest. "It was eight."

"And what time does he arrive at the office?" Shaun asked.

"The office?" Emma frowned. "I don't know. I don't work at his office. I work on his campaign."

Shaun wrote quickly in his pad. "Did he stay with you all night?"

"I just told you." She curled her lip into a sneer.

"Eleven to eight," Shaun read from his notes. "But did he leave at any point in the night?"

"Of course not," Emma answered.

"How do you sleep?"

"Pardon me?"

"When you're asleep, are you dead to the world?" Shaun asked. "Or does every little noise wake you?"

"Somewhere in the middle, I guess," she said.

"So, it's possible Mister Delacruz could have left and returned while you were sleeping without your knowledge."

"No," she said. "That isn't possible."

"How can you be sure?"

"I'm sure."

Shaun studied the woman's face. Her jaw was set, her eyes narrowed. She was ready for a fight and the detective wondered why.

"That's all I have for now," Shaun said. "But keep yourself available in case we have more questions."

She huffed and stood. "If you don't mind, I need to get back to work."

"Of course," Shaun stood and smiled. "You have a nice day."

39

The department was buzzing with activity when Maureen stepped off the elevator. She was holding her phone to her ear as she made her way to the conference room where Jack was bent over stacks of papers, wielding a highlighter, and marking lines of information on two separate pages at the same time. Shaun waved in greeting when she entered but continued his phone conversation. Maureen took a seat and pulled some files to her as she talked to the person on the other side of the line. Both calls ended at almost the same time.

The two detectives placed their phones on the table and looked at one another. Jack raised his head to the silence, his eyes darting back and forth between them. "Is someone going to speak?"

They both started and then stopped.

"You go," Maureen said.

"No, you go," Shaun replied.

"Oh, Lord," Jack sighed. "Maureen, you go."

"Showing favoritism, I see," Shaun smiled broadly.

Jack rolled his eyes.

Maureen chuckled. "Well, that was Doctor Silvia Osborn, Sharon's primary physician for the past three decades. According to the doctor, Sharon's cancer was news to her. The chief had not reported any symptoms that would have warranted testing for the disease."

"So, it's unlikely she knew," Jack concluded. "Which means she didn't hire someone to put her out of her misery."

"Unless she went to another doctor without her primary knowing," Maureen said. "Although I doubt that happened."

"What about you?" Jack spoke to Shaun. "Who were you talking to?"

"One of the officers that has been helping with video searches," Shaun responded. "He found a video doorbell across the street from Vince Abrams' home. It shows Abrams pulling out of his drive thirty minutes after the chief was killed. It would be nearly impossible for him to have killed her and get home unseen, clean up, and leave again in thirty minutes."

"So we clear him." Jack nodded. He laid his highlighter down. "The DNA under Sharon's nails did not provide a hit in the database."

"Of course not," Shaun said. "That would have been too easy."

"Well," Jack continued. "It did help with eliminating Ian Fielding. He's in the database. Which means we don't need to know his whereabouts."

"That's good," Maureen sighed. "Because I was having trouble with that."

"It also clears Dave Bartlett," Jack said.

"The neighbor with the motorcycles?" Shaun asked.

"Yes," Jack acknowledged. "He's a fireman and the DNA of first responders are also in the database."

"That leaves us with," Shaun looked at the whiteboard. "Dan Pollard. Randy Keyes. Carl Delacruz. And our mystery cheater."

"Not a mystery anymore," Maureen said. "Turns out the chief had an affair with Logan Carr."

"Reggie's friend, Logan Carr?" Jack raised an eyebrow.

"That's what her sister told me," Maureen said.

Jack moved to the whiteboard, erased the question mark representing the mystery man, and wrote Logan's name. "Sharon's husband had all but dropped off our suspect list. That information pushes him back to the top?"

"Do we think Reggie knew his wife and best friend were an item?" Maureen asked. "Because that might make the difference."

"I don't think he did," Shaun spun his chair for a better view.

"Based on what?"

"Based on the fact that, after he discovered his wife's body," Shaun said, "Reggie called 9-1-1, and then Logan Carr. I don't see him doing that if he knew they had slept together."

"Personally," Maureen said. "I think he's more likely to want to kill Logan than his wife."

"Or both," Shaun said.

"I think this puts Reggie and Logan pretty high on the list," Jack said.

"It does give both of them a strong motive," Maureen agreed.

"The forensics on Randy Keyes' clothing came back," Jack announced. "They said the shooter could not have been wearing them. Only transfer GSR and no high-velocity splatter. He's looking less like a suspect and more like a neighbor giving aid."

"Remove two," Maureen sighed. "Add two."

"Doesn't feel like progress, does it?" Jack rearranged the photos of the suspects, rewriting their names under the respective new locations. When he was finished, all of those who were cleared were on the left side of the whiteboard. Those who were not cleared, but not considered primary, were on the right. Top center were the photos of Dan Pollard and Carl Delacruz. Next to them was Logan Carr's name. "These are the three we focus on. I was just going through phone records for the chief and Delacruz. There were a lot of exchanges between the two. He claimed all of their arguments occurred in meetings and in the media. If he wasn't the one she was having an affair with, we need to know what these calls were about."

"What I don't get," Shaun leaned back in his chair, "the chief used to be narcotics and then homicide. Yet Vince Abrams claimed she was the one who got him banned from bidding on city jobs. And she was going after Delacruz publicly. What was her beef with them?"

"Good question," Jack pointed at his partner. "You look into that. Was she investigating them? And why?"

"I'll need her files to know that." Shaun pointed back.

"I'll get you access," Jack agreed. "Meanwhile, ballistics came back and as we expected, the chief was killed with her own gun. Also, the blood on the doorbell was the chief's, and they were able to get a print, but there wasn't a match in the system."

"Are we thinking the killer tried to ring the doorbell?" Maureen scrutinized her colleagues. "Because why would he use gloves when he attacked her, then remove them to ring the bell?"

"Why ring the bell at all?" Shaun added.

"When we talked to Randy, he said he didn't go to the door after finding Sharon," Jack said. "So, if it wasn't the killer, that would mean there was another possible witness. The electrician said he saw someone running away from the chief's house. It's possible he didn't see the murderer, but the other witness running after trying to ring the bell."

"Someone else saw her first," Shaun said. "Checked on her then rang the bell to get her help, but ran away because they didn't want to be involved?"

"Maybe they witnessed the actual murder and were afraid of getting involved," Maureen suggested. "Didn't want to have to testify."

"If such a witness exists," Jack said. "We need to find them."

"We should talk to the electrician again," Maureen said. "If we suggest the person he saw might be a neighbor out jogging, someone might come to mind."

"We should also show him a photo lineup." Jack gestured to the whiteboard. "Show him the three suspects along with three others and see if he picks anyone out."

"I'll put one together," Shaun said.

"What do you want me to work on?" Maureen asked.

Jack sighed. "The security footage from Emma Acosta's gated community that Shaun requested came in."

"You want me to scan video?"

He shrugged.

"You owe me." She sat forward. "Send it to me."

40

J ack," Chief Grimes directed the detective to a chair. "Come in. Have a seat."

The friendly greeting would have been better received if the man hadn't made Jack wait nearly an hour to enter. He sat, as requested, but on the front edge of the seat, ready to make his escape. "We need . . ."

"Give me an update, Jack," the chief interrupted. "Where are we on this?"

"What do you want to know, sir?"

"Do you have a suspect?"

"We've narrowed it down to three," Jack said.

"Three?" Chief Grimes frowned. "Can't you narrow it down any further? We need a result. We need to close this."

"I assume you want us to arrest the actual killer." Jack's response was sharp.

"There's no need for you to take that tone," the chief said.

"You think I don't know we need to close this?" Jack said. "You think we aren't trying to narrow it down to one suspect?"

"Detective Mallory!" The chief rose to his feet. "I know this case has you under a lot of pressure. But remember who you're talking to."

Jack sat rigid, staring at the man's chest rather than his eyes. "We have three primary suspects, sir. We're following leads and conducting interviews. If it is one of these men, we will prove it."

"And if it's not?"

Jack raised his eyes to meet the chief's gaze. "Then we move on."

"What do we know about the suspects?"

"One is a family friend," Jack reported. "One is a former neighbor."

"And the third?"

"A politician."

"A politician?" The chief sat once more. "Are you serious? Who?"

"Carl Delacruz," Jack said. "They had a very public dislike for one another. And I have reason to believe it carried over to the personal."

"You think they were involved?"

"No, sir." Jack shook his head. "But I believe there was more to their rift than just political disagreements. My team is looking into it."

"Why are you here?"

"I need permission to search the chief's office." Jack stood. "Her home office as well."

Chief Grimes hesitated for only a moment. "Granted. Reginald should allow you into her home office. If you need a warrant, let me know. I will request it myself."

"Thank you, sir." Jack spun and was out of the office before the chief could say anything more.

41

Detective Weatherby set a very strong cup of coffee next to the computer on Jack's desk, which she had commandeered in his absence. Logging into the system, she waited as the spinning circle in the center of the screen let her know things were loading in the background. She had taken three drinks of the liquid caffeine before the generic logo was replaced with her desktop menu.

Accessing her email, she located the video files that Detective Travis had forwarded to her. The complex where Emma Acosta lived had three entrances. Each one had a camera pointed at the cars as they entered and another at the cars as they left. Six videos covering a twenty-four-hour period. Six days of video to scan. She rubbed her eyes and made a mental note to make Jack pay.

The videos were not labeled. Their file names were just a series of letters and numbers with nothing indicating which entry they were from, nor if they were the coming or going angle. Maureen sighed heavily as she started the first one. It was one of the incoming camera views. She fast-forwarded until a vehicle came into view, at which point she stopped the image and played it at normal speed. She froze the image on the best shot she could get of the driver. After comparing it to the photos of Carl and Emma that were taped to the edges of the screen, she moved on to the next.

Most times, there were long periods when no car passed in front of the camera. When there were cars, it was one at a time. The driver would pull up to the gate, enter their code, wait for the gate to open, and drive in. She considered that it would be easier to just find out when Emma's code was used and check those times on the videos, but from eight o'clock in the morning until six in the evening, the gates were open and no codes were required.

Maureen was fast-forwarding when the math hit her. She stopped the video and picked up her phone. Jack answered on the first ring. "Jack, I have one-hundred and forty-four hours of video to scan. This computer's fast-forward only goes at six times the normal speed. It's going to take me twenty-four hours to get through it all. You need to get me help."

"I'll see what..."

She hung up and turned back to the screen. She knew what he was going to say and knew he would follow through. No need to drag it out. A drink of coffee, a brief stretch and she leaned toward the screen, pressing play.

About a quarter way through the first video, a faint shadow crossed the desk. Stopping the fast-forward, she looked to see where the shadow had come from. Side by side, two rookie uniformed officers stood silently watching her.

"We were told to report to you," the female rookie said.

"Thank you, Jack," Maureen muttered under her breath.

"What was that?" the male rookie questioned.

"Nothing." Maureen pushed away from the desk and rose to her feet. "Let me get you set up."

A few minutes later the female was sitting across from her at Shaun's desk. The male was a couple of rows away at the desk of a detective who worked nights. Each had one of the videos cued and copies of the photos next to them. A brief instruction and the three of them were face to screen.

The next two hours were filled with computer key clicks, yawns, eye rubs, several cups of coffee, and restroom breaks. Jack appeared briefly to retrieve his service weapon from his desk before leaving the building. Shaun stopped by long enough to get his coffee mug off his desk, scowling at the rookie working there.

"Don't worry about him," Maureen assured the woman after Shaun retreated to the breakroom.

The rookie did not respond, until she said, "I think I have something."

Maureen came around the desks and leaned over the rookie. On the screen was the image of a car entering the complex. The time stamp read six-seventeen. There was a woman in the driver's seat, leaning out to enter her code for the gate. The detective pulled the photo of Emma off the computer's edge and held it to the screen. There was no doubt they were the same woman.

Maureen wrote down the file name and the time stamp. She noted that Emma was entering the complex, probably after work. With a hand on the rookie's shoulder, she said, "Nice work."

The rookie smiled triumphantly.

"Don't get too excited," Maureen warned. "We still need to know if she left again, or if the man entered at any point."

The smile faded and the two of them returned to the task at hand.

42

As soon as Jack told him they had the okay, Shaun settled into Chief Hutchins' office. He sat in her seat and fleetingly imagined himself as the highest-ranking detective in homicide. Once the moment had passed, he realized how much more comfortable her chair was than his. Dismissing the thought he pulled open the top drawer on the left side of her desk.

Inside he found office supplies, neatly arranged. The second drawer was filled with incident reports and evidence logs from the past week waiting for her review and signature. The third drawer, deeper than the others, held hanging folders that contained various blank forms. Each folder was clearly labeled to identify the form within.

The center drawer contained a pull-out surface holding the keyboard and mouse to her computer. He closed it and moved on.

The top drawer on the right side was empty. Shaun assumed, like his, that the space was reserved for her weapon while she was in the office.

Below that was a drawer with case files. Shaun pulled them out and set them in front of him. He opened each file and skimmed its contents before setting it aside and doing the same to the next. The files were cold cases, some dating back to her days in narcotics. When he had gone through each one, Shaun returned the files to the drawer as he had found them.

He reached down to open the bottom drawer, but it didn't budge. Thinking it stuck, Shaun pulled harder to no result. The drawer was locked. He quickly searched each of the other drawers again, hoping to find a key. None turned up.

There were two filing cabinets on one wall and a credenza opposite them. Shaun searched the credenza first, finding manuals and old awards the chief had received over her years of service. The storage in this piece of furniture was nowhere near as neat as the desk. Shaun closed it up and moved on to the filing cabinets that, like the bottom drawer of the desk, were locked.

With no keys in her desk, they must have been on the chief's key ring that she carried with her. Shaun left the office, glancing toward Jack's desk where Maureen was viewing video footage. At his desk was a uniformed woman. A few desks away, another uniform sat with his eyes transfixed on the screen in front of him. Shaun took the stairs to the basement level where he would find the evidence lockup.

The officer inside the cage looked up with a bored expression when the detective entered. There was no change when Shaun stepped up to the service window.

"What can I do for you, detective?"

Shaun was convinced the man was holding back a yawn. "I need to access the evidence from Chief Hutchins' shooting."

The officer slid a clipboard to him. "You know the drill."

The detective pulled out a pen and started filling out the request form. The officer leaned on his elbows with his face in his hands, waiting.

"How long have you been down here?" Shaun shoved the clipboard back to the other.

The officer studied the request before setting it aside. "Two weeks."

"I would like to tell you it gets better." Shaun had spent time in the cage when he returned to work after being shot. "But it doesn't."

"I wasn't getting my hopes up." The officer turned away. "Be right back."

Shaun watched him walk into the maze of shelves that held the evidence of cases dating back decades. Once a year, older cases were reviewed to determine if the evidence needed to be held. This helped keep things from piling up too much. Theft cases usually saw the property returned to the original owners, when possible, whereas the evidence in murder cases was kept until all appeals were exhausted. Cold cases were kept indefinitely.

"It wasn't even put on the shelf yet." The officer appeared, carrying two evidence boxes.

Shaun thought of the scene and wondered how two boxes had been filled. He opened the first and found the chief's handgun, photos of the scene, copies of reports, and every scrap they had collected from their search of the area around the shooting. The second box contained the chief's clothes, including the vest she was wearing, which took up most of the space.

Shaun reached inside and pulled out the smaller bags until he found what he was looking for. The bag holding her keys was heavy. The woman had a lot of keys. The detective held them up for the officer to see. "That's all I need."

The officer took the request form and tore the top copy off, putting it on another clipboard hanging on the wall. The second copy he dropped into the box the keys had been in. "Alright then."

Shaun felt for the man, but at the same time knew that when he was assigned to the cage, he had brought things to occupy him during the down times. He had managed to complete three of the novels on his must-reads list. He had also spent time studying for his detective exams.

The man settled into the chair provided to him and leaned back against the wall. Shaun shook his head and started back upstairs. He stopped by his desk to get his coffee mug. The officer sitting at his desk barely acknowledged him. He made a quick stop in the breakroom to fill his mug before returning to the chief's office.

Armed with keys, Shaun sat at the desk once more and tried key after key until he found the one that unlocked the bottom drawer. Triumphantly, he pulled the drawer open. Anticipating a treasure trove of information, he was disappointed to find three bottles of various alcohol and glass tumblers.

He pushed the drawer closed and locked it up. He sighed and looked at the two filing cabinets. He checked her ring, having used similar cabinets and knowing what the keys would look like. There were four. Rising to his feet, it took no time at all to access the drawers.

Inside he found just what he expected. Each drawer was nearly stuffed with files. Disregarding schedules, personnel files, and other administrative information, he was able to focus his search on two of the eight drawers. They contained case files of both open and closed cases that she had a hand in.

Shaun quickly found a file with Vince Abrams' name. He pulled the folder and put it on the desk. Returning to the cabinet, he continued thumbing through the tabs, expecting to find a similar file on Carl Delacruz. After two thorough searches, he could only conclude there was nothing to find.

With a heavy sigh, Shaun fell into the chief's chair and spread the Abrams file across the surface of the desk. He read page after page of witness statements, interview notes, and engineering reports. It was substantial and every indication was that Vince Abrams was indeed cutting corners and providing substandard results. What the file did not explain was why the then narcotics detective was the one investigating the case.

43

Logan Carr opened his front door to Detective Mallory and his smile fell instantly. The quick change in expression left the man with a dopey look that almost made Jack smile.

"Mister Carr," Jack said. "I have a few more questions for you. And your wife, Alecia, isn't it?"

"It is," Logan muttered. "Let me get her."

"That's okay," Jack waved him off. "I need to speak to you separately."

"Oh, okay."

"Do you have somewhere we can go to talk in private?" Jack asked.

"Sure," Logan looked nervously over his shoulder. "We have an office. Follow me."

Jack fell in step behind the homeowner, taking in the surroundings as they walked. The home decor suggested someone who knew what they were doing, though it wasn't the detective's taste. Logan led him to one of the bedrooms that was furnished with a desk and chair on one side, a sewing machine and worktable on the other.

The homeowner sat heavily in the desk chair, leaving the sewing bench for the detective. Jack perched on the edge of the seat facing the man, who spun his chair so that his extended legs were just inches from the detective's. He slouched comfortably and waited.

"I need to know your whereabouts at the time of Sharon's death," Jack started.

"We already went through all this," Logan protested.

"Actually, we never discussed where you were," Jack corrected. "But we're discussing it now."

"You think I killed Sharon?"

"Answer the question," Jack said. "Where were you at the time of Sharon's murder?"

"I was here." Logan pointed at the floor.

"You told me earlier that your wife, an ER nurse, was at work," Jack reminded the man. "Can anyone confirm you were here?"

"No." There was a slight shake of his head.

"So, no alibi."

"Why?" Logan pleaded. "Why do you think I would have hurt Sharon?"

"We already established your motive," Jack said. "She was going to tell your wife about the affair you were having."

"I wouldn't kill her for that."

"What you didn't tell me," Jack continued. "Was that the affair was between you and Sharon."

"What?"

"The affair Sharon had while she and Reggie were separated was with you." Jack leaned forward. "That's what Sharon was going to tell your wife. Not only would it have ruined your marriage, but it would also have destroyed your relationship with your best friend. You had to keep her quiet. You had to kill her."

Logan sat slack jawed. "I didn't kill her. And I didn't sleep with her."

"I'm told you did," Jack said.

"Told?" Logan knotted his brow. "Told by whom?"

"Sharon's sister gave your name."

"Wendi?" Logan appeared confused. "Why would she say that?"

"You told me that you and Sharon dated before she chose Reggie," Jack said. "Maybe the two of you decided to give it another go?"

"No." His response was sharp. "No way."

"To put your own question to you," Jack said. "Why would Wendi say that unless Sharon told her?"

"I can't explain it." Logan sat up straight for the first time. "You have to understand. When Sharon and I dated, we learned very quickly that we weren't meant to be together. But she and Reggie were. Like Alecia and I were. Reggie and I are best friends. Alecia and Sharon were good friends. Sharon and me? We tolerated each other for Reggie's sake."

"Tolerated each other?" Jack cocked his head. "You told me your relationship with Sharon was good until recently, due to the affair. Are you now saying that's not the case?"

"Our relationship was good," Logan insisted. "Just not good enough to want to sleep together and risk ruining our marriages."

"But you did just that," Jack said. "Both of you did. You both had affairs that put your marriages at risk."

"I know!" Logan ran his hand through his curly hair.

"So you can understand why I need proof that it wasn't the two of you together."

"It wasn't."

"Then who, Mister Carr?" Jack asked. "Who did you have your affair with?"

"You have to understand," Logan pleaded. "It was a one-time thing."

"I need a name, Mister Carr," Jack demanded.

"Why?"

"I need to confirm what you're saying," Jack explained. "If you were having an affair with a woman other than Sharon, I can take you off the list."

Jack knew that, just because the man was sleeping with another woman, it would not exclude him from having a relationship with Sharon as well. But talking to the other woman might help him determine if the man in front of him was a player.

"Her name was Laura, or Lori," Logan grimaced. "Maybe Lauren."

"You don't know?"

"Listen." Logan clasped his hands together. "I was at a conference. We were in meetings all day. Went for drinks after. We all got a little wasted. It was a bad moment. This one woman and I . . . I don't even know how it happened. We woke up in my room. She grabbed her things and left. I never saw her again."

"She wasn't at the conference?"

"I thought she was," Logan shrugged. "But I never saw her."

"Did you look for her?"

"I did." Logan's head dropped. "I wanted to be sure to avoid her. So, I looked for her so I could steer clear. Maybe she was doing the same thing and avoided me. I don't know. Maybe she wasn't even there for the conference."

"So, there's no way to verify your story."

"You can ask Reggie," Logan looked up. "I told him everything as soon as I got back. That's when Sharon overheard me. Or maybe Reggie told her. I'm not sure."

"I'll need the dates and location of the conference." Jack adjusted himself on the sewing bench, wondering how anyone could sit on the thing long enough to sew an outfit together.

"Sure thing."

"Would you go let your wife know I need to speak to her?"

Logan stood. "You're not going to tell her are you?"

"About your infidelity?" Jack looked up at him. "No."

The man nodded, opened the door, and stepped out. Jack took the opportunity to look around the room. On the desk side, there were numerous books on shelves, the main topic of which was infrastructure. The majority were about bridges. Some covered integrity and design, others were photo books of bridges throughout the ages. There were books on roads, intersections, tunnels, and the like. One photo book covered on and off-ramp loops both old and new.

The other side of the room was focused around the sewing machine and the work table beside it. Spools of thread, bolts of cloth, scissors, measuring tapes, pins, and stacks of patterns filled the space. On the table itself was a piece of cloth spread out with a pattern pinned to it, waiting to be cut out and sewn together. He was standing over the table when Alecia Carr stepped in.

"Misses Carr." He held out a hand. "I'm Detective Jack Mallory."

She took his hand briefly, before pulling hers back inside the sleeves of the oversized cardigan sweater she was wearing and wrapped herself up tight, before perching on the sewing bench.

Jack stepped to the desk chair and sat. "You like to sew?"

"It's a hobby," she said. "I find it calming after a long day at the ER."

"I think I would find it frustrating," Jack chuckled. "Do you sew your own clothes?"

"I make my scrubs sometimes," she said. "Mostly I sew for the children in the family."

"I see."

"What does this have to do with anything?" Alecia asked.

"I'm sorry," Jack said. "Nothing. I was just curious."

"And why are you here?" Alecia was direct. "I assume you're investigating Sharon's murder. Why are you here instead of out there looking for her killer?"

"I am investigating her murder," Jack nodded. "That's why I'm here."

"What?" She straightened. "You think I did it? Or Logan?"

She looked at the door.

"We don't just interview suspects." Jack was careful not to confirm or deny what she was asking. I need to ask you some questions as a friend of the victim. You were friends, were you not? Logan gave me the impression you were close to the victim."

"We were friends." She gave a sad smile. "What do you want to know?"

"Tell me about the relationship between Sharon and Mister Hutchins." Jack poised his pen over his notepad.

"Well, they met in college," Alecia said. "We all did. They were inseparable at times. It was annoying at first. But as I became more involved in my nursing studies, I wasn't around as much. Then they introduced me to Logan. Everything just fell into place. We did almost everything together."

"We being you, Sharon, Reggie, and Logan."

"Yes," Alecia said. "Whenever I wasn't studying, I was with them."

"Then things progressed," Jack said. "Did you all graduate together?"

"I was a year behind them," Alecia shook her head. "For a year I saw them primarily on the weekends, some evenings."

"After you graduated you still hung out together?"

"Of course," Alecia said. "We were friends. That's what friends do."

"And who married first?"

"Sharon and Reggie," she answered. "Shortly after I graduated."

"And you and Logan?"

"Three years after them."

"Why did you wait so long?" Jack asked. "If you were so close?"

"My parents didn't want me to get married so young and refused to pay for a wedding," Alecia said. "We saved up and paid for it ourselves."

"What did your parents think of that?"

"I won't discuss my parents," she said. "They have nothing to do with what happened to Sharon."

Jack nodded. "The detective in me. Always wanting to know everything."

"I understand."

"Okay, so they married. Then you married," Jack summarized. "What next?"

"Sharon got pregnant with Brian." There was sadness in her voice.

"What about you?" Jack asked. "You don't have children, do you?"

"No."

"Was that by choice?"

"It just wasn't in the cards," she said.

"Did Logan want kids?"

"Yes."

"And you?"

"Yes."

"It just didn't happen?"

"No, detective, it didn't." The sadness turned to frustration. "Again. What could that possibly have to do with Sharon's murder?"

"I'm just trying to get a sense of her home life," Jack explained.

"Her home life or mine?"

Jack paused and nodded. "The four of you remained close. Do you have other friends from college that you all kept in contact with?"

"Logan and I don't," she said. "You would have to ask Reggie if they did."

"Surely you had gatherings," Jack suggested. "Either here or at the Hutchins' home."

"Yes," she said. "Of course."

"Did you or they ever invite others?"

"Of course we did," Alecia said.

"And you never saw anyone you knew from school?" Jack asked.

"Not that I recall," she said. "Why are you asking?"

"About a year ago," Jack leaned forward. "Sharon and Reggie separated."

"I'm very aware," Alecia said. "It was a hard time for them."

"I'm sure it was," Jack nodded. "But Sharon had an easier time of it."

"Why would you say that?" Alecia crossed her arms.

"Well," Jack raised an eyebrow. "Because she had an affair."

"How did you know that?"

"Because Reggie and Logan both told me," Jack said. "In fact, Sharon's sister told me she was having an affair with Logan."

"That's ridiculous," Alecia dismissed.

"Why?" Jack asked. "Because you trust your husband?"

"No," she said. "I mean, I do trust my husband. But it's ridiculous because I know who she had the affair with."

"You do?"

"We talked nearly every day," Alecia said. "We told each other everything."

"Who was it?"

"I don't think I should tell," Alecia said. "It's been a year."

"Do you know for sure that he hasn't been holding a torch for her?" Jack asked. "Do you know for sure that he hasn't been angry since she went back to Reggie, just waiting for his time to get revenge?"

"No."

"Then give me a name," Jack said. "I need to investigate every possible suspect, every possible motive."

The woman sighed heavily, weighing her options. "Fine. But I don't want to be involved."

"Easy enough," Jack said. "The name?"

"Detective Hardy or Hardman," she said. "Something like that."

"Detective Kirk Harding?"

"That sounds right," she smiled. "Do you know him?"

"I do." Jack rose to his feet. "Thank you. I'll let you get back to your day."

"I hope you catch him, detective." Alecia stood as well. "Whoever did this. I hope you put him away for a long time. Sharon didn't deserve this."

"No, she didn't." Jack was somber. He left the house without so much as a glance at the homeowners. His mind was elsewhere. He had been reading up on Captain Hutchins. That was how he knew the name, Kirk Harding. They had been partners when Sharon had been in narcotics.

44

Maureen sat in Detective Mallory's chair with her head resting on his desk. Hours upon hours of surveillance video had taken a toll on her eyes. The two rookies working with her had returned to their respective departments to be assigned other duties.

"You asleep?"

"I'm awake!" Her head jerked up and she stared through thin slits at Jack, sitting next to her on the edge of his desk. "Oh, it's you."

"That's some greeting." Jack pushed off his desk. "What did you find?"

"Right." Maureen became alert and spun her chair to face him. "We watched every minute of footage on every camera in and out of the complex."

"And?"

"We found Emma entering the complex at six-seventeen," she said. "After work."

"As expected."

"Then we found her leaving again at seven-twenty," she said.

"An hour later?"

"No." Maureen shook her head. "The next morning on her way back to work."

"Also expected," Jack said. "What about Delacruz?"

"No sign of him coming into or leaving the complex."

"And you didn't see her at any other time?"

"No."

"So, they lied."

"Unless they have a secret entrance or he scaled the wall," Maureen said. "It appears so."

"And if Delacruz lied," Jack concluded. "It means he has something to hide."

"One thing bothers me," Maureen stood and stretched. "If he was going to lie, why say you're with your mistress? Wouldn't it be better to say you were at home? I mean, if his alibi gets out, his wife is going to know about his indiscretions."

"My guess," Jack shrugged. "His wife wouldn't lie for him."

"Good for her."

The two of them moved to the war room where they stood in front of the whiteboard.

"Now the questions are." Jack pointed at the man's photo. "Where was he? What is he hiding? Did he kill Chief Hutchins?"

"Seems like for every answer we get, we have three more questions," Maureen said. "What about Reggie's friend? Logan Carr, wasn't it? Did he confess to an affair with the chief?"

"According to him," Jack said. "His affair was with a woman at a conference. Didn't even remember her name."

"And you believe him?"

"I didn't," Jack admitted. "Until his wife told me who the chief actually had her affair with."

"Anyone on our suspect list?"

"No." Jack grabbed a marker and wrote K. H. in an empty space. "But he is now."

"K. H.?" Maureen looked at Jack. "He doesn't have a name?"

"Not one I want everyone seeing," Jack said. "It's Detective Kirk Harding."

"From narcotics?" Maureen's eyebrows rose. "No kidding? No wonder you don't want his name up there."

"I don't want too many knowing he's a possible. I don't need word getting to him before I question him," Jack said. "I'm going to talk to him alone."

"That's a good idea," she agreed. "If it comes to nothing, you don't want to embarrass the man."

"That's what I was thinking."

"I can clear out," Maureen said. "I have to talk to Emma Acosta about why she lied to us."

45

Shaun was brushing lint off his pant leg when the door to the Hutchins' home opened. Brian, the chief's son, took a brief look at the detective and turned away, calling for his father. Shaun stood at attention until the man arrived.

"What do you need?" Reggie asked.

"Detective Travis," Shaun announced himself.

"I know who you are," Reggie said. "Why are you here?"

"First," Shaun said. "Your neighbor said he saw someone running away from your home that morning. Possibly the murderer, possibly a witness. I was wondering if you knew of anyone in the neighborhood who jogged in the early mornings?"

"You think someone running away from my wife's murder might have just been a jogger passing by?"

"We don't want to be chasing this suspect if they aren't an actual suspect," Shaun nodded. "And if it was the suspect, a jogger might have seen something."

"I don't know anyone who jogs." Reggie's voice was flat. "What else do you want?"

"We're looking at the possibility that your wife's murder might have something to do with a case she was associated with," Shaun explained.

"Okay?"

"Did the chief keep any case files here at the house?" Shaun asked. "Or notes maybe?"

"I don't know," Reggie said. "She's got filing cabinets, but I don't know what's in them."

"I have her keys." Shaun held them up for him to see. "Mind if I take a look? It could help our investigation."

"Knock yourself out." Reggie stepped aside. "Might save me the trouble of cleaning them out later."

"Yes, sir." Shaun stepped inside. "Anything personal I find, I will separate from work-related files."

"Fine," Reggie waved him on. "Just don't make a mess."

"I'll be careful," the detective promised.

Reggie guided him to the office, making a point to identify the filing cabinets in question. Shaun tried the remaining keys on the ring he had taken from the chief's belongings and was able to unlock both. He nodded to Reggie who grimaced and turned away, leaving Shaun alone with eight drawers of files.

Sharon Hutchins had been a detective for almost twenty years. The first filing cabinet was crammed full of case notes and copies of files, most of which had been closed years ago. There were also copies of cases that remained unsolved and slated to cold case status. These showed more wear than the others, suggesting the chief had pulled them out and reviewed them regularly.

Shaun took each file out, thumbed through its contents, and made notes before returning it to its place and moving on to the next. He was determined that not a single page would be out of place when he was done.

In the third drawer, he located a file that was full of handwritten notes and letters. He was about to put them back, thinking them to be private, when he saw a drawing in the corner of one page. He pulled it out to examine it more closely.

The image was almost childlike in its simplicity and style. But the subject was clear. The disproportioned drawing depicted a man stabbing a woman in the neck. Violent red lines represented blood spewing from the wound.

Shaun opened the file to examine the rest of the papers held within. Dozens of similar drawings were shuffled together with handwritten block-letter notes. Again, word choices and misspellings suggested the author was a child. And again, the subject matter was violent and threatening. As Shaun used his phone to photograph the pages, he wondered why none of them had been in the chief's file of threatening letters at the department.

He arranged the pages as they had been and returned them to the folder they had been bound in. Tucking them under his arm, he left the office in search of Reggie. He found the widower sitting on the couch staring at the television even though it wasn't on.

"Mr. Hutchins," Shaun said as he entered the room.

"What now?"

"I was wondering if you could tell me about these." Shaun held out the folder. "I don't understand why none of these are in her threatening letter file in our department."

Reggie eyed the folder warily before taking the offering. He laid it in his lap and opened it, exposing the disturbing contents. His eyes widened. "Why the hell did she save these?"

"You recognize them?"

"Yes." The man's voice changed, an undertone of anger creeping in.

"Do you know why they aren't in our files?" Shaun asked.

"Because they're none of your business," Reggie shifted in his seat. "That's why."

"I don't understand," the detective said. "If the chief was being threatened, it is our business."

"She wasn't being threatened."

"Those notes and drawings suggest otherwise." Shaun gestured to the folder.

"These." Reggie waved the folder. "These are a dozen years old or more."

Shaun was silent for a long moment. "Twelve years? Why would she keep a folder if they're so old?"

"That's what I want to know." Reggie placed the folder on the couch next to his leg. "I thought she got rid of these years ago."

"Who are they from, Mister Hutchins?" Shaun asked. "It could be that they found her again. We should follow up."

"Find her?" Reggie laughed. "He never lost her."

"I don't understand," Shaun said again.

"If you must know," Reggie lowered his voice. "Brian had anger issues when he was young. He went through therapy. He's good now. Doesn't even remember this stuff."

"You're sure?"

"I'm sure," Reggie snapped. "Our son did not kill his mother."

Shaun stared at the folder but did not ask for its return.

"Do you need anything else?"

"No, sir," Shaun shook his head. "I'll get back to it."

"You do that."

Shaun hesitated just a moment before retreating to the office. Returning to where he had last been, he was relieved to be almost finished with the first cabinet.

He pulled the bottom drawer open and searched inside. It contained more case notes and copies, each of which Shaun reviewed and returned.

He checked his watch and saw that an hour had passed him by. With a sigh, he moved to the second cabinet.

The top drawer stuck and required a little finesse to open. Inside were bottles of alcohol similar to the contents of the desk drawer in her office. Shaun slid the drawer shut. In the second he found loan documents, insurance papers, and numerous other home-related papers. Finding nothing that would get anyone killed, he moved on.

The third drawer was solely dedicated to a single case. It was an apartment building collapse that should have never come across the chief's desk, particularly since she was still in narcotics at the time. Thumbing through the initial pages of the first folder, Shaun quickly discovered why she had taken an interest in the case. The residents and ultimate victims of the failed building were all working girls, ten in all. Shaun read on.

From the papers Sharon had gathered and the notes she had made, it was clear that the apartment building had been used as a brothel. All the girls were from other countries, undocumented, and probably forced into prostitution. A tragedy compounded by what inspectors in the aftermath called inadequate footings.

The building gave way during the early morning hours when there were no johns in the building. The only victims were the poor women living and working there. Shaun flipped through the pages. It appeared no charges were ever filed. No one was ever held accountable for the deaths of the ten women.

The next folder contained dozens of photographs of the rubble that had once been the building in question. The front half of the structure had broken away and come to rest in a pile one-quarter of its original height. It was heartbreaking to look at.

The third file contained more of Sharon's research. One document, near the top, identified the company responsible for the building's construction: Abrams' Construction Inc. It was Vince Abrams' company.

The next document contained the city inspection for the building, several pages long. Each stage of the process had been signed off on, from the footings to the end. Not one violation was ever noted, not even a minor one. But the most interesting detail was the name of the inspector, some ten years prior to the collapse; Carl Delacruz.

46

"Thank you for coming in, detective." Jack waved a hand at a seat at the end of the conference table.

Kirk Harding took the cue and sat, rolling in tight to rest his arms on the surface. He glanced at the whiteboard before turning his attention to Jack. "Whatever I can do to help. Sharon didn't deserve this."

Jack sat on the side of the table nearest the board. Jack noticed the peek. He imagined the look would have been longer had he not erased the detective's initials.

"It's our understanding that you and Chief Hutchins were partners in narcotics," Jack started.

"Seven years," Kirk confirmed. "Before you guys stole her."

"Do you know of any cases the two of you worked on that might have put one of your suspects on the path to murdering her?"

"You're asking if anyone we arrested was angry with her?" The detective laughed. "Tell me, have you ever arrested someone who wasn't angry with you?"

"Just a routine question, detective," Jack said. "We're trying to make a list of suspects. Does anyone come to mind?"

"Well, of course perps come to mind," Kirk said. "Some even made threats. But most times nothing comes of it."

"I'm aware," Jack said. "Would you check on the ones that you think might act on their threats and send me a list of the ones that could be possibilities?"

"Sure," Kirk nodded. "I can do that."

"I would appreciate it," Jack said. "Now, I was hoping you could give us some insight into something."

"What's that?" Kirk shifted in his seat.

"It seems the chief had a couple of ongoing issues with men that had nothing to do with narcotics," Jack said. "I was wondering if you knew what her fight was with a Vince Abrams or Carl Delacruz."

"I know she had problems with them," Kirk said. "But she was looking into them on her own. It started shortly before she became chief. She told me she was on to something but didn't want to involve me until she was sure."

"She never gave you any indication what it was about?"

"Like I said," Kirk repeated. "She wanted to be sure. You think that's what got her killed?"

"We don't know," Jack admitted. "We're trying to gather information."

"Well, I hope you get them," Kirk said.

"We will," Jack assured him.

"Anything else?" Kirk turned his chair. "I really need to get back."

"One more thing." Jack stopped him.

Kirk turned back and looked at the detective. "What's that?"

"Tell us about your relationship with Shannon," Jack said.

"My relationship?" Kirk looked Jack in the eyes. "Am I a suspect?"

"We have been told that about a year ago, while Shannon and her husband were separated, the two of you had an affair," Jack said. "Any truth to it?"

Kirk pursed his lips and looked down at the table. "It's true."

"How long did it go on?" Jack asked.

"How is that relevant?"

"What we need to know is when it ended," Jack said. "If it ended."

"I see," Kirk said. "None of this leaves this room."

"We can do that," Jack agreed.

"When they split." Kirk sat back. "Shannon came over to talk. We were friends and talked a lot over the years. Anyway, she came over. We talked. We drank. One thing led to another."

"How long?"

"It lasted about a month," Kirk looked down at the floor. "But we knew we weren't meant to be together. We made better friends. So, it ended. Shortly after that, she went back to Reggie. She and I never discussed it again. Kind of messed up our friendship too. But that was the way it was."

"That was it?"

"I didn't kill her in a jealous rage," Kirk said. "If that's what you're asking."

47

Detective Weatherby walked into Carl Delacruz's campaign headquarters and scanned the women's faces in search of the one that had been taped to the side of her computer screen for hours. It was not hard to locate Emma Acosta standing behind a table loaded with posters and flyers. There were a couple of people standing across from her, receiving directions for where and how to display the items they held.

Maureen stepped into cue behind them and waited for the woman to finish. After a brief 'do it for the cause' speech the two volunteers headed for the door to start their day.

"I don't think I know you." Emma's voice was sickeningly upbeat. It reminded Maureen of a girl she went to high school with, a cheerleader who was always playing the part. "Are you here to volunteer? Or learn more about Mister Delacruz?"

Maureen smiled, holding up her shield.

"Another one?" Emma's demeanor changed. "How many of you are there?"

"Detectives?" Maureen put her identification away. "Dozens."

"Do I have to speak to them all?"

"No," Maureen grinned. "Just Mallory, Travis, and myself."

"I see." Emma started straightening the items on the table even though they did not need it. "And what? They thought I might open up to a woman?"

"Something like that," Maureen crossed her arms. "Is there somewhere we can talk?"

"Carl's out on a meet and greet," Emma nodded. "We can use his office."

The two of them walked toward the office in the back of the room. Just before stepping in, Emma stopped.

"Paul," she called out. "Can you handle things for a bit? This woman and I need to talk."

"Sure thing, Emma," the young man said.

Inside, Emma settled into Carl's seat behind the desk with her elbows on the surface and her hands clasped together in front of her. "What can I do for you, detective? I think I told the other two just about everything."

"You did tell them everything," Maureen agreed. "Except the truth."

"Pardon me?"

"You told them that the night before and the morning of Sharon Hutchins' death," Maureen said. "Carl Delacruz was with you at your home."

"I did."

"Your complex has cameras at every entrance," Maureen informed the woman. "Coming in and going out. And we watched that video, hours and hours of video. We checked every car. And although we saw you enter and leave, we never saw Mister Delacruz. Why do you think that is?"

"You said yourself." Emma crossed her arms across her chest. "There were hours and hours of video. Perhaps you just missed him."

"There were several of us scanning the images," Maureen countered. "It's unlikely we would have missed his entrance and his exit."

"Maybe he hid from the cameras," Emma offered.

"Are you suggesting he ducked down as he drove through?" Maureen asked. "I think a driverless car would stand out. Don't you?"

"If he wasn't the driver," Emma said. "He could have hidden from view."

"So, were you driving?" The detective leaned in. "And be careful here. You never mentioned it before now, and it's hard to believe you had forgotten a grown man hiding in your backseat."

She opened her mouth to respond, then closed it again. A moment later she said, "He wasn't in my car. But that isn't to say he drove himself. One of his staff may have driven him."

"You think the volunteers on his campaign would have driven their candidate, hiding in the backseat, to a secret rendezvous with his mistress?"

"Maybe." Emma did not sound as confident as she had. "He has other staff though. Bodyguards. Even drivers. It's their job to drive him places."

"If we ask them," Maureen said. "Are they going to admit driving him to your place that night?"

"Maybe."

"Emma!" Maureen snapped. "I know you're trying to help him. But think. If he wasn't with you, he should have been home with his wife. If he's not asking her to be his alibi, he wasn't there. So, where was he?"

Tears were forming in the corners of the woman's eyes.

"This is a murder investigation, Emma." Maureen turned the screw a little more. "Where was he that he is having to ask you to lie for him? If he goes down for murder, you will go down for accessory. Do you understand that?"

"Accessory?"

"You're lying for him," Maureen said. "That makes you involved."

Emma shook her head. "He wouldn't kill anyone."

"Are you sure about that? I mean one hundred percent sure?" Maureen asked. "Because if he wasn't with you and he wasn't with his wife, where was he?"

"I, uh …"

"Emma Acosta, was Carl Delacruz with you the night before and morning of the murder of Sharon Hutchins?" Maureen raised her voice. "Yes or no?"

Tears streamed down her cheeks as she closed her eyes and shook her head. "No."

48

Detectives Jack Mallory and Shaun Travis were in the conference room when Maureen arrived. The two detectives turned to her when she entered, looking very much like they were guilty of something.

"What?"

"Nothing." Jack scowled.

"We bet on whether you would get Emma Acosta to crack," Shaun admitted.

"You did what?" Maureen put her hands on her hips.

"Don't listen to him," Jack said. "How did it go?"

She looked at the two men who seemed to be waiting with great anticipation. "Carl Delacruz was not with Maureen when the chief was killed."

"I knew it," Jack clapped. "Good job."

Shaun held out a ten-dollar bill which Maureen snatched out of his hand.

"Hey, that's mine," Jack said.

"You bet against me?" Maureen stared Shaun down.

"He wasn't going to." Shaun pointed at Jack.

"He better not." Maureen grinned.

"So that leaves Delacruz without an alibi." Jack moved to the whiteboard and moved the politician's photo back to the suspect list. "What did you find?"

"Looking at the chief's papers," Shaun said. "I found that she was investigating a building that collapsed resulting in deaths."

"We knew that," Jack said. "Any indication why she was the one looking into it?"

"The victims were prostitutes," Shaun said. "It's possible the chief knew some of them from her work in narcotics."

"So she was trying to get justice for them," Maureen said.

"I haven't gotten through it all," Shaun said. "But it looks like that may have been her motivation."

"Something just doesn't add up," Jack said. "I want to see what she had."

"It's on my desk." Shaun hooked a thumb in that direction.

"For now, let's move on." Jack looked at the whiteboard.

"What about Logan Carr?" Maureen asked. "Since he wasn't the one who had the affair with Sharon."

"But he did have a one-night stand," Jack reminded. "And Sharon was threatening to tell his wife. I'm curious how she found out."

"Don't know if it means anything," Shaun said. "But Brian Hutchins had anger issues as a child."

"As a child?" Jack turned to his partner. "Or still?"

"As far as I know it was only while he was young," Shaun said. "Reggie says he's fine now."

"His father says?" Maureen questioned.

"He could be protecting his son," Jack said.

"True, but," Shaun said.

"But you don't think so?"

"I don't know," Shaun admitted. "I suppose it's possible."

Jack moved the boy's photo to the suspect list. "We're supposed to be eliminating suspects. Not adding them."

"Speaking of adding," Maureen said. "How did it go with Harding?"

"Detective Kirk Harding admitted having the affair," Jack crossed his arms. "But swears it ended a long time ago."

"And you believe him?"

"There was no call history between the two in recent months," Jack said. "And he was working the night shift when she was killed. Doesn't clear him, but does make it less likely to be him."

"And you don't want to put a fellow officer on the board?" Maureen questioned.

"Not unless we eliminate everyone else," Jack said.

"And how do we do that?"

"The witness. The one who found her." Jack pointed to the board. "Randy Keyes. Have we shown him a photo lineup yet?"

"Not yet," Shaun answered.

"Let's expand it," Jack said. "All of our suspects on one board. See who he picks out. Obviously, you leave him out."

"He knows Brian," Maureen said.

"I think if it was Brian he saw, he would have known it," Jack said. "We leave him out as well. See if he picks one of the others."

"I can put it together," Maureen offered. "You want Carl Delacruz, Vince Abrams, Dan Pollard, and Logan Carr on the board?"

"And Kirk Harding."

"I thought you didn't want him on the board." Maureen spun her chair to face him.

"I don't want him on this board." Jack pointed at the whiteboard. "On a photo line-up, he's just another face."

"That gives me five," Maureen said. "How many others do you want?"

"Let's do ten, total," Jack said. "Five suspects. Five randoms. That should make it fair. Hopefully, he'll recognize one of them."

"Okay." She stood. "I'm off to make a line-up."

"Shaun," Jack stopped his partner from leaving the room. "Let's have a look at the files you found on Delacruz and Abrams."

"I'll grab them and bring them in."

49

Shaun carried the stack of files into the conference room and dropped them onto the table between Jack's seat and the one he fell into.

"That much, huh?" Jack eyed the pile.

"She was very thorough," Shaun said.

"Let's see how thorough." Jack took the top file and opened it.

Shaun grabbed the next one and laid it on the desk before him. "What are we looking for, exactly?"

"Anything that might explain why Sharon kept this locked in a filing cabinet at her home instead of using it to bring charges against them." Jack smiled. "Simple as that."

The two men read file after file, taking notes of any detail they felt relevant along with dates and times. The chief's investigation spanned years. There were notes from interviews with witnesses and experts whose identities were concealed by using code names. Verifying the information would be a daunting task unless somewhere in the files they could find a list of their real names.

"So, this all started twelve years ago when the former Moonlight Motel collapsed." Jack sat forward and stretched the kinks from his back. "Ten women and two men died. Later identified as victims of human trafficking and two of their keepers. From what I read, Sharon knew some of the victims."

"She spent a lot of time researching the building." Shaun referenced his notes. "The motel itself was only in business for less than three years. There were so many bad reviews about the plumbing and ventilation issues that no one wanted to stay there. There were a few complaints that stated on windy days the building seemed to sway."

"Sway?"

"That's what they said," Shaun confirmed. "Anyway, five years after it was built, the building was sold for a fraction of the original value."

"Was there any mention of who bought it?"

"A JP Investments," Shaun read. "But she was never able to identify actual owners. JP Investments only exists on paper."

"That fits," Jack said. "It was about that time that the place became a brothel of sorts, with the women literally living where they worked. And it was only two years later that the structure failed and the whole place came down."

"It only lasted seven years," Shaun said. "How badly was the place built?"

"From the report by the National Institute of Standards and Technology, the footings were not poured to the specifications of the architect and engineer." Jack held up the document. "They said the question was not whether it would fail, but when."

"How is it no one was ever brought up on charges?"

"The victims weren't important enough." Jack was somber. "And someone must have had a hand in stalling the investigation. Sharon started, but being narcotics, she wasn't given the latitude to continue."

"But she started again," Shaun said. "What triggered that?"

"Five years ago." Jack stood. "A balcony separated from a building, killing the couple who were enjoying the night air. It seems that Sharon was looking into any structural failures, looking for similarities to the Moonlight Motel. A notation of the construction company not following the architect's and engineer's specifications caught her eye."

"Abrams Construction Incorporated."

"That's the one." Jack nodded. "Our friend Vince Abrams came under the spotlight."

"How did it tie into the first collapse?" Shaun asked. "There was no mention of Abrams Construction in the earlier reports."

"No. The Moonlight Motel was built by American Commercial Construction." Jack flipped through papers until he found what he was looking for. "ACC closed its doors shortly after it completed the project. And Sharon uncovered that the owner of ACC was Vince Abrams."

"Seriously?"

"She also found that Delacruz, who was a building inspector for the city for fifteen years, was the one who signed off on the work," Jack said.

"You're kidding?" Shaun sat up. "And the chief found out?"

"Apparently."

"If she was going to expose them," Shaun looked at Jack. "That's motive."

"The question is why hadn't she exposed them already?" Jack frowned.

"Maybe she needed more proof?" Shaun suggested. "Or do you think she was blackmailing them?"

"She was instrumental in Abrams' business going under," Jack shook his head. "That's not the action of someone blackmailing him."

"Unless he didn't pay," Shaun offered.

"Maybe," Jack said. "But from what I know of Sharon, she wanted justice, not money. I'm guessing she tried to go after them and was shut down. Politics can be an enemy of justice."

"Since, she couldn't go after them with the law," Shaun summarized, "she went after Abrams' business and Delacruz's reputation."

"Which is another motive," Jack said. "And Delacruz no longer has an alibi."

"But Abrams' was confirmed," Shaun said. "So we focus on Delacruz?"

"First of all," Jack said. "Technically, his truck has an alibi. Anyone could have been driving it. And second, either one of them could have hired someone. I don't think either of them is the type to do their own dirty work."

"Then what's our next step?"

"I need you to get warrants for the financial records of both Abrams and Delacruz," Jack said. "I'm going to go brief the Chief of Ds."

50

When Detective Weatherby arrived at the construction site where Jack and Shaun had met with Randy Keyes, she endured catcalls from some of the crew as she made her way to the foreman. The man was quick to inform her that the electrician was not there. He had completed the current phase of the assignment just that morning and would not be back for several days when the next phase would begin.

"Where would I find him?" she asked.

"He's a contract employee," the foreman said. "He works for the electric company that won the bid, not for me. I don't know where he is, nor do I care. As long as he's here when I need him."

"How do you reach him?"

"Look." The man was losing patience. "I don't have anything but a phone number. Check with his company. They can tell you where he lives, what assignment he might be on, maybe even his favorite food. Just get off my site and let me get back to work."

Maureen returned to her car and sat looking up at the concrete structure, wondering if the construction company building it was related to Vince Abrams in any way. She pulled out her phone and called the number for the company Randy Keyes worked for.

"Yes," she said when the woman answered. "I'm Detective Maureen Weatherby and I am trying to locate one of your employees. Randy Keyes."

"Randy?" The woman became curious. "What has he done?"

"Just need to ask him some questions," Maureen said. "Could you tell me where he's assigned today, please?"

"Just a minute." The woman became silent, only the clicking of a computer keyboard letting the detective know she hadn't hung up. "Randy is on a construction site on Riverfront Drive today."

"That's where I'm at," Maureen informed the woman. "They said he finished up this morning."

"News to me," she said. "If he isn't there, you might check his home."

Maureen ended the call and, with one last glance at the construction site, drove away. After a twenty-minute drive, she came to a rolling stop in front of Randy Keyes' house. The morning the chief had been killed, she had not been available, so she had not been to the crime scene. She put her car in park and sat for a time, staring at the Hutchins' home.

When she finally exited her vehicle and approached the house, she noted two details. There was a 'For Sale' sign in the front yard and there was a utility truck in the driveway. Standing on the front porch, she rang the doorbell and waited.

The door opened slowly and just enough for the man inside peered out. "What do you want?"

"Detective Weatherby." She held up her badge. "May I come in? I have some questions."

"Two other detectives," Randy said, "they already questioned me. I told them everything I know."

"I understand," Maureen said. "But we have just a few more questions. It won't take long."

"Fine," Randy huffed. He opened the door the rest of the way. He was still wearing his company coveralls. "Come in. But excuse the mess."

Maureen walked into the house noting the boxes stacked everywhere. The walls were bare and most of the furniture was covered with boxes or items waiting to be packed. "I saw your sign out front. Are you moving away?"

"Away?" Randy glanced around. "No. Just downsizing. I can't really afford this place now that my wife is gone."

"So sorry," she said. "When did she pass?"

"She didn't die." Randy's voice strengthened. "She left me."

"Also sorry."

"Can we just get on with this?" the homeowner asked. "I need to finish packing."

"Sure, okay." Maureen opened the file folder she was holding. "In your statement, you said you saw someone running away from the scene."

"Yes," Randy sighed. "I already told the others about it."

"If I showed you a photo line-up," Maureen continued. "Do you think you could pick them out?"

"I don't know," Randy wavered. "It was dark and they were wearing a hoodie. I didn't get a very good look."

"Would you mind trying?" Maureen asked.

"I can try," he said. "Just can't promise anything."

Maureen grinned and nodded, knowingly. She pulled out two pieces of posterboard. Each board had five portraits on them, pulled from DMV photos. The suspects were all there, with the exception of Brian Hutchins, mixed with some random images. She put them side by side on the kitchen counter, one of the few surfaces available. "Take your time. Do any of these men look familiar?"

Randy bent over and studied the faces with scrutiny. "Yes."

"Which one?" Maureen felt hopeful.

"Well," he pointed. "That's Dan Pollard. He used to live across the street. And that one is that politician, Carl something. Are they suspects?"

"I just need to know if any of these men is the one you saw fleeing the scene the morning Sharon Hutchins was killed."

Randy looked again. "I'm telling you, it was dark. I didn't get a good look at the man. At the time I thought it was just a jogger, not a murderer."

"You're sure?"

"I'm sure it could be any of them or none of them," Randy said. "I'm sorry. But I can't just pick a picture. I didn't get a good look and I could never be positive I was picking the right one."

"In case your first thought was correct," Maureen said, "and it was a jogger, not the killer. Do you know any of your neighbors who might fit the body type you saw?"

"I don't know, detective," Randy said. "I just don't know."

"Thank you for your honesty." Maureen gathered the boards and slid them back into the file. "Good luck with your move. And please contact us with your new address when you do, just in case we have more questions."

"The others told me the same thing," Randy said. "I will let you know."

The electrician followed her to the front and locked the door behind her when she left.

Maureen paused in the driveway and looked toward the location where the murder had taken place. The chief's car was still parked there. The detective tried to imagine Randy Keyes coming out of his home early in the morning with no streetlights. It would have been nearly impossible to see the face of someone running on the street.

She was curious why the man had run past the electrician instead of away. Had they not heard Randy leave his house? Or did they have to go that direction to get to their getaway vehicle? She spun on her heals and knocked on the door. It opened almost immediately.

"What now?"

"That morning," Maureen asked. "Did you see a car? I mean, if the killer ran from the scene, you would assume they ran to their car. Did you hear an engine start? Or see headlights?"

Randy thought for a moment. "I don't recall. But by then I had seen Sharon and gone to offer aid. I didn't see anything more."

"Is it possible you were able to see her because headlights shone on her?"

"I suppose it's possible," Randy said. "I don't remember."

"Thanks for your time." Maureen walked away as the door closed and locked behind her again.

51

Jack was made to wait outside Chief Grimes' office for twenty minutes. The detective grumbled to the man's assistant numerous times and stood to leave. He was tucking his files under his arm when the phone on the woman's desk announced an internal call. She grabbed the receiver and after two quick 'yes, sir's she dropped the phone and looked at Jack.

"He'll see you now."

"It's about time," Jack growled and changed course for the office door. He pushed his way in and charged up to the Chief of Detectives where he sat behind his over-sized desk. "If you want me to take the time to come give you updates, you need to take the time to see me. I can't be sitting out there for half an hour while there's a killer to be caught."

"Are you finished?"

Jack stood with his jaw clenched.

"I know you're under a lot of stress trying to find Sharon's killer," the chief said. "But when you come to my office you need to remember who I am and address me accordingly. Is that understood, detective?"

Jack continued to clench his jaw.

"Jack." The chief's voice raised a notch. "Is that understood?"

"Yes, sir." His jaw remained clenched.

"What news do you have?"

"Sharon was investigating a building collapse that killed a dozen people," Jack reported.

"Why have I not heard of this?"

"It happened over a decade ago," Jack said. "She was in narcotics and some of the victims may have been women she had crossed paths with."

"Why wasn't it investigated at the time?" the chief asked. "Why was she looking into it now?"

"It seems the original investigation may have been blocked," Jack said. "She looked into it at the time and found evidence of sub-par construction and the work being signed off by a building inspector who may have been bribed. But when she approached her superiors, she was told to drop it."

"She had evidence?"

"Yes, sir," Jack said. "She may have uncovered something recently and was threatening to expose those involved."

"You think she was killed to keep her silent?"

"That's a possibility." Jack straightened. "I need you to know we are requesting warrants for financial documents back at the time of the possible bribes and for possible payment to a hitman."

"Okay." The chief narrowed his eyes. "That seems like the right path. Why do you need to let me know?"

"The building inspector at that time," Jack said. "He is now Councilman Carl Delacruz."

The chief closed his eyes. "You can't be serious. Are you sure?"

"I've seen his signature on the inspections," Jack said. "And he lied about his alibi."

"If he hired a hitman," the chief looked up. "Why would he lie about his alibi?"

"We don't know, yet," Jack said. "There is always the possibility that he killed her himself."

"You don't think a sitting councilman," the chief said, "up for re-election, no less, would risk it all by committing a high-profile murder, do you?"

"No," Jack admitted. "That's why I'm looking into the hitman possibility. But if it came out he was taking bribes, his time in office would be over anyway. So, he may have taken his chances. Plus he told his mistress to tell us he was at her place, which he wasn't. And he wasn't at home with his wife. That leaves the question of where he actually was at the time Sharon was killed."

"Tread lightly, Jack." The chief sighed heavily. "If you've got any of this wrong and it comes back on us, it could be the end of both our careers."

"And if we're right," Jack countered, "he'll be facing murder charges, or at least conspiracy to commit murder. Not to mention the fourteen counts of accessory to murder."

"Fourteen?" The chief furrowed his brow. "I thought you said a dozen people died in the collapse."

"Two more died when a balcony fell off the side of a building," Jack clarified. "Same man owned both construction companies and Delacruz was the inspector for both projects."

"Is there anything else?"

"That about covers it," Jack said. "Now, if you'll excuse me, I need to get back to my team."

52

Talk to me." Detective Mallory walked into the conference room and both of the detectives looked up. "Come on. Where are we at on the warrants?"

"Requested, but no word yet," Shaun said.

"Which judge did it go to?"

"Blake."

"That's good," Jack nodded. "He won't mess around."

"His clerk said he would catch him as soon as he recessed for lunch," Shaun said.

"Good." Jack turned to Maureen. "How did the line-up go?"

"Randy Keyes was at home packing today," Maureen said. "I told him we would need his forwarding address."

"Thank you," Jack said. "And you showed him the line-up?"

"Of course," Maureen said. "He recognized Dan Pollard, his former neighbor, and Carl Delacruz."

"Either of them the person he saw that morning?"

"He said it was dark and he didn't get a good look," Maureen said. "He couldn't be sure and didn't want to wrongly accuse anyone. When I stood in front of his house I checked the line of sight. I don't think he could have identified his own mother without any streetlights."

"His own mother?" Shaun questioned. "Really?"

"You know what I mean," Maureen said. "There's no way he would make a reliable visual witness."

"We suspected that," Jack said. "And if a hitman was involved, he wouldn't be known to us anyway."

"One thing I did find odd was the getaway," Maureen said.

"How so?"

"If the man he saw running away from the scene was the killer," Maureen said. "That means the man ran past Randy, risking being seen, instead of running away from him."

"Maybe he figured he wouldn't be seen in the dark," Shaun said. "So he took the most direct route to his car."

"That's what I thought," Maureen agreed. "But Randy didn't remember hearing a car start or seeing headlights. With no streetlights at that hour, headlights, even taillights would be noticeable."

"What does that tell us?" Jack asked.

"Either the killer lived in the neighborhood," Maureen said, "or he parked a long way from the Hutchins' home," Shaun finished.

"Which would make you ask again," Maureen said. "Why did he risk running past anyone?"

"It was dark," Jack said. "Maybe the killer didn't see Randy come out of his house."

"Or maybe the man running was just that," Shaun said. "Someone unrelated to the case out for a morning jog."

"If that's the case, he may have witnessed something without even knowing what it was," Jack said. "We need to identify who it was so we can question them."

"A jogger could have come from two or three miles away," Shaun said. "They would be nearly impossible to find. And we aren't even sure there's anyone to find."

Jack's cell rang. He pulled the phone out and answered, "Mallory."

He listened to the caller for a good amount of time before he thanked them and disconnected the call. He turned to Shaun. "That was Kirk Harding. Apparently, we upset him when we questioned him to the point he forgot he had an alibi. Says he was here processing a suspect with his partner at the time of Sharon's murder."

"That's a pretty good alibi," Maureen commented.

"And easy to confirm," Jack agreed. "Shaun, would you do the honors? Just call down and find out if anyone saw him here. Even better, did he sign the paperwork?"

"I'll call from my desk." Shaun left the room leaving Jack and Maureen alone with the whiteboard.

"What do you want to do for dinner tonight?" Maureen asked.

"Can we pick something up on the way home?" Jack asked. "I could use a quiet night in."

"Sounds good to me." She tilted her head and smiled.

"What?"

"Nothing."

"It's never nothing." Jack turned to the board. "Any ideas how we track a hitman without any DNA, fingerprints, or witnesses?"

"Follow the money," she said. "I know we aren't telling anyone about us, but I think Shaun knows."

"He's a detective." Jack glanced in the direction of his partner. "If he doesn't know, I would be disappointed. We're getting financials on Delacruz and Abrams. If that doesn't show us anything, how else can we track him?"

"Or her." Maureen shrugged. "Women can be hitmen too."

"And how do we track her?"

"Phone calls?" she suggested. "Some form of communication had to transpire between the hitman and the person hiring him, even if it's just to set up a meeting."

"Phone calls, texts, message boards, dark web," Jack rambled off a list. "We have their phone records. We may have to get their computers."

Shaun returned, sitting heavily in the chair he had vacated only moments before. "Harding's alibi checks out. He was processing a suspect. He filled out the paperwork at almost the exact same time as Sharon's murder."

Jack moved to the whiteboard and erased the question mark that represented Harding. "It's good to be able to clear someone."

"While I was at my desk, the warrants for Vince Abrams' and Carl Delacruz's financial records came through," Shaun said. "I've already sent the requests."

"Going back fifteen years?"

"That's what you asked for." Shaun crossed his arms.

"Maybe we'll finally be able to connect some dots." Jack stared at the four remaining faces in the center of the whiteboard. "We need to exhaust these others as well. Just in case it wasn't these two."

"The one who didn't want Sharon exposing his affair?" Maureen said. "The son with anger issues? Or the one who hated her for helping his wife leave him and get a restraining order?"

Jack stood, hands on hips, staring at the photos of the two men and boy corresponding to Maureen's descriptions. "Okay, Shaun, when the financials come in, start sifting through them for large withdrawals or deposits. Maureen and I are going to pay Mr. Pollard a visit."

53

Detectives Jack Mallory and Maureen Weatherby parked in front of Dan Pollard's home. The green sedan was parked in the driveway with the hood up. Behind it, on the street side, was an old gray compact pick-up. There were numerous dents on the driver's side door and bed. Rust was eating away at the wheel wells and along the bottom of the cab and bed. What paint there was showed signs of peeling and fading.

The two detectives exited their vehicle and started up the driveway. Jack pulled his phone out and dialed. "This is Detective Mallory. Can you run a plate for me?"

He read the tag number from the truck and held the phone to his ear as they climbed the porch. The screen door was still lying on the ground where it had fallen during Jack's last visit. They knocked on the door and waited. No one came to the door.

"Car suggests he's here," Jack said. "But if it's not running, who knows."

"Truck says someone's here," Maureen added. "Maybe he saw us and just isn't coming to the door."

Jack knocked again, more forcefully.

"You still there?" the voice in Jack's ear asked.

"Still here," Jack relaxed his body and turned to the truck. "What have you got?"

"Tag is registered to a stolen Honda Civic," the woman replied.

"Really?" Jack grinned. He hung up and turned to Maureen. "Does that look like a Honda Civic to you?"

"Not even close."

"Looks like we have something to bring him in on," Jack said. "Why don't you check around back, in case he just didn't hear us knock."

"Will do."

"Maureen," Jack stopped her. "Be careful. He may have already killed a cop. Assume he's dangerous."

Maureen smiled. "I'm always careful."

The female detective started around the house following the driveway toward the garage in the back yard.

"Jack?" She turned back. "Did you hear that?"

Jack was already on the move. He had heard. It was the distinct scream of a woman in distress. It had come from the neighbor's house. Dan Pollard would have to wait.

The two detectives approached the front door quietly. They heard a child wailing, mixed with shouting. They could tell the voice was male, but could not make out the words over the child. Standing on the porch, Jack tried the doorknob. It turned easily in his hand and the door swung freely on its hinges. Everything was suddenly louder and more clear.

"Stop it!" a woman shouted. "Dan! You're hurting me!"

"You think this is hurting you?" The male shouted back. "This is hurting you!"

The sound of flesh hitting flesh was distinct. Jack moved only a millisecond before Maureen. The two of them raced down the short hallway with guns at the ready. Following the repeated sounds of the assault in progress, they burst through the last doorway into a bedroom.

Dan Pollard stood over the now unconscious woman. He held her hair with one hand, his other was balled into a fist, raised to strike again. He looked up in shock at the intruders. Seeing the guns trained on his chest he released the woman who fell to the floor with an audible thud.

Jack rushed, grabbing Dan's arm and twisting him around. He shoved the man against the wall and held him there as he put his weapon away and worked his cuffs onto the suspect's wrists. When it was clear there was no more threat, Maureen holstered her weapon and fell to her knees to check on the victim. In the corner of the room, the child was curled in a ball, still wailing.

"She's alive," Maureen reported. She pulled her phone out and dialed. "Detective Maureen Mallory. I need an ambulance and a wagon, now."

She gave the address, put away the phone, and returned her attention to the woman. She looked up at Dan. "What's her name?"

Dan just sneered in reply.

Jack twisted upon his arm. "She asked you a question."

Crying out in agony, Dan said, "Missy."

"Missy what?" Jack asked.

"I don't know," Dan said. "Missy. That's it."

Jack used his size to move Dan toward the doorway. He shoved the prisoner through the opening and walked him to the living room.

"Missy?" Maureen spoke to the woman. "Can you hear me?"

There was no response.

In the living room, Jack forced Dan to sit and held him at gunpoint while he searched through papers on the kitchen counter. He found a small stack of bills. He called out, "Missy Faulkner."

"Missy Faulkner," Maureen repeated. She held her fingers to the woman's neck. The pulse was weak. "Missy! I need you to fight, Missy. Your son needs you to fight."

Maureen looked up to the child. The wailing had turned to sobs. His entire body shook as he cried. There was a sadness in his eyes, a bruise on his face. "Jack! I think he hit the boy."

Jack turned on Dan, who shrank at the look on the detective's face. "Is that true? You hit a defenseless child?"

Dan pulled back even more, resembling to some extent the child in the corner of the bedroom.

"When she wakes, you know she'll tell us," Jack said. "It would be better for you if you told me now."

"Better how?"

Jack took a step forward.

"Okay," Dan whined. "Yes. I did it. But..."

"Shut up!" Jack yelled, not wanting to hear what the man might think would be a good excuse for abuse.

Sirens drowned out all other sounds in the neighborhood as they converged on the small house. Officers arrived first and Jack happily transferred custody of Dan Pollard, telling them to book him on two counts of assault and that he would add more when he got to the station.

As they were leaving the house, paramedics entered with their equipment. Jack directed them to the victim and suggested they would need a gurney. Jack remained in the living room. Moments later, Maureen came down the hall holding the boy to her chest. He was still whimpering.

"Child services is on its way," Jack informed her. "They'll help find relatives."

Maureen looked up at him with her head tilted to one side.

"Sorry," he said. "Habit. I forget you deal with kids of missing parents."

"Not missing this time," Maureen sighed. "They seem to think she'll pull through. What he did to her."

"No wonder his wife left him," Jack said. "Sharon may have saved her life."

"And lost hers for her efforts," Maureen added.

"He's just climbed to the top of the suspect list." Jack put his hand on Maureen's shoulder. "You okay? That was a lot to take in."

"I'm fine." Maureen rested her cheek on his hand briefly. "I've located several kidnapping victims in this condition. Some even worse. Not that it gets any easier."

"When protective services arrive, we can go fill out the paperwork," Jack squeezed her shoulder gently then dropped his hand. "Then I'll take you to dinner. Dan can stew in his cell tonight. We'll talk to him in the morning."

54

With warrants in hand, Shaun collected financial documents from Vince Abrams' home and Carl Delacruz's accountant. The former took two boxes whereas the latter required a half dozen. Vince grumbled about having to dig the files out of storage where Carl's accountant threatened legal action if everything was not returned in proper order. In both cases, Shaun merely handed them the warrant and thanked them.

In the department's garage, Shaun borrowed a flatbed cart that was used for delivering packages. Loading the eight boxes, he pushed them into the elevator and rode up with them. He abandoned the cart along the wall next to the door to the conference room while he logged into his computer and then email. There he found bank and credit details on both individuals which had been requested earlier in the day.

While they printed, Shaun carried the two boxes containing the Abrams' papers inside the room and placed them on the far end of the table. Three more trips and the Delacruz boxes were stacked on the near end. A quick run to retrieve the documents he printed and he was ready to begin.

He opened boxes and sorted the contents, spreading them across the back side of the long table which had, to that point, remained clear. The surface filled quickly and there were still three boxes to go on the Delacruz side. Having moved the chairs away while he worked, the detective dragged one back and sat in front of his haul.

What Shaun learned within minutes of starting was that it was a good thing he had not become an accountant because he hated reading financial documents. He rubbed his eyes and looked away from the stacks of papers. In doing so, he caught sight of the flatbed he had borrowed still parked outside the door. With a slight grin, he determined it needed to be returned right away.

The detective pushed the down button and waited for the elevator. Only seconds passed before the doors parted. Jack and Maureen were there and exited, stepping to one side to allow Shaun to board.

"You find anything?" Jack asked as they crossed paths.

"Can't talk," Shaun said. "I have to get this back to the garage."

Jack stared back at him as the doors closed. With his partner out of sight, he turned to follow Maureen to the conference room. "What do you suppose that was about?"

"I would guess he has nothing to tell you." Maureen shrugged. "Either that or the person he borrowed that flatbed from is a scary, scary man."

Jacke entered the conference room and scanned the table, covered with documents. "Oh. Now I get it."

"Get what?" Maureen circled the table for a closer look. "He's been busy."

"Busy sorting everything," Jack said. "Not going through the numbers."

"You're saying he's trying to avoid going through all this?"

"Not avoid," Jack said. "But definitely delay."

"I can help, but I'm going to need coffee." Maureen came back around the table. "You want some?"

"Sure," Jack nodded. "But I can get my own."

"What?" she looked up at him. "You worried someone will think you're sexist for letting me get you a cup of coffee?"

"Something like that."

Maureen put a hand on his chest. "You can get me one next time."

She left the conference room in the direction of the break room. Jack shifted his attention to the whiteboard. As he looked at each photo, he considered the information they had gathered on them. Each was a viable suspect, but they had not yet discovered that one piece of evidence that would make them primary, though Dan Pollard was close. Jack was still staring at the board when Maureen and Shaun entered.

"Look who I found in the break room." Maureen handed Jack one of the cups she was carrying. She followed his gaze. "What are you thinking?"

"I think we're missing something."

"When are you going to interview Pollard?"

"You mean we," Jack looked at her. "Don't you?"

"After what he did to that woman," Maureen inhaled deeply. "In front of her kid, no less. I don't think you want me in there with him. If he tries to say it was her fault, I might kill him."

"All the more reason to have you there," Jack grinned. "He might talk if he thinks he's in danger."

When she didn't respond, he said, "Anyway, to answer your question, I thought I'd give him another thirty minutes or so."

"Well, that gives us some time to help Shaun." She clapped her hands together. "Let's get to it."

55

Dan Pollard slouched in the chair inside the interview room with his arms crossed over his chest and his legs stretched out in front of him. He wore a scowl on his face and only gave Detectives Mallory and Weatherby a cursory glance when they entered.

Jack sat in one of the seats across from their suspect while Maureen leaned against the wall, not wanting to be any closer to the man than she had to be. Dan looked up at her and sneered.

"Worried I might bite?" He looked her up and down.

"You even think of touching me and you'll be in a body cast," Maureen replied.

"Aren't you a feisty one?" he grinned.

Maureen took a deep breath, clenching her fists.

Jack slapped his hand down on the table causing the man to jump and look at him. "Mister Pollard. I would think someone in your situation would want to be on their best behavior."

Dan narrowed his eyes at the detective. "What situation is that?"

"We caught you beating Missy Faulkner," Maureen said.

"Assault," Dan said. "Hardly a situation."

"Attempted murder," Jack said.

"That requires intent," Dan spread his hands. "I deny I was trying to kill her."

"Felony Assault then," Maureen said.

"That's so hard to convict," Dan grinned. "My lawyer will be able to plead it down."

"You seem to know a lot about this," Jack commented.

"Did you forget how we met, detective?" Dan said. "I learned a lot from our time together."

Jack had previously arrested him for assault in a bar fight. He was beginning to think that wasn't Dan's first time.

"Tell me," Jack leaned forward. "Why were you trying to kill Ms. Faulkner?"

"I told you," Dan said. "I wasn't trying to kill her."

"Then why did you put her in the hospital?"

"Oh, detective," he sat up. "The last time I saw her, she was at home. I think you sent her to the hospital."

"Jack." Maureen pushed off the wall and took a step toward Dan.

"Detective Weatherby." Jack held out a hand. "He isn't worth it."

"I'm so worth it." Dan pursed his lips.

Maureen took another step, stopping when she reached Jack's arm. Dan flinched ever so slightly before sitting back. Maureen returned to leaning against the wall.

"Let's talk about Chief Hutchins," Jack said.

"What about her?"

"We still need to know where you were at the time of her murder," Jack said. "Because we know you weren't at home."

"You aren't pinning that on me." Dan tapped the table with his forefinger.

"From where I see it," Jack said, "you have a motive. You don't shy away from violence. And most importantly, you don't have an alibi, which gives you opportunity."

"I didn't kill her," Dan insisted. "I may have wanted to, but I didn't."

"Like Missy Faulkner?" Maureen asked.

"No," Dan snapped. "Not like Missy. I didn't touch Sharon Hutchins."

"Then where were you?" Jack demanded. "Without an alibi, you're our number one suspect."

Dan clenched his jaw. "I didn't kill her. I wasn't going to kill Missy. If I was going to kill anyone, it would be Julia."

"Your ex?" Jack sat forward.

"She's the reason for all my problems," Dan said. "World would be better off."

"You're blaming the wife you abused." Maureen stepped up to the table and leaned toward him. "She's the problem?"

Dan looked up at her. "All of you ..."

"Enough," Jack interrupted. "Rodney."

The door opened and a uniformed officer opened the door. "You ready?"

"Take him away before he ends up hurt," Jack acknowledged.

Rodney stepped in, ordered Dan to his feet, cuffed him, and led him out of the room.

"What do you think?" Maureen sat on the edge of the table.

"He doesn't want to tell us where he was that morning," Jack said. "He could be our guy. But we need something to put him at the scene."

"Did they ever run the print on the doorbell against his?"

"Should have," Jack said. "But I'll have them double-check."

56

Shaun sat in the center of the far side of the conference table with his head resting in his hands as he read page after page of financial spreadsheets, a job for a forensic accountant, which the department currently did not have. Jack and Maureen helped him for a short time before leaving to interview Dan Pollard and he was happy to see them return.

"I miss Betty," Shaun announced as they entered. Betty Greenburg had been the department's forensic accountant for eighteen years before she retired.

"I bet you do," Jack said. "Chief Hutchins told me they were close to hiring a replacement."

"Can they start today?"

"That was about three months ago," Jack admitted. "So probably not."

"Why even tell me that?"

Jack chuckled. "Find anything useful?"

Maureen rounded the table and took a chair two down from Shaun.

"I did actually," Shaun sat up straight and stretched his back. "Vince Abrams did not hire a hitman."

"How can you be sure?" Jack asked.

"Vince Abrams is broke," the detective said. "He can't even pay for his mortgage, let alone a murder for hire. He and his wife have filed for bankruptcy and haven't made any large withdrawals."

"Any chance he has cash hidden somewhere?" Maureen asked. "Or assets he could have sold off under the radar?"

"It's all possible," Shaun admitted. "It wouldn't show up in his bank statements or his taxes. But if he had it, I think he would have paid his mortgage."

"Not if he knew he would still lose the house," Jack said. "If he was getting behind on his payments, he might decide to skip a couple more and put that money to use elsewhere."

"You're saying he hired a hitman for six grand?" Shaun questioned.

"A down payment maybe," Jack suggested. "If he blamed Sharon for losing his business, I'm sure he blamed her for losing his house. That just increases his motive."

"How does he pay the rest?" Maureen asked.

"What?"

"If the six thousand was a down payment for the job," Maureen clarified. "How does he pay the rest after the job is done? I would assume the killer wouldn't offer a monthly finance plan."

"We should look into whether he has any assets not listed in what he gave us," Jack said. "Particularly things that are easy to sell off. He may be trying to get the rest of the money that way."

"I can do that," Maureen offered. "I've done a lot of property searches while looking for kidnap victims."

"Thanks," Jack said. He turned back to Shaun, "What about Delacruz? Anything helpful with him?"

"Have you noticed how much there is to go through for him?" Shaun looked up at his partner.

"Aren't you done?"

"No," Shaun said. "I'm not done."

"I just thought," Jack said, "since you were resting your head when we came in."

"I wasn't resting my head," Shaun defended. "I was holding my head up while I was reading financial reports. You know how boring spreadsheets are?"

"What if Delacruz paid the rest?" Maureen suggested. "They may have been in on it together."

"Then we need to find proof of it." Jack pointed at the papers on the table. "I'm going to talk to Tony in the lab about Pollard's fingerprints."

57

The lab seemed busier than usual when Jack walked in. A half dozen white coats were walking around. Another three or four stood at workstations, bent over whatever piece of evidence they were trying to extract information from.

"Fire in the hole!" Tony's voice was heard above all other noises in the room. Two muffled gunshots rang out drawing Jack's attention to the bullet recovery water tank in the corner of the lab. Tony had already unloaded and set the firearm on a tray and was retrieving the two bullets from the tank.

Jack bypassed the other technicians and made his way to Tony's side. With weapon and bullets on the tray, the technician turned to the detective.

"Detective Mallory?" he said. "Did I tell you I had something for you?"

"No." Jack followed the man to his workstation. "Just have some questions."

"Then what can I do for you?"

A young female in a white lab coat stepped backward and stumbled forward again when she bumped into the much larger detective. She fumbled to keep the object of her attention from falling to the ground. Catching it at the last possible second, she let out a long sigh before turning to the human wall. "Sorry."

"No problem," Jack grimaced. He turned back to Tony. "What's with all the new bodies?"

"Students," Tony rolled his eyes. "They are here to learn."

"You don't have one following you," Jack observed. "Seems you would have the most to teach them."

"I had one." Tony turned back to his station. "I was deemed too impatient and grumpy."

"You're too grumpy?" Jack grinned.

"I yelled at the kid for accidentally destroying a sample," Tony shrugged. "Sure I had more samples, but what if I hadn't? You don't destroy samples."

"You're not grumpy," Jack assured him. "You're passionate and care about the job."

"Exactly," Tony agreed. "But I'm better off without a student following me around. Anyway, you were about to tell me why you're here."

"The Hutchins' case," Jack said.

"I know what case you're working on," Tony said. "What about it?"

"The bloody print on the doorbell," Jack said.

"Not the best quality print," Tony said. "But I've made matches with less."

"I need you to run the print against a suspect we brought in earlier today."

"He wasn't in the database?"

"He should have been," Jack said. "I arrested him myself a few months back. But I want you to run it against a fresh sample."

"For that, I would need a fresh sample," Tony said.

"Like I said," Jack said. "We brought him in earlier today. His prints were taken then."

"So you didn't just bring him in for questioning," Tony nodded. "You arrested him. Shouldn't you have matched the prints first? Unless he confessed. But then, why would you need to match his print?"

"We arrested him on another charge," Jack clarified. "I just want you to run his prints against the one on the doorbell."

"Prints don't change, you know?" Tony quizzed.

"Do I need to find someone else to run them?"

"Geez," Tony huffed. "And they say I'm the impatient one."

"Can you do it, or not?"

"You know I will," Tony said. "What's the suspect's name?"

"Dan Pollard."

Tony wrote the name down. "Now if you'll excuse me, I have to check these bullets against a triple homicide."

58

Maureen searched through property tax records under Vince Abrams' name and that of his construction company, creating a list of every asset she could find. It was an extensive list, as the company owned equipment and real estate with a total value in the millions.

Setting that aside, she went through the financial records to create a second list of all the assets Vince still claimed to own. A much shorter list than the previous one, it took Maureen about half the time to compile as the first.

All that remained was the task of paring down the first list by marking out anything on the second and determining ownership of all assets remaining. As the company had folded, many of its assets had been sold off to pay creditors. Maureen would have to determine which ones so they could be removed from the list.

It was a tedious process that took hours to complete until she ultimately had a small list of properties that Vince claimed were no longer assets but also had no record of being sold. Finishing, she rewarded herself with a yawn and full body stretch. Her satisfaction was not only in a job well done but also in the appreciation that she had not been tasked with Shaun's work.

Two seats away from her, the young detective shuffled papers from stack to stack as he read every entry on every spreadsheet, cross-referencing with documents provided to back up the entries looking for anything that was not as it should be. While Maureen worked next to him, progressing through the pages before her, Shaun struggled to remember which spreadsheets he had completed and which he had not.

More than once, in frustration, he covered his eyes with the palms of his hands and pressed as if attempting to keep his eyeballs from popping out of the sockets. Each time, he uncovered his eyes and went straight back to work.

After Maureen stretched, she looked at Shaun who was again bent over a spreadsheet guiding his eyes with a finger as he read the line items.

"It doesn't look like Jack is coming back," Maureen announced. "What do you say we go grab a bite?"

Shaun turned away from his work to meet the other's gaze. "Should we?"

"Eat?" Maureen grinned. "It's actually encouraged."

"I mean, you know," Shaun glanced toward the door of the conference room. "You and Jack."

"Shaun?" Maureen laughed. "Are you going to make a move on me?"

"No." He was taken aback. "Of course not."

"Do you think I'm planning to make a move on you?"

"No."

"Then let's call it two colleagues going to get some food," she suggested. "We can even discuss the case if that will make you feel better. But I'm starved."

"I guess I am too."

"Great." Maureen stood. "Where do you want to go? And let's take separate cars so no one gets suspicious."

"What?"

"Kidding," she said. "But I do need to take separate cars. After we eat, I have to go talk to Vince Abrams about some missing assets."

59

Halfway between the lab and his car Jack's phone rang. He stopped just shy of stepping off the curb to answer.

"Mallory."

The call was brief. A nurse informed him that Missy Faulkner, the young mother that Dan Pollard had beaten to unconsciousness had wakened. With that news, Jack jogged to his car and steered toward the hospital.

When he reached the intensive care unit the same nurse buzzed him in and walked with him to the patient's room.

"We didn't expect her to regain consciousness this soon," the nurse smiled. "She's quite the fighter."

"How is she doing mentally?" Jack asked. "Does she remember anything?"

"She asked where she was," the nurse answered. "And she asked for Calvin, whoever that is."

"Her son." Jack grimaced. "He's probably the reason she's fighting so hard."

"The doctor asked me to tell you to keep it brief." The nurse stopped in front of Missy's room. "He's worried too much interaction might distress her."

"I only have a few questions," Jack assured her. "If she's able to answer them."

She nodded and pushed the door open. The two of them entered together. The first thing Jack noticed was the familiar sound of machines tracking her vitals. In the center of the room, a hospital bed stood at an angle with monitors on one side and an IV pole on the other. In the bed, hidden by sheets and blankets, was Missy Faulkner, curled in a fetal position. Her eyes were closed when they entered but opened slightly by the time they reached her side.

"Missy?" The nurse spoke to her in a soft, friendly tone. "There's someone to see you."

"Calvin?" Missy's raspy voice was barely audible.

"I'm afraid not." The nurse patted her patient's arm. "It's a detective."

Missy's head shifted, though not enough to make a difference. Bruises covered the left side of her face and bandages were wrapped around her head.

"I'll take it from here," Jack said. He dragged a chair from the wall until he was able to sit near her head. He rested his elbows on his knees so that she could look directly at him without moving. "Hi, Missy. I'm Detective Jack Mallory."

A tear formed in the corner of her eye. "Calvin?"

It suddenly occurred to him that she had no way of knowing what happened after she lost consciousness. "He's safe. We have him in protective custody. If you have family, I can reach out to them for you."

She closed her eyes and allowed herself a small smile.

"Missy?"

Her eyes opened again.

"Do you remember what happened?"

She blinked slowly. "Yes."

"Can you tell me?"

"Dan." She closed her eyes and Jack thought she had drifted to sleep. They opened again and she said, "Beat the crap out of me."

"He did," Jack said. "Do you remember why?"

A bandaged hand emerged, clasping the edge of the blanket, trying to pull it higher. Jack moved to help, tucking the cloth under her chin.

She gave him a grin that faded quickly. "Questions."

"You have questions for me?"

Eyes closed again; she shook her head almost unperceptively.

"Your fight was over questions?" Jack said.

A nod.

"I don't understand."

"Ex-wife," Missy said.

"You asked about his ex?"

"And murdered..."

"And the murdered policewoman," Jack finished. "You asked him whether he beat his ex and murdered Sharon Hutchins?"

Missy nodded.

"That's why he did this to you?"

She nodded.

He put his hand over hers. "You get some rest. I'll see if I can arrange for someone to bring your son to visit you."

She closed her eyes and the corner of her lip curled into a smile.

60

The waitress set a basket containing Maureen's burger and fries in front of the detective. She then slid an identical basket across the table to Shaun.

"Anything else I can get you?" She was pleasant, but not in the artificial way some could be.

"I don't think so," Shaun replied.

"We're good, thank you," Maureen added. She sipped from the soda that had been delivered earlier then started salting her fries.

Shaun took the ketchup bottle and squeezed a small mound of the contents into his basket. "You said you have to ask Abrams about some missing assets."

"That's right." She popped a couple of fries into her mouth.

"You think he may have sold them to pay someone to kill Chief Hutchins?" Shaun lifted his burger and examined it for a starting point.

"It's possible," Maureen said. "It's also possible that it's a clerical error or he sold them to pay off debt. That's why I have to talk to him."

"I'm just wondering about whether Delacruz could have done something like that, too." Shaun stopped rotating the burger. "There are six boxes of financial papers. Trying to find a transaction that may have been to pay a hitman is like looking for a particular piece of hay in a hay pile."

"You want me to help you go through the rest of his finances?"

Shaun chewed and swallowed. "I can't ask you to do that. You need to talk to Abrams."

"He'll still be there when we're done," she said. "I'll help you. It'll go twice as fast that way."

"That would be great." Shaun smiled and took a large bite of his burger.

They ate for a time in silence until Maureen decided she needed a distraction.

"How are you and Liza doing?" she asked.

"Good," he said.

"I know this job can be hard on relationships," she said.

"The hours aren't the best," Shaun agreed. "But then, her hours are inconsistent. There have been days when she leaves for work around ten and doesn't get off until two in the morning."

"That's a long day." Maureen raised an eyebrow. "I suppose that only happens on your days off."

"And murders only take place on hers," Shaun nodded. "That's what it seems like anyway. But when we are together it's great."

"Good for you," Maureen raised her glass as if to toast him. "It's good to have someone to go home to."

"Like you and Jack?" Shaun said.

"Exactly," Maureen said. "Speaking of Jack. I haven't heard from him in a while."

61

Detective Mallory's phone buzzed twice while he was on a call trying to arrange for Missy Faulkner's son to be taken to her for a visit. He had a feeling that seeing the boy and knowing that he was safe would go a long way toward her recovery.

He also made a call to Missy's sister. The injured woman wasn't sure it would do any good as the two had not spoken in nearly a decade, having had a falling out when Missy was at her lowest. She had wanted to reach out and make amends but never had the courage to do so. Her sister did not even know about Calvin.

When there was no answer, Jack left a brief uninformative message asking that the woman call him back about a police matter.

He checked his call log and saw that the two buzzes were missed calls from the lab. He hit the phone icon to return the call and waited.

"Forensics lab." The voice was too high for a man and too low for a woman.

Jack did know it was not Tony's distinct voice. "Is Tony available?"

Without a response, Jack heard the phone being placed on a table, then the non-gender voice saying, "Tony! Phone!"

The detective waited for what seemed far too long for the technician to make his way across the lab. He was deciding that Tony wasn't even there when he heard fumbling and ultimately a person.

"This is Tony."

"This is Mallory."

"I've been trying to reach you," the technician declared.

"Which is why I called," Jack countered.

"So, I ran the doorbell print against the man you have in the cell and there was no match," Tony announced.

"You're kidding?"

"I don't kid about forensics," the man said.

"You once told me that a murder suspect's DNA came back as the president," Jack reminded the man.

"Okay, I might kid, on occasion," Tony backpedaled. "But not this time. There was no match."

"And the boot prints came back as a match to the boots the electrician was wearing when he found Sharon," Tony said. "Um, the victim."

"Boot prints?" Jack's ears perked. "No one told me there were boot prints?"

"I just test the evidence," Tony defended. "I didn't collect it. Besides, like I said, it came back to be the electrician's boots. And since he found her, it makes sense he would leave prints."

"Still," Jack muttered. "This shouldn't be the first time I'm hearing about it. Are there photos? I don't even have photos."

"I can check," Tony said. "I'm sure there are."

Jack's phone beeped, notifying him of another call. He guessed it to be Shaun or Maureen and ignored it. "Who collected the boot evidence?"

"I'm not letting you assault one of my techs," Tony said.

"I'm not going to assault them," Jack said. "I just want to know why they didn't think it was important that the lead detective should have all the evidence. Maybe ask what else they didn't give me."

"Four years ago," Tony said. "The, uh, the John Harris case."

"For one thing," Jack said. "That was four years ago. I'm better now. And second, they didn't forget to give me evidence. They lost evidence. Entirely different."

"Just the same," Tony said. "I will get anything you don't have and send it your way."

"Who was it?"

"I'll talk to you later, detective." Tony hung up the phone.

62

B ack in the conference room, Detectives Travis and Weatherby divided the pages of Carl Delacruz's finances and started working their way through them, highlighting any movement of money that could not be easily explained and cross-referencing with the records of the many expense reports.

It was tedious, frustrating work made more so by the fact that every time they thought they had found something that might equate to a payment to the phantom hitman, they found a legitimate expense report that explained it away. After two hours of mind-numbing effort, they sat back to examine what they had found.

"Nothing ties Carl Delacruz to a payment to a hitman," Shaun grumbled.

"He either wasn't involved," Maureen rubbed her eyes, "has money hidden away for such a reason, or he did it himself."

"His alibi did fall through." Shaun looked up at the whiteboard. "We still don't know where he was that morning."

"He's hiding something." Maureen moved some papers around until she found the one she was looking for. "He refuses to say where he was and got his mistress to lie for him."

"Until you found out he wasn't there," Shaun said.

"And he has some shady transactions," Maureen passed the paper to the other. "One of which is a monthly payment of one thousand dollars to a P.S."

"Maybe P.S. is our hitman," Shaun suggested.

"No," Maureen shook her head. "The payments go back months. You don't make installments in advance to a killer. Too much of a paper trail. And what hitman would offer financing? They would want their money so they could distance themselves from their clients."

"How many months?"

"What?"

"How many months back do the payments go?" Shaun clarified.

"Uh." Maureen flipped through previous statements. "Seven."

"Seven months ago Carl started making payments for something." Shaun started moving papers. "Is there any way to trace them?"

"That's just it," Maureen said. "They were cash withdrawals. They were entered in the ledger as being P.S. It could be a business or a person. We don't know."

"There was something else about that time." Shaun continued to search until he found what he was looking for. "Here it is."

"What?"

"Eight months ago, Carl bought a car." Shaun set the page in front of Maureen.

"So," Maureen said. "I show car payments on the ledger."

"And a townhome." Shaun placed another page over the first.

"Listed as investment property in the ledger," Maureen said. "Payments followed. Neither of those is where the thousand is going."

"Are you sure?" Shaun looked her in the eyes. "A car and a townhome. At the same time."

Maureen sat up. "You think he has another mistress."

"One that he gives a grand a month to," Shaun said.

"And a place to live and a car to drive." Maureen picked up and studied the documents. "But if he was there, why didn't he use them as his alibi? He must not have been there. He just picked the one he thought would be most likely to lie for him."

"Which didn't work out for him," Shaun said. "It's true, if he was there, he would most likely have used them as his alibi, but I think it may still be worth looking into."

"You want to pursue a lead that we know won't produce any results?"

"They may not be his alibi," Shaun conceded. "But they may know what he did that morning. And if the thousand dollars is going to them every month, then we'll be able to take that off our list of unknowns."

63

While Jack was talking to Tony, he received another call that went to voicemail. It was not, as he suspected, Shaun or Maureen, but rather Missy Faulkner's sister, Brenda Wilkenson. In the message she left, she asked the detective to meet her at her place of employment.

He turned his car around and drove the fifteen minutes to a small advertising firm. Inside he waited for the receptionist to finish a phone call.

"How may I help you?" The woman looked up as she dropped the phone onto its cradle.

"Brenda Wilkenson."

"Do you have an appointment?"

Jack showed his shield.

"Is she in trouble?" The woman lowered her voice.

"Could you let her know I'm here?" Jack ignored the question.

"One moment." She pursed her lips and picked up her phone again.

Jack moved away and began looking at the posters that lined the wall. Each one represented an ad campaign the company had developed. He recognized a couple of them.

"Detective Mallory, is it?"

Jack turned at the sound of her voice. The woman standing before him looked like a healthier, more vibrant version of Missy Faulkner. "Mrs. Wilkerson?"

"Your message didn't explain why you wanted to see me." She crossed her arms defensively.

"Is there somewhere we could speak in private?"

"That serious, huh?" She turned, giving the receptionist a side glance. "We can go to my office."

They walked the short distance to her office among stares from her co-workers. Inside, she turned to shut the door behind them before circling her desk and sitting.

"Can you tell me, now, why you're here?"

Jack sat across from her. "I need to talk to you about Missy."

Taken aback, Brenda choked on her words. "Don't tell me she's dead."

"No," Jack assured her. "She's not dead. However, she was assaulted and hospitalized."

"Oh." Deep concern flashed on her face, fading quickly to apprehension. "Was it one of her drug addict friends?"

"No ma'am," Jack said. "My understanding is that she's been clean for over five years."

"What?" She looked confused. "Why didn't she let me know?"

"I can't tell you that," Jack said.

"Who did this to her?"

"Her neighbor," Jack answered. "He's a dangerous man. A suspect in another case."

"Is he in custody?"

"Yes."

"Good. That's good," Brenda said. "Can I ask you a question?"

"Of course."

"You're a detective," she said. "It can't be normal for a detective to notify the family of an assault. Why are you here?"

"True. It's not normal," Jack nodded. "Like I said. The man who hurt her was a suspect in another case. We happened to arrive during the assault. It made me feel a little responsible for her. When I asked her who to call, she gave me your name."

"After ten years? I'm surprised," she said. "Is she going to need help with her recovery?"

"It's more complicated than that."

"I don't understand."

"She may need help with her recovery," Jack said. "More than that, though, she needs help with her son."

"Her son?" Brenda sat up. "You're saying she has a son? I have a nephew?"

"You do."

"How old is he?"

"Almost three," Jack said.

Brenda fought against the tears that were forming. "Three years and she never told me."

"The boy is going to be placed with child protective services until Missy is able to leave the hospital," Jack said. "Unless a family member can take him in."

"Wait," she turned to the detective. "Is that why she gave you my name? She trusts me to take care of him for her?"

"Yes, ma'am," Jack said. "I understand if you need to talk to your husband."

"He's my nephew, detective," she said. "Of course, we'll take him in. I just have one question."

"His name is Calvin," Jack said.

"Two questions then," she said. "Can I see her?"

64

J ack grumbled when he answered Maureen's call.

"What's that about?" she asked.

"Getting a lot of calls today," he said. "What's up?"

"Haven't heard from you in a while," she said. "Everything okay?"

"Everything's fine," he said. "Is that why you called?"

"No," she confessed. "I wanted to see if you were at a point where you could pay Vince Abrams a visit."

"I can head that way," Jack said. "Any particular reason?"

"He has some assets that are no longer showing on his portfolio," Maureen explained. "But there's no record of them being sold. Could be nothing. Could be he hid the sale so he could use the cash for something sinister."

"Like paying for a hit?"

"That's a possibility," she confirmed.

"I'll talk to him," Jack said.

"I'll send you the details," Maureen said. "Shaun and I are going to follow up on another lead."

"Anything I should know?"

"Delacruz bought a car and a townhome eight months ago," she said. "He also started making a thousand dollar a month payment seven months ago. Thought the two might be related."

"I doubt he's keeping a killer on stand-by," Jack said.

"I know, but we wanted to check it out," she said. "Cross all our T's so we don't miss anything. If it comes to something, I'll let you know."

Shaun was driving and turned onto the street where the townhome was located. They scanned the house numbers until they found the right one. In front was the same make and model of the car listed as being purchased at nearly the same time. The two detectives looked at one another, their interest piqued.

Shaun pulled in next to the car. "How do you want to do this?"

"Straight forward," Maureen said. "We knock and see who answers."

The two of them exited the vehicle and walked up to the door. Shaun pressed the doorbell and they waited. It only took a minute for the door to open a crack. A woman in her mid to late twenties peered out at them.

"Hello?"

Maureen took the lead, raising her shield for the woman to see. "Detective Weatherby, ma'am. This is Detective Travis. Could we have a minute of your time?"

The door opened a bit more. "What's this about?"

"Are you the homeowner?" Maureen asked.

"Yes." She wrinkled her brow. "Well, not technically."

"Not technically?" Shaun asked. "What does that mean?"

"I live here," the young woman answered. "But I don't own the place."

"So you're renting?" Shaun asked.

"Something like that," the woman said.

"Do you pay rent or don't you?" Maureen asked.

"No."

"You live here," Shaun said. "But you're not the owner and you don't pay rent?"

"That's right."

"So you live with the owner," Maureen concluded.

"Not exactly." It almost came out as a question.

"So who is the owner?" Shaun asked.

"It's complicated." The woman seemed to be second-guessing herself.

"Let's try something easy," Maureen said. "What is your name?"

"Pamela," she answered. "Pamela Stuart."

"P.S." Shaun said.

"Those are my initials," the woman agreed.

From somewhere in the townhome the sound of a child crying caught the attention of the three of them.

"Oh, I'm so sorry," Pamela said. "Do you mind coming in? I need to get the baby."

"The baby?" Maureen glanced at Shaun.

"Yes." Pamela moved away from the door. "Excuse me. I'll be right back."

The two detectives stared at one another, then stepped inside, closing the door behind them. They stayed in the entryway until she returned with a child cradled in her arms. She swayed the baby back and forth while talking in a soothing voice as the crying faded away to silence.

The woman smiled triumphantly and whispered, "Follow me."

They followed her to the living room where she sat on a glider and used her legs to stay in constant motion. "He can be fussy sometimes. But he loves to rock back and forth."

"How old is he?" Maureen asked.

"Six months," Pamela answered while smiling at the child.

"And his name?"

"I call him C.C.," the woman was using a sing-song voice, maintaining eye contact with the baby who smiled back at her.

"Short for?"

"Chase Carlton."

"Carlton?" Shaun blurted.

"He's Carl Delacruz's child, isn't he?" Maureen asked.

The woman stopped gliding. "So, you knew all along who owns this place?"

The child fidgeted and Pamela pushed with her legs to set herself back into motion.

"You're receiving a thousand dollars a month from him," Maureen stated.

"How do you know that?" Pamela was perplexed. "No one is supposed to know."

"We're detectives, ma'am," Shaun responded.

"I suppose you are," Pamela grimaced.

"You heard about the police chief being murdered?" Maureen asked.

"Of course." She had a grave expression. "It's all they talk about on the news."

"That morning," Maureen continued. "Was Carl Delacruz with you?"

"He stayed the night," she said. "We were having breakfast when we heard about it."

"That's why he wouldn't tell us where he was," Shaun said.

"What?" Pamela's eyes widened. "You thought Carl did it?"

"His name came up," Shaun confirmed.

"He couldn't have done it," the woman said. "He's so gentle and kind. He would never hurt anyone."

"I think we're done here." Maureen smiled at the baby. "He's a cute kid. Looks like his mother."

"Thank you," Pamela beamed.

The detectives showed themselves out and remained silent until they reached their car.

"Oh my God," Maureen exclaimed. "A wife, a mistress, and a second mistress with a kid."

"If this comes out, he's finished," Shaun said. "His wife might divorce him. The first mistress runs his campaign."

"And he would rather be a murder suspect than let it out," Maureen said. "I'm so glad you talked me into this."

65

B ecause Vince Abrams told him, the last time they spoke, that he would not answer any more questions without his lawyer present, Jack called ahead to warn the man he was on his way. The former contractor grumbled but agreed to call his attorney. To Jack's amazement, a silver Mercedes pulled into the driveway at the same time the detective did.

The two drivers exited their vehicles moments apart. The woman in the Mercedes was tall, blond, and dressed like a wealthy businesswoman. She stood beside her car as Jack took his time climbing out of his.

"You must be Detective Mallory." The woman held the handle of her briefcase with both hands, as it dangled in front of her.

"And you are?"

"Natalie Olson," she answered. "Mister Abrams' attorney."

"You made good time." Jack started for the house.

"I happened to be in the area." She fell into step next to the detective. "May I ask what this is about?"

"Your client didn't tell you?" Jack was amused.

"He said something about being a murder suspect." Natalie kept her eyes on the ground, careful to avoid cracks in the pavement as she walked in heels. "But I've known him a few years now. I assume he's joking."

"Don't you attorneys charge by the hour, even on the phone?" Jack turned to her. "Is he in the habit of joking with you?"

"Well, no," she said. "But ..."

"He's not joking now," Jack said.

"Really?" Natalie stopped walking for a beat before starting again. "You can't be serious?"

They reached the front door and Jack knocked loudly. "A woman is dead. Your client's name came up during the investigation and we haven't been able to rule him out."

The door swung away and Vince Abrams stood in the opening. He looked from one to the other. "Well, I see you've met."

"We arrived at the same time," Natalie said.

"Come on in." Vince stepped aside. "We can use the dining room."

"Can we have a moment?" The attorney looked at Jack.

"Sure thing," Jack said. "Where's the dining room?"

Vince pointed to a doorway just a few feet away. Jack started for it. He wasn't yet there when he heard Natalie's hushed voice.

"I'm not a criminal attorney, Vince."

"I'm not a criminal," the homeowner replied.

Jack entered the dining room and the voices became murmurs. It was obvious from the tone that there was some disagreement between the two parties.

The detective was admiring the family photos that lined the walls when the other two walked in. Vince took a seat and his attorney sat next to him. Jack took his cue and sat across from them, placing his notepad in front of him.

"This is your meeting, detective," Natalie said. "What is it you want to know?"

"As you are aware," Jack addressed Vince, "you provided us with financial statements."

"You what?" Natalie sat forward.

"They had a warrant," Vince assured her. "What of it? I don't have anything to hide."

"Funny you should say that," Jack checked his notes. "According to what we found, you have three assets that appear to be hidden. It shows that you claim to no longer own them, however, there is no record of you selling them."

"What?" Vince leaned forward. "What assets?"

"How does this have anything to do with murder?" Natalie questioned.

"The assets are," Jack read from the notes he made while talking to Maureen. "One bulldozer. One heavy-duty pickup. And twenty-five acres of land."

Vince chuckled.

"Something funny?" Jack asked. "You appear to be hiding assets."

"It's hard to hide twenty-five acres, detective," Vince said.

"True," Jack said. "But if you sold the land, you could be hiding the money, or what you did with the money."

"What does this have to do with murder?" Natalie insisted.

"He thinks I sold this stuff to finance a hit on Chief Hutchins," Vince explained.

"Seriously?" she looked at the detective.

"Until we know where the assets are," Jack said.

"Well, tell your researchers to take another look at the sale of my company," Vince said. "The bulldozer and heavy-duty were both part of that deal. I no longer own them and the money is accounted for in full. Went to creditors as I recall."

"And the land?"

Vince sighed and looked at Natalie. She leaned in and the two whispered to one another for a moment. When they parted, she seemed to be upset with the man.

"I sold the land," he said.

"And the money?" Jack asked.

"I sold the land to my son," Vince said. "For one dollar. Just before everything fell apart."

"You were protecting assets from the dissolution of your company?" Jack asked.

"I was getting some land I had promised my son to him," Vince said. "He deserved that."

"You know how that looks," Jack said.

"He's answered your questions about the assets, detective," Natalie said. "He didn't sell any assets to pay for a murder."

"That may be true," Jack admitted. "But that doesn't mean your client didn't find another way."

"He's been more than cooperative, Detective Mallory," Natalie said. "Unless you have any relevant questions, I think this interview is over."

66

J ack sat in a corner booth at a diner he frequented. His waitress had served him many times over the years, knew to give him space, and was familiar with his signals for when he was ready to order or needed a refill of his drink. Because of this, the detective would ask to be seated in her section and tipped very well. Because of that, she was always glad to see him.

Today she set his plate in front of him, smiled, and moved on. He reached for the salt and pepper, seasoning heavily before taking his knife and fork to the entree. He was halfway through the meal when the entrance opened and Maureen turned toward him. Moments later, Shaun followed the same path.

Maureen sat and slid into the booth until her thigh was touching Jack's. Shaun centered himself across from the two of them.

"Any luck?" Jack asked between bites.

"Delacruz has a second mistress with whom he has a son," Maureen said.

"Really?" Jack stopped chewing. "I look at the guy and wonder how he ever got a wife. How does he have two mistresses?"

"He's not that bad," Maureen said. "And he has charisma, which is how he got elected. Plus, having money doesn't hurt."

"So, you're into him?"

"Lord, no." Maureen scrunched her face. "I'm just saying I can see where others might be."

"How did you find her anyway?" Jack asked.

"That was all Shaun," Maureen turned to the other detective.

"I just followed the money," Shaun shrugged.

The waitress appeared with a drink refill for Jack. "Can I get you two anything?"

"I'm buying," Jack said.

"Now I'm sorry we already ate," Maureen smiled. "But I'll take a cola."

"Same for me," Shaun added.

The waitress nodded and went to get the drinks.

"You were following the money?" Jack gestured to Shaun.

"Delacruz bought a townhome and a car around the same time he started making those thousand-dollar payments to an unknown party," Shaun explained.

"We went to the townhome and found the car in the driveway," Maureen said. "The mistress inside."

"Good job," Jack said.

"If she's to be believed," Shaun said. "Delacruz was with her when the chief was killed."

"Do you think she'd lie for him?"

"If she's worried about losing her home, car, and allowance, she might," Maureen said.

"How do we prove it?" Jack asked. "One way or the other?"

"His phone," Shaun suggested. "We looked at who he called. But we only checked for phone pinging in the area of the chief's house that morning. Assuming he's innocent and had no reason to turn his phone off, his phone would ping in the area of the townhome, if that's where he was."

"Good," Jack nodded. "You check that out. Meanwhile, I learned that there were shoe prints found at the scene."

"Why haven't we heard this before?" Shaun asked. "Where was it found?"

"A bare patch of dirt in the yard between Sharon's and the neighbor's driveways," Jack answered.

"And they didn't tell us until now?" Maureen said.

"The prints were consistent with the boots the electrician was wearing when he found her," Jack continued. "Noting unexpected. But what I want to know, is why there were no other prints found."

"Maybe the killer was careful to only step on grass," Shaun said.

"In the dark?" Maureen questioned.

"We've been assuming that the killer rushed her from behind," Jack said. "The most logical move, given her training. But if he was hiding behind the electrician's truck, why aren't there any other prints? And if he wasn't, then where was he hiding?"

"Even in the dark," Maureen said. "It's unlikely she wouldn't have seen someone coming from behind her car."

"Exactly," Jack said. "And the only other option would be they were hiding near the house and followed after she passed them."

"On the driveway, there would have been the sound of footsteps," Maureen said. "No way she didn't turn to see who was behind her."

"Which leaves us with Sharon not only knew her killer," Jack concluded. "But trusted them."

"That would eliminate everyone still on our list," Shaun said.

"She didn't really have to trust them, did she?" Maureen straightened. "Trusting someone with your money and trusting them with your life are two different things. She didn't have to trust them to turn her back on them. She just had to see them as not being a threat."

"You have a point," Jack agreed.

"Did you get anything out of Vince Abrams?"

"He accounted for the properties in question," Jack said. "I'm having them checked, but it doesn't look like he secretly sold anything to get a wad of cash for a hit. Which means if he was involved, he would have had to do it himself."

"She might not have seen him as a physical threat," Shaun said. "Especially if he wasn't armed."

"But he was seen on video leaving his home a half-hour after the murder," Jack reminded. "The only way for it to have been him was if he left through the back and took another vehicle to her place. Then he would have to kill her, return home the way he had come, clean up, and leave his home in his truck in half an hour."

"The camera was on the street," Maureen pointed out. "Not his house. He could have taken his truck and left through another exit on his land. But half an hour is cutting it short."

"Unless our timeline is off," Shaun said.

"The timeline is based on witness statements," Jack waved a finger at Shaun. "We need to try to get more precise. Talk to Reginald and get an exact time Sharon left the house. Talk to the electrician to get the exact time he found her. Maybe Abrams had more time than we thought."

"Seems unlikely," Maureen said. "He would have to plan it out perfectly."

"We should drive from Abrams' place to Sharon's and see how long it takes to get there," Jack suggested. "That way we have a number to compare to what we learn."

"Agreed."

"Shaun, you check Delacruz's phone records," Jack said. "We'll take the interviews."

Jack waved a hand to the waitress. She came to the table and dropped his ticket on the table then cleared the dishes. "Thanks for coming."

"See you next time," Jack responded.

The three detectives stood and left. Maureen waited by the door while Jack paid. When they stepped out into the evening air Jack said, "We can leave your car here and pick it up later."

Moments later they were headed to Vince Abrams' home once more.

67

J ack steered the car onto the main road after leaving Vince Abrams' street. Maureen, sitting next to him, had set a timer from the time they drove by the former contractor's home.

"Do you really think he did it?" Maureen asked. "Abrams I mean."

"We're running out of suspects," Jack sighed. "I'm hoping one of the ones we have left did it. Otherwise, we're back to ground zero."

"It's just..." Maureen looked at a car they were passing. "Even if he had more time, enough time. Taking a back way out of his home would suggest premeditation. Yet, he used her own weapon on her. He would have to have a lot of confidence to think he could disarm and shoot her. He would have had to know the power would be off."

"He was a contractor," Jack reminded. "He would know how to shut off power."

"True," she pursed her lips. "It's just, the timing would have to be almost exact to pull it off."

"Well," Jack said. "After this, we may be able to clear him, if there was no time to get the job done."

"And if there was time?"

"Then we have to determine where he parked," Jack said. "How he got to her driveway unnoticed, where he hid waiting for her, as well as what route he took to get away."

"Oh, is that all?" Her sarcasm made Jack grin.

"Piece of cake," he said.

They arrived at the chief's house and Maureen stopped the timer. "Thirty-five minutes."

"That makes it a very tight window." Jack parked the car in front of the Hutchins' home. "Now let's find out how much time he had to work with."

They walked up the driveway. Jack stared at the empty space where the chief's car had been. He then examined the grassy divider between the driveway they were on and the next one over. There were several patches of dirt, mostly on Randy Keyes' side. Behind the electrician's truck still seemed the most obvious place for the killer to hide. But there should have been footprints.

They reached the front porch and Maureen rang the doorbell, on which Jack focused his gaze. The bloody fingerprint was another unanswered question. Who tried to ring the bell after coming into contact with Sharon's blood, the killer? Why would a killer take the risk? A passerby? Then why didn't they try harder to get the victim help?

The door opened and Brian stood there with a somber expression. Without a word, he left the door open and walked away. Jack and Maureen exchanged a glance then entered the home. Following the sound of a television, Jack walked toward what he knew to be the family room and kitchen.

"Who was at the door?" Reginald's voice, rising above the television volume, seemed hollow. There was no answer.

As the detectives stepped into view, Reginald was rounding the island. He stopped in his tracks and frowned when he saw them.

"Brian opened the door." Jack scanned the room for the teenager. "Not sure where he went."

"Anyone but his closest friends," Reginald's eyes were as hollow as his voice, "he just goes to his room until they're gone."

Jack nodded his understanding.

"What brings you here, detective?" Reggie pulled a barstool away from the island and sat. "Are you here to accuse me of murdering my wife again?"

"We have a few more questions," Jack said. "We need to get more exact on our timeline."

"You have a suspect?"

"We have a person of interest," Maureen confirmed. "But we have to establish that he had time to commit the crime."

"The crime?" Reggie considered the words. "You mean when he killed my wife?"

"You know we do," Jack said. "We need to know if there is any way you can give us an exact time that Sharon left the house. We need to get as accurate as possible."

"The exact time that I last saw Sharon alive?" Reggie contemplated. "Seems I should know that, doesn't it?"

"Do you?" Maureen prompted.

"Let me think," he said. "It wasn't the most pressing thing on my mind that morning."

"Take your time," Jack said. "It's important we get this right."

"Six-twenty-two." It wasn't Reggie who answered.

The three of them shifted their eyes to the doorway leading to the stairs. Brian was leaning against the molding.

"Six-twenty-two?" Maureen repeated. "Are you sure about that?"

"I'm sure," Brian said. "Does that help you catch them?"

"It might," Jack walked toward the boy. "What makes you so positive? That's a very exact time."

"I was playing one of my games," Brian held up his phone. "When she said she was leaving, I happened to look to see how much time I had before I had to leave for school. It was six-twenty-two."

"You're sure, son?" Reggie asked.

"I said I was," the boy huffed.

"That's good," Jack said. "That helps us a lot."

"It'll help you catch him?" Brian asked.

"I hope so."

"When you do," Brian said. "You're going to shoot him, aren't you?"

"Brian?" Reggie came out of his seat. "That's not what your mother would want."

"What she would want?" Brian said. "She didn't want to be killed. This is about what I want."

"It won't bring her back," Reggie said.

"I know that, dad," Brian said.

"I'm not going to shoot anyone," Jack said. "Unless I have to. I'm sorry. But I promise we will catch whoever did it."

"Whatever," Brian grumbled, rolled his body off the doorframe, and started for the stairs.

"Sorry about that," Reggie said. "He's taken all of this rather hard."

"Understandable," Maureen said. She put a hand on the father's arm. "You should have him talk to someone."

Reggie sighed heavily. "I know. I will."

"Thank you for your time," Jack said. "We'll get out of your way."

"You are going to catch them, though," Reggie said. "Aren't you?"

"We are," Jack assured.

"Okay." Reggie nodded. "You do that."

The homeowner turned to the kitchen to return to where he had been when the doorbell rang. The detectives took their cue to show themselves out. They locked the front door and pulled it closed.

"Six-twenty-two," Jack said. "It's dark. And it isn't an emergency. How long for her to walk to her car?"

"Say, a minute to get out of the house," Maureen said. "Let's walk it."

"You're about her height," Jack said. "Similar stride. You walk it. I'll follow."

"Okay." Maureen pretended to close the door again. Then turned down the sidewalk. "It would have been hard to see, but I would have walked this path thousands of times. So, cautious, but not too slow."

Jack trailed behind. "Round the car. And stop at the door. About there."

"Another minute, minute and a half." Maureen checked her watch.

"That puts us where?" Jack asked. "Six-twenty-four, twenty-five?"

"So, now how long does it take to disarm and kill a trained police officer?" Maureen asked.

"He came up behind her," Jack said. "Probably body slammed her into the car. Then there would be a struggle where she would try to go for her gun, then ultimately try to keep him from pulling it out of its holster. There's no telling how long that would take. She wouldn't give up on protecting her weapon. Once he started, he couldn't give up. If he did, he'd be going to jail."

"So how do we figure it out?"

"Timeline," Jack said. "We talk to Keyes. Close the timeline."

68

Detective Travis left the diner, drove to the station, and was sitting at his desk within twenty minutes. He attached a city map to a bare wall in the conference room, retrieved some pins from his desk, and used them to mark the homes of the chief, Carl Delacruz, Emma Acosta, and Pamela Stuart. He also pinned Carl's work office and campaign headquarters.

Shaun opened the folder containing the politician's phone records and pulled out the pages representing the week leading up to the chief's murder. He separated the day before and the day of the killing and set them aside. With the remaining records, he went line by line adding a pin for every ping indicated in the records. There were dozens and the process seemed to take forever. But he did not stop until he had completed the task.

When he was done, he stepped away, dropping the pages on top of the folder they had been delivered in. Leaning against the table, he studied his handiwork. The largest number of pings were located at Carl's home, followed closely by those at Carl's campaign office. Third was the neighborhood where his assistant, Emma, lived, which contradicted her statement that they had only transgressed one time. Next was the townhome where they had found Pamela Stuart. A couple of dozen more pins were spread across the map individually. But most significant was the fact that there were no pings in the area where Chief Hutchins lived.

With a frustrating sigh, he picked up the records for the day before and the day of Sharon's murder. Using a different color pin, he repeated the process. The data showed that Carl's phone had indeed been at Pamela Stuart's place, or at least in the area, starting the night before until late the next morning. It did not prove Carl's presence since he could have easily left the phone with his mistress while he went to commit the crime. Unfortunately, his whereabouts were going to be harder to establish.

Concentrating on the data showing what towers the politician's phone pinged off of, Shaun traced the path Carl most likely took while driving to the townhome. He then searched for traffic camera data coinciding with the times searching for Carl's car. Under the assumption that whether the man was oblivious to the upcoming crime, or if he was establishing an alibi, he would take the main roads, the detective was able to locate the car quickly enough. It was also easy to identify the driver as Carl. He used the same method to locate Carl leaving the area the next morning, well after Sharon's time of death.

The more difficult task was plotting all of the alternate routes that could be taken in and out of the neighborhood, in case the man left his phone behind while he went to murder the chief. It was daunting, as there were dozens of paths that could be taken and the timeframe was broad. It could take hours to locate the car. Even longer to go through all of the footage, if Carl never left the townhome during the time in question and therefore nothing to be found.

After locating the cameras likely to have caught Carl leaving or returning to the townhome if he was trying to avoid being noticed, Shaun narrowed his search to the five that seemed most promising. The detective cued the images and began watching them one at a time, fast-forwarding when there were no cars on the screen and slowing to identify each vehicle as it passed. Searching the footage of the first camera took nearly two hours to complete.

With a fresh cup of coffee, Shaun started the second.

69

Jack and Maureen stood on Randy Keyes' front porch waiting for the man to come to the door. After about thirty seconds, Maureen pressed the doorbell again.

Jack looked back at the driveway where the man's company truck was parked. Possibly, the man's personal vehicle was parked in the garage. It was also possible he wasn't home. Jack knocked loudly on the door.

A few minutes later, the door opened and Randy Keyes looked at them confused. "Detective, isn't it?"

"Mallory," Jack confirmed. "This is my colleague Detective Weatherby."

"We met." Randy nodded to the woman. "What can I do for you? I thought I answered all of your questions."

"We are following a lead," Jack explained. "We need to establish a more precise timeline. We're hoping you can tell us the exact time you came out and found the victim."

"The exact time?"

"Yes, sir."

"I don't know," Randy said. "I mean, my power was out, so all my appliance clocks were off. I don't know what time it was when I left the house."

"Can you do your best?" Maureen asked. "We are trying to determine if a suspect was capable of killing her."

"You have a suspect?" Randy said. "That's good. Let me try. I mean, I didn't look at my phone for the time. And when dispatch called, it was on my landline, so I can't check the time there."

"Anything that can narrow the time down would help," Jack said. "We need to be sure we aren't wasting time on the wrong man."

"That would be bad," Randy agreed. "You think he might not be the guy? That would be frustrating. Let me think. I woke up because of the quiet. You know. The power went off, everything was so quiet it woke me."

"What time was that?" Jack asked. "When you woke?"

"I don't know," Randy said. "I think I did check my phone then. Six maybe?"

"Then what did you do?" Jack prompted.

"What did I do?"

"Did you sit and have a cup of coffee?" Maureen asked.

"I didn't have coffee," Randy said. "No power. Couldn't make any."

"Did you get dressed? Take a shower?" Maureen pressed.

"I took a shower," Randy answered. "Then I got dressed and waited for the inevitable call to go help with the power outage."

"Taking a shower and getting dressed," Jack said. "Something you do nearly every day. How long does that take you?"

"Twenty, twenty-five minutes, maybe," Randy said.

"And how long after that did you get the call?" Jack asked.

"Five or ten," Randy shrugged. "I wasn't tracking the time."

"So you woke around six," Jack recounted. "Then twenty-five to thirty-five minutes later, you got the call?"

"Maybe," Randy said. "But I can't be sure. Give or take, that sounds about right."

"It's a start," Jack said. "Thank you for your time."

"No problem," Randy said. "Sorry I wasn't more of a help."

"You still have my card?"

"Sure."

"If you remember anything, give me a call," Jack said. "Any time, no matter how insignificant you think the detail might be."

"I will," the man promised. "I want to help you catch this guy."

When the detectives were back in their car, Jack said, "Let's call it a night. But tomorrow, we need to call the electrical company's dispatch and find out when they called Randy. That'll give us the time we need."

"Don't forget," Maureen said. "We need to pick my car up from the diner."

70

The elevator doors opened and Detectives Mallory and Weatherby stepped out. The two of them made small talk while making their way to the breakroom. Jack set himself to the task of preparing coffee. Maureen gathered their mugs and put them on the counter.

"When Shaun gets here, we'll do a quick review." Jack kept one hand on the carafe and watched the brewed liquid pouring from the filter basket.

"I kind of feel guilty," Maureen said. "He had a lot of video to go through."

"You did your time on the campaign assistant's apartment complex."

"She's going to be pissed when she finds out Carl had a kid with, and bought a townhome for, another woman," Maureen grinned.

"You're not telling her." Jack poured the coffee. "I don't need anything coming back on us if the guy turns out to be innocent."

"But she deserves to know," Maureen protested. "And he deserves the aftermath."

"I'm sure they do." Jack placed the carafe back on the warming plate. "But it won't come from us."

"You're no fun." Maureen sipped from her coffee.

The two detectives left the breakroom and turned toward the conference room where they had set up their murder board. Halfway there, Jack noticed Shaun at his desk, head down.

"He's here early." Jack pointed.

"What is he doing?" Maureen looked toward the young detective. "Is he sleeping?"

"I think he is." Jack scrutinized his partner's body position. He looked around the empty desks in the room and grinned.

"What are you smiling about?"

"Nothing," Jack shrugged, though his grin did not fade. The detective changed directions so that he would pass directly in front of Shaun's desk.

Reaching his destination, Jack stopped and slapped his open palm down on the surface of the desk, inches from the sleeping man's face.

Shaun jumped up, his hand reaching for the weapon normally in his shoulder holster. Because he was in the department, it was secured in his desk. His head moved from side to side searching for the danger, his eyes settling on his grinning partner.

"You and Liza stay out too late last night? Jack asked.

"Liza?" Shaun looked from Jack to Maureen. "What time is it?"

"Eight-thirty," Maureen said. "Were you here all night?"

"She's going to kill me." He reached for his phone. "Give me a minute." Shaun walked away, raising the phone to his ear.

"Did they move in together?" Maureen watched him retreat.

"No." Jack shook his head. "But I think they stay together most nights."

"That was fast," Maureen said.

"They started dating before we did." Jack walked toward the conference room.

"Yeah." She fell in step to follow him in. "But we're old."

Jack spun around and gave her a look.

"Compared to them," she hunched her shoulders. "We are."

"What are you?" Jack challenged her. "Six years older than Shaun?"

"Five."

"Five?" Jack repeated. "And you're old to him?"

"Of course."

"But I'm six years older than you." Jack crossed his arms. "You're making me feel old."

"That's because you are." Maureen winked. "Now let's catch a killer."

The two detectives moved into the conference room where they stood in front of the whiteboard. That is where Shaun found them when he returned.

"She said she's not mad," Shaun groaned. "But that's not what it sounded like."

"Young love," Maureen smiled. "You better treat her like a queen next time you see her."

"Number one rule," Jack said. "Always call."

"Aren't you divorced?" Shaun said.

"I didn't follow the number one rule." Jack patted Shaun's shoulder. "Okay, let's get to work solving this thing."

Everyone's focus was on the board.

"Starting with Carl Delacruz." Jack pointed at the politician's photo. "You were here all night, Shaun. What did you find?"

"His phone pinged at Pamela Stuart's house all night." Shaun directed their attention to the map he had used to visualize the data. "I found him, on camera, entering the neighborhood late the evening before the murder. And leaving late the next morning."

"Nothing in between?"

"If he left and returned in the night," Shaun reported. "He knew how to avoid the cameras."

"How would a politician come by that kind of information?" Maureen asked.

"Not easily," Jack said.

"Are we clearing him?" Shaun asked.

"Not completely." Jack approached the board and moved Carl's photo across the board. "We'll move him farther down the list."

"That leaves Vince Abrams and Dan Pollard at the top of the list," Maureen announced. "My money is on Pollard."

"He does seem most likely," Shaun agreed. "Openly hated the chief, knew where she lived. And most importantly, not opposed to using violence against a woman."

"You may be right," Jack said. "But without evidence, it doesn't matter. We need to pursue them both. In Abrams' case, it means determining whether he even had time to kill her. We know when Sharon left her house. And we know about when Randy Keyes found her. If the hooded man Keyes saw running through his yard was the killer, then Abrams couldn't possibly have gotten back to his home in time to be seen leaving again on camera. If the hooded man isn't our perp, then we need to know exactly when our electrician came out of his house."

"What did Keyes say?" Shaun asked.

"He says he didn't know what time it was because of the power outage," Jack said. "His company called his landline with his assignment, so he couldn't look it up. We need to contact his employer and see what time that call was made."

"I can do that." Shaun pushed off his half-sitting position on the table next to where the others stood.

"You sure you're up to it?" Jack asked.

Shaun frowned. "I'm not a rookie anymore, Jack. I can handle a phone call."

"I was referring to the fact that you just pulled an all-nighter."

"Oh," Shaun glanced at Maureen. "Okay. Yeah, I'm fine. I'll get right on it."

"You do that," Jack said.

The young detective rose from his seat and walked out to his desk.

Jack turned to Maureen. "What is up with him?"

"You're his partner, Jack," Maureen said.

"I'm well aware."

"Well, I've been here a lot on this case," Maureen said. "And we've gone on a lot of interviews together."

"You think he wants to conduct more interviews?" Jack scowled.

"No," Maureen sighed. "That's not what I'm saying."

"Then what?"

"I think he wants to be your partner," Maureen answered.

"Which he is," Jack sighed right back at her.

"He wants to be in on the interviews with you," Maureen said. "Sit in the car with you during stakeouts. That's how he wants to be your partner. I'm in the way."

"He's jealous?"

"Shhhh," Maureen looked toward the squad room. "Not of me. Of the time I've had with you on this case."

"Great," Jack grumbled. "Not what I need right now."

"I could be wrong." Maureen gave him an awkward grin.

"Or you could be right." Jack looked out the door to where Shaun sat at his desk, phone to ear.

71

Detective Travis sat at his desk, phone to ear, with his head bowed and resting on his free hand. It had only taken a moment to look up the name and phone number of Randy Keyes' employer. Contacting them was another matter.

The first two attempts had resulted in a busy signal. Both times, he hung up and dialed again. Now on the third try, he was greeted with ringing. His triumph was short-lived when he realized no one was answering. In frustration, he slammed the receiver down on its cradle and stood.

Taking angry strides to the breakroom he poured himself a cup of coffee before returning. Sitting heavily on his chair, he glanced toward the conference room where Jack and Maureen were deep in conversation. He checked the number and called a fourth time. On this attempt, the phone was answered on the first ring.

"Full Current Electric." The woman had a twang in her voice. "What can we do to light your day?"

"My name is Detective Shaun Travis." He paused, caught by surprise. "Uh, I need to speak to someone about one of your employees. Can you connect me with someone in charge of dispatch?"

"Today, that would be me." She was hesitant. "You say you're a detective?"

"Yes, ma'am."

"You're the second detective to call in a week," she stated.

"That first call was me as well," Shaun said.

"You already called?"

"Yes, ma'am."

"And you're calling again?"

"Yes, ma'am."

"You're looking into another of our electricians?" she asked.

"No, ma'am," Shaun corrected. "Same one."

"Randy," she said. "You need to know where he is again? Cuz he didn't come in today."

"He didn't?"

"No, sir."

"No matter," the detective dismissed. "I actually need to speak with you."

"Me?"

"Yes, ma'am," Shaun said. "About Randy Keyes."

"I don't know him very well," the woman responded.

"I'm more interested in your knowledge as a dispatcher."

"Oh, okay." She sounded relieved. "What do you want to know?"

"Are you aware of the police chief that was murdered?"

"Oh, yes." She lowered her voice. "That was terrible."

"I need to know what time Randy Keyes was contacted to help with the power outage in her neighborhood," Shaun said.

"Well, I wasn't working that morning," she said. "Give me a minute and I'll look it up."

"Thank you," Shaun said. He turned his chair to face the conference room where Jack and Maureen were now sitting, still talking.

"Hello, detective, are you still there?" The woman came back online.

"I'm here," Shaun assured her.

"I'm a little confused."

"How so?"

"Well, you asked what time Randy was dispatched to help with the power outage."

"Yes."

"We didn't dispatch him that morning because he was already on an assigned job." The woman paused before continuing. "But he was called for a power outage in that same neighborhood six weeks ago."

72

Detective Mallory stood at the whiteboard rearranging almost everything. He cleared the middle of the board and placed the photo of Vince Abrams at the bottom center. At the top center, he placed the portrait of the electrician.

"What do we know about Randy Keyes?" Jack took a step back.

"He lied to us," Shaun said.

"He lied to us," Jack repeated. "Why? Does it mean he killed Sharon? Or is he hiding something else?"

"Wasn't he cleared?" Maureen asked.

"He was," Jack nodded. "The forensics on his clothing showed only trace amounts of gunshot residue. And the blood was determined to be transfer from assisting the chief. There was no high-velocity spray. If he shot the chief, how did he do it? Did we search his house?"

"Yes." Shaun pulled the notes on the search. "We looked for gloves. But none were found to have blood on them."

"Did he wash them?"

"They searched the washer and dryer." Shaun skimmed the page. "Nothing."

"He's the one who told us about the man in the hoodie running from the scene," Maureen said. "It could have been an effort to put us off his trail. But what if he was the one wearing the hoodie? He might have been making himself a witness in case someone else in the neighborhood mentioned seeing a man in a hoodie."

"Then where is the hoodie?" Jack asked. "Where are the gloves?"

"Every inch of that neighborhood was searched." Shaun crossed his arms. "Every trashcan. Every Shed. Every bush. If Randy discarded anything, he would have had to get it out of the search radius."

"The timeline." Jack snapped his fingers. "We built a timeline to determine if Abrams had time to get back home in time to be caught on video. But we used information given to us by Randy Keyes."

"Who has lied to us about when he received a phone call he never actually received," Maureen added.

"Our timeline is skewed," Jack acknowledged. "Now we need to know how much time passed between the shot that killed Sharon and when Reggie heard Randy yelling for help. So, when was the shot fired?"

"A few neighbors said they heard what sounded like a gunshot," Shaun reviewed his notes. "None could give an exact time that they heard it."

"We know when Sharon left the house." It was Jacks's turn to check his notes. "Six-twenty-two. And the 911 call was made when?"

"Close to seven," Maureen said.

"Thirty-eight minutes." Jack thought aloud. "He would have had to attack her as soon as she started to unlock her car. When you walked it, it took three minutes. Leaving us thirty-five. Could Randy Keyes shoot Sharon, then get out of the search radius and back in thirty-five minutes?"

"Sure." Shaun was hesitant. "But wouldn't he run the risk of someone seeing him leave or return?"

"Not if he was on foot," Maureen pointed out.

"The Bartlett's dogs barked at something behind their house," Shaun remembered. "It could have been him. But from the way they described it, this was before the shooting."

"On foot," Jack reasoned, "he would have had to run, find a place to stash the hoodie and gloves, and then run back. He would have been out of breath. Could he call for help while catching his breath?"

Shaun and Maureen both shrugged.

"What about motive?" Jack asked. "Does he have one?"

"He and his wife are going through a divorce," Shaun suggested. "Maybe Sharon was helping her the same way she helped Julia Pollard."

"When we met with Samantha Keyes, we didn't ask her about the relationship between Randy and Sharon," Jack grumbled. "She was so convinced he couldn't have done it; I didn't see the need to ask."

"You think you missed something?" Maureen asked.

"We need to get some answers," Jack said. "Then we bring Randy Keyes in for questioning."

"He didn't report to work today," Shaun said.

"We divide and concur," Jack concluded. "Shaun talk to Dave Bartlett again. Maureen get in touch with Samantha Keyes and ask what I didn't. I'll talk to Reginald. Then we bring in Randy."

73

Jack pulled up in front of Reginald Hutchins' house and parked at the curb. He and Shaun climbed out of the car and met on the sidewalk.

"I'll take Reginald," Jack repeated. "You talk to Dave Bartlett. We'll meet here at the car before approaching Keyes."

Shaun nodded and turned away, walking down the sidewalk toward the Bartlett home. As he passed by, he glanced up to Randy Keyes' house, the 'For Sale' sign standing dominantly in the front yard. From his brief look, he could not determine if anyone was in the house though the electrician's truck was not in the driveway.

He continued to the next house and turned up the driveway. Reaching the front porch, Shaun rang the doorbell and pounded his fist on the door. It only took a few minutes for Michelle Bartlett to answer.

"Can I help you?" she asked. "Aren't you the detective that was here the other morning?"

"Yes, ma'am," Shaun answered. "Is your husband home?"

"He's in the garage," she answered. "Can I ask what this is about?"

"I have some follow-up questions?" Shaun explained. "Would you get your husband?"

"I'll be right back," Michelle said. She left the detective standing in the doorway as she walked through the house to the garage. A few minutes later, she returned with Dave walking behind her wiping his hands on a towel.

"Detective," Dave greeted. "I thought we answered all your questions."

"When I spoke to you the other day," Shaun said. "You mentioned your dogs barking at the back door."

"They did," Dave agreed.

"I need you to think back," Shaun said. "How long after the power outage did they start?"

"Funny thing is," Dave looked to the ground. "The first time they barked, it was like ten minutes before the outage."

"Before?" Shaun could not hide his surprise. "You're positive?"

"Yes." Dave nodded. "I was listening to the radio and a song I like came on. Then the dogs just go nuts. Drowned out the song. I went in to yell at them and they were at the back door."

"Before the outage?"

"Like I said," Dave confirmed.

"Why didn't you say this before?" Michelle asked.

"I forgot," Dave shrugged. "You know. After the power went out they stared in again, so when we talked to you detectives, that's what I remembered."

"How long after?" Shaun demanded.

"How long after what?" Dave asked.

"How long after the power went out did the dogs start barking?"

"I don't know," Dave sighed. "Maybe ten minutes."

"And the third time," Shaun pressed. "The time the dogs barked in the middle of the room. How long after the second time did they start again?"

"Five or ten minutes," Dave said.

"And nothing after that?"

"They went crazy with all the sirens," Michelle said.

"And when you guys knocked on our door," Dave added.

"Thank you for your time." Shaun half-jogged down the driveway.

74

Jack sat across from Reginald Hutchins in his living room. The man's son, Brian, was in the kitchen making something to eat.

"Have you found him?" Reggie asked.

"We may be getting close," Jack answered.

"So, no."

"We need to ask you some more questions," Jack said.

"You still think I did it?" Reggie locked eyes with the detective.

"No." Jack shook his head. "I need to ask you about your neighbors, Randy and Samantha Keyes."

"What about them?" Reggie frowned. "Did they have something to do with Sharon?"

"Are you aware that Sharon had helped Julia Pollard get out of her abusive marriage?" Jack asked. "And helped her get a restraining order against Dan?"

"Of course I did." The man seemed offended at the suggestion he didn't. "What does that have to do with the Keyes?"

"The Keyes are going through a divorce," Jack explained. "Did Sharon have any part in helping Samantha get out of that relationship, like she did with Julia?"

"No," Reggie shook his head.

"You're sure?"

"Sharon would have said if she did," Reggie insisted. "The only thing was when Sam was accusing Dave of killing her cat. I mean she was helping Dave. But in the end, when she proved it wasn't Dave, Sharon talked to Sam and everything calmed down."

"Was she able to determine who killed the cat?"

"My wife was killed." The man's demeanor changed. "Why are you worried about a dead cat?"

"Just answer the question," Jack demanded.

"You know Sharon," Reggie said. "I'm sure she did."

"She didn't tell you?"

"No."

"Randy never mentioned it?" Jack asked.

"Randy and I were never talkers," Reggie said. "I tried to be friends, for Sharon. But we weren't the same, he and I."

"What does that mean?" Jack asked.

"I got this from Sharon," Reggie clarified. "But Randy and Samantha were high school sweethearts. Married young. She went on to college. He went to trade school. She landed a good career. He bounced from job to job. She outgrew him."

"You think he resented her?"

"I don't know," Reggie said. "But Sharon told me Sam was unhappy. Then they found out they couldn't have kids. She had tests and found out she was fine. But Randy refused to get tested."

"More strain on the marriage."

"So her cats became her babies," Reggie said. "Two beautiful purebred Persians. When the one was killed it was like she lost a child."

"Was Randy jealous of the cats?"

"I don't know," Reggie scrunched his face. "But it wasn't long after the cat was killed that she left him. Wait. Do you think he did it? Sharon, I mean, not the cat."

"We aren't saying that," Jack said. "We're just trying to get a picture of the neighborhood dynamics. Do you think Randy might be selling the house to get away from his neighbors?"

"No." Brian was standing behind them.

"What do you know about it?" Reggie asked.

"I was outside one day and overheard him telling the real estate agent that the judge was making him sell," Brian explained. "He had to split the assets with Mrs. Keyes. He said he couldn't afford it anymore anyway."

"He never fit in here," Reggie said.

"Why do you say that?" Jack asked.

"This is a white-collar neighborhood, detective. Randy was blue-collar all the way. Damn, the man wore those coveralls all the time. We even had a neighborhood barbecue, and he showed up wearing those coveralls."

"The coveralls from work?"

"Those," Reggie nodded. "Sometimes his own. But always coveralls."

75

Maureen found Samantha Keyes at work. The woman was reluctant to step away to talk to the detective, but Maureen can be very convincing. A few minutes later the two of them were sitting across from one another in a small meeting room.

"Why are you here?" Samantha asked. "I already answered your questions. I don't know anything more. I don't know anything about Sharon's murder."

"You and your husband are divorcing," Maureen said.

Samantha stared at the detective, her mouth open.

"Mrs. Keyes?"

"What does my divorce have to do with anything?" Samantha argued.

"Did Sharon Hutchins help you?"

"Help me?" Samantha tightened her brow. "With my divorce?"

"We know that she helped Julia Pollard get away from her husband," Maureen explained. "We just want to know if she helped you in the same way."

"She helped Julia?" Samantha's expression softened. "I didn't know. Good for her."

"But she didn't help you?"

"No," Samantha said. "Of course not. Randy was nothing like Dan Pollard."

"So Randy had no reason to be upset with her?"

"Randy? No." Samantha shook her head. "Well I mean."

"You mean what?" Maureen pressed.

"Well I guess Sharon did help me end my marriage in one way," Samantha gave a half-grin.

"In what way?" Maureen asked.

"When she told me that Randy was the one who killed my cat," Samantha stated.

"Your husband killed your cat?"

"He did," Samantha teared up. "Sorry."

"He killed your cat," Maureen repeated. "Then let you believe your neighbor did it?"

"Can you believe it?" Samantha sniffed. "Of course, he claimed it was an accident."

"Then why let you think Dave did it?"

"Exactly," Samantha said.

"Did you ask him?"

"He said he was afraid to tell me because I wouldn't believe it was an accident," Samantha chuckled. "He knew Dave hated cats and when I blamed Dave, he thought he'd be in the clear. 'No harm. No foul.' His words."

"Then Sharon stepped in," Maureen said.

"She sure did," Samantha chuckled again. "I mean it was a cat. He meant a lot to me, but no one else. So when Sharon started asking questions, investigating the death of my cat, it was surreal. A police chief investigating the murder of my cat."

"How did Randy take it?"

"The investigation?" Samantha smiled. "He kept talking about how stupid it was. A waste of time. Everyone knew Dave did it. Why waste the energy finding out what we already knew."

"And when she told you Randy had done it?"

"Oh, my God," Samantha took a deep breath. "Randy denied it, of course. But the evidence didn't leave a lot of room for doubt. Then he was mad at Sharon for interfering, for proving he did it. Then it was my fault for having cats to begin with. It was never his fault."

"And what happened next?"

"The next day, I saw a divorce attorney," Samantha said. "The day after that Randy was served with papers while at work. I had taken the day off and packed my things with the help of my brother and some friends."

"He gets served at work," Maureen said. "Then comes home to an empty house."

"It wasn't empty," Samantha defended. "I only took my things and a few furniture pieces that I wanted to keep."

"But you weren't there," Maureen sighed. "To him, it was an empty house. When my colleagues talked to you, you told them you didn't think Randy could have done this to Sharon."

"He's not a violent guy," Samantha assured her.

"He killed your cat."

"I, uh," Samantha stammered.

"He killed your cat," Maureen repeated. "And I think he killed Sharon because she told you he did. He blamed her for your divorce."

Maureen's phone rang. The intrusion startled them both.

"Just a minute," Maureen pulled her phone out, saw Jack's name on the screen, and answered. "Jack?"

"Where are you?"

"I'm with Samantha Keyes as we discussed?" Maureen turned away from her interviewee. "Why?"

"Randy Keyes is our man," Jack announced.

"He blamed Sharon for Samantha leaving him," Maureen said. "The chief proved that he killed her cat. But that doesn't prove murder."

"Shaun thinks he turned off the power," Jack said. "Ran down the back alley to the box and returned to meet her coming out of her house."

"He must have known she would come out," Shaun yelled to the phone. "He was dispatched for an outage a few months ago. She must have come out of the house when he did. Gave him the idea."

"The man wears coveralls everywhere," Jack added. "But the clothes he submitted for testing were slacks and a shirt. He must have stripped out of the coveralls and returned to the scene."

"Coveralls?" Maureen said.

"Coveralls?" Samantha repeated. "What about them?"

"Does Randy wear them?" Maureen asked.

"All the time," Samantha answered. "Probably would have slept in them if I didn't complain about them so much."

"Confirmed on the coveralls," Maureen spoke into the phone. "Do you have him in custody?"

"No," Jack replied. "He's not at home. I think you should take Samantha to the station. Just to be safe."

"Agreed," Maureen said. "Samantha, get your jacket. We're going downtown for a while."

"You think he did it?" She seemed to deflate. "Don't you?"

"He's a person of interest," Maureen nodded. "Now let's go."

Samantha picked up her purse and went to the closet to get her jacket. Slipping it on, the two of them moved to the front door.

"On our way, Jack," Maureen said into the phone as she opened the door.

On the porch, dressed in coveralls, was Randy Keyes. In one hand he held a pistol. "Going somewhere?"

76

"Maureen!" Jack shouted into the phone for a second time. There was no response and a moment later the line went dead. The detective stomped down on the accelerator making the car lurch forward. Beside him, Shaun held the armrest to stabilize himself. Jack glanced in his partner's direction. "Call for backup."

Shaun knew exactly what that meant. Randy Keyes was at his ex-wife's house along with their colleague. The fact that the call was disconnected could only mean that Maureen was in trouble. Shaun pulled his phone out and called dispatch, explained the problem, and requested anyone that was available.

The way Jack was driving at full acceleration weaving in and out of lanes, they would be there in about ten minutes. The problem was that they had no way of knowing if Maureen had ten minutes.

Flying through an intersection against the light, sparks flew as the right side of Jack's car scraped the front end of a small SUV. Seconds before, the driver slammed on their brakes when they saw the speeding sedan coming at them. Jack cursed and Shaun sighed in relief, but they did not slow down.

Racing through Samantha Keyes' neighborhood proved more challenging as there were numerous sharp turns and the risk of children being on the street was high. Jack scanned for any sign of movement as he maneuvered past parked cars and other obstacles, while Shaun eyed the driver of every vehicle they passed looking for their suspect.

Reaching the last turn, Jack slid around the corner, braking hard when Samantha Keyes' home came into view. Randy's electrician's truck was parked at an angle, blocking Maureen's car. There was no sign of anyone in front of the house. As Jack rolled to a stop at the end of the driveway, he could not see any movement from inside the house.

The detectives left their doors open and moved toward the home with weapons in hand.

77

Move back," Randy ordered. He waved the gun from woman to woman as he herded them into the living room. He looked around the room and turned to his soon-to-be ex-wife. "Good God, Sam. Look at what you've done with this place. It looks like you've lived here for years."

"Randy?" Samantha's voice cracked. "What are you doing? Since when do you have a gun?"

"You wouldn't believe how easy it is to get one of these." Randy rotated his hand and observed the weapon. "I mean, they'll let anybody buy one."

"Mr. Keyes," Maureen said. "Why don't you put that down? You don't want to hurt anyone."

He twisted the gun back around and pointed it at the detective. "You think you know what I want? How could you? You don't know me."

"Randy," Samantha pleaded. "Please."

"You know." Randy directed his attention to his wife. "Our house used to have that lived-in feel. But now...you know what it's like now? It's full of boxes. Our whole life. Just packed away in cardboard boxes."

He stepped forward and placed the gun against Samantha's head. The woman let out a small scream that turned into a whimper. With her eyes closed, she begged, "Please. Please, don't do this."

"Randy." Maureen held her hands at shoulder height, waving them from side to side, wanting to take his attention from Samantha without having him look down. Her service pistol was holstered at her waist. He either hadn't noticed or didn't care. "Don't do something you'll regret."

The man turned to the detective as if seeing her for the first time. "Regret? What would I regret? We've been married twenty years. She took that away. She took my life from me. And do you know why?"

Samantha began to sob.

Randy glanced at her and then back to Maureen. "Do you know why?"

"Randy," Maureen remained calm. "You're scaring her. Put the gun down."

"It was a cat," Randy said. "She threw everything away because of a cat."

"That's not true," Samantha cried.

"I told you it was an accident," Randy yelled. "I told you I didn't mean to kill it. But you didn't believe me. You cared more about that cat than you did for me."

"No," Samantha insisted. "That's not true."

"You heard her," Maureen said. "She believes you. She believes it was an accident. Don't you Samantha?"

"Y-yes." Samantha held her eyes shut, tears running down her face.

"No," Randy nodded his head. "You didn't believe me. You don't."

"I do, Randy." Samantha opened her eyes. "I believe you."

"You're just saying that so I won't shoot you," Randy said.

"No." Her eyes welled up. "I believe you."

"You don't believe me," Randy insisted. "You can't believe me. You're too smart for that."

"I don't understand," Samantha said.

"It wasn't an accident," Randy laughed. "I hated those cats. The way you cared for them. And ignored me. I only regret that I didn't kill them both."

"Oh, Randy," Samantha sobbed.

"Where is it?" Randy demanded. "Where is your other precious little baby?"

"Randy," Maureen tried to snap him back. "Put the gun down, Randy. Let's talk this out."

"You," Randy swung the gun on the detective. "You're just like her."

"Like Samantha?" Maureen wanted to keep him focused on her. "How am I like her?"

"No," Randy said. "Not like Sam. Like Sharon. You're just like meddling Sharon."

"Is that why you killed her?" Maureen asked. "Because she was meddling?"

"Everything was fine while she," Randy turned the gun on Samantha again. The woman held her hands up and wailed. "When she believed Dave killed the cat, everything was good."

"You had to know the truth would come out," Maureen said. "Eventually."

"It wouldn't," Randy argued. "No one would have ever known had it not been for her. Sharon ruined my life. She had to pay."

"You killed her?" Samantha asked between sobs.

"She ruined our lives, Sam," Randy tried to explain. "I had to fix it. I fixed it for us."

"You killed Sharon to fix things?" Maureen softened her voice. "To fix your marriage?"

"Yes."

"Because you want Samantha back?" Maureen continued. "To come home?"

"That's all I want," Randy agreed.

"Then why are you holding a gun on her, Randy?" Maureen asked. "Can't you see she's terrified?"

"She wouldn't listen to me." Randy faced his wife. "I just needed you to listen."

Outside, Detectives Mallory and Travis reached the front porch and stood outside the door listening. They could hear voices but could not make out any words. Jack reached out and gingerly tried the knob on the door. It turned freely. He took a deep breath and hoped the hinges wouldn't give them away. Stepping forward, he guided the door all the way open and the two men entered the home.

The voices were clearer, tense, and at times angry. In defiance of the way Jack drove to get there, he moved with cautious, smooth motions. Shaun was a half-step behind him on the opposite side of the short hall.

Reaching the room from which the voices came, Jack chanced a quick peek around the corner before pulling back. Randy had his back to them but he held a gun pointed at Samantha Keyes' face. They had to be careful and strategic. He peeked in again, this time stepping across the opening to the other side of the doorway. He made eye contact with Maureen as he went. Once there, Shaun stepped into the space he had vacated and they waited for a signal from inside.

Maureen caught the movement in the corner of her eye and looked over just as Jack repositioned himself. Her eyes snapped back to Randy who was still focused on Samantha. The detective took the opportunity to take a small step back and away from the other woman.

"What are you doing?" Randy spun on her.

"She's listening, now," Maureen assured him. "She's hearing what you're saying. Aren't you, Samantha?"

"Is that true, Sam?" Randy softened as he spoke to his wife, almost tender. "Are you hearing what I'm saying?"

Samantha only quivered, tears running down her face. The tenderness faded from Randy's eyes as he used the gun in his hand to point at her.

"Are you listening to me or not?" he yelled. Samantha shrank in fear.

"She is, aren't you, Samantha?" Maureen spoke to her as if she were a child. "Tell him you understand."

Something registered in her mind. She stopped sobbing, sniffed and nodded. "I understand. I'm listening and I understand."

Maureen took another step back. Randy's neck snapped in her direction along with the gun. "You're moving again. Why are you moving?"

"I'm giving you space, Randy." Maureen held her hands out. "I want you to know I'm in no way a threat to you."

Detectives Mallory and Travis watched on, unable to intervene without putting the hostages at risk. Twice, Jack watched Maureen move to distance herself from the crazed man waving a gun. She was a smart detective with good instincts. She wasn't trying to retreat to safety. She was putting space between herself and Samantha Keyes. Jack motioned to Shaun to be ready.

Using hand signals, they prepared to move as soon as the situation dictated. Jack would move to the left toward Maureen while Shaun took the right and Samantha Keyes. They double checked their weapons and Jack held up three fingers for a countdown to a synchronized assault.

"I know what you're doing!" Randy yelled. "You're trying to get away."

"No." Maureen kept calm and focused on the man's eyes. "I'm not going anywhere."

"That's right," Randy nodded.

Jack lowered one of his fingers.

"Think of Samantha," Maureen pointed at the cowering woman. "You want her to remember how things were before, right? You want her to forgive you. Take you back. Look at her. She's scared to death. You're doing that."

"She knows I won't hurt her," Randy argued. "She's not scared of me. It's you. I need to protect her from you."

"Randy," Samantha's small voice was almost inaudible. "No. Don't hurt anyone else. Please."

A second finger lowered.

"She's trying to manipulate us, Sam," Randy said. "You can see that, can't you?"

"It doesn't matter," Samantha fought back tears. "Whatever it is she is or isn't doing doesn't matter anymore. It's just you and me."

"You do understand," Randy gave the woman a knowing smile. "We don't need anyone else."

As the last finger collapsed into Jack's fist, the two detectives lunged from the hallway into the living room shouting for their suspect to drop his weapon. Anguish consumed Randy's face as his head snapped toward the charging men, multiplied ten-fold when the explosion of a gunshot filled the room.

Maureen spun and fell to the ground. Jack did not think, only reacted to what he saw. He squeezed the trigger of his service pistol and Randy was thrown back by the impact of the bullet striking him. The ringing in their ears from the gunfire was overwhelmed by the screams of Samantha Keyes. Shaun wrapped his arm around the woman's shoulders and guided her out of the room.

Jack kicked Randy's fallen gun across the room before dropping to his knees next to the female detective.

78

S haun entered the room and took cautious steps toward where Jack appeared to be sleeping in an uncomfortable looking recliner. The senior detective raised his head to the sound of his footsteps.

"Sorry," Shaun whispered. "How is she?"

"She's fine." Maureen spoke with her eyes closed.

"You're awake," Shaun stated the obvious.

"As fine as she can be," Jack elaborated. "All things considered."

"What do the doctors say?" Shaun asked.

"They say I'm fine," Maureen said.

"They said she was millimeters from joining Sharon," Jack muttered. "She was lucky."

"I wouldn't say lucky," Maureen disagreed.

"She's going to be off work a while," Jack reached out and took Maureen's hand.

"How long?"

"Six months," Maureen grumbled.

"If things go well," Jack added. "Could be longer."

"Six months," Maureen repeated. "Maybe five."

"I like your confidence," Shaun smiled.

"I'm a fast healer," she assured him. "And he's going to help me."

"I am?" Jack feigned shock.

"You better," Maureen sneered. "You're the reason I was on this case to begin with."

"I thought it was because you volunteered," Jack gave her hand a gentle squeeze.

"Only because you two couldn't close it alone," she chuckled, followed by a wince of pain.

"That's what you get," Jack grinned.

"Hey, Shaun," Maureen changed the subject. "This guy's been napping for the past two days. What happened with Keyes?"

"He has a long recovery ahead of him," the young detective said.

"Seems fair," Maureen scoffed. "He admitted shooting Chief Hutchins. I thought we cleared him because there was almost no GSR on his clothes. And no blood splatter."

"Coveralls," Jack spoke up. "We learned that he wore coveralls all the time. His company had issued him five pairs. A search of his home and work locker only turned up four. A forensics examination of his truck found small amounts of Sharon's blood in one of the locked compartments. Apparently, after he shot her, he stripped of the coveralls and stored them in the truck, disposing of them later."

"It was his fingerprint on the Hutchins' doorbell," Shaun reported. "His plan was to say he found her and ran to the door to get help. But when he touched the doorbell, he realized he got blood on his hand when he removed his gloves. He panicked and ran back to the body to explain the blood on him."

"Funny thing was trying to ring the doorbell at all," Jack said. "The man's an electrician and didn't think about the bell having no power. And he's the one that cut the power to begin with. The Bartlett's dogs barking at their back yard was him running back home after he turned it off."

"He cut the power?"

"There was an actual power outage about six months ago," Jack explained. "When he was called to work on it, he saw Sharon coming out of her house. They exchanged pleasantries, with Sharon mentioning she was going to work in case she was needed. That's where his idea was born."

"All because she proved he killed his wife's cat," Maureen sighed.

"He blamed Sharon for everything," Jack said. "Even though it was all on him."

"I almost forgot," Maureen said. "How is Samantha?"

"Understandably shaken," Shaun answered. "She's planning to move again."

"Poor woman."

"She wanted me to tell you how much she appreciated you being there when he came for her," Shaun said. "And how sorry she was for..."

"For getting shot?"

"Okay," Jack said. "I think that's enough shop talk. She needs her rest."

"You're probably right," Maureen lay back and closed her eyes. A moment later she was sound asleep.

THE END

Thank you for reading!

Dear Reader,

I hope you enjoyed reading **Death Before Dawn** as much as I enjoyed writing it. At this time, I would like to request, if you're so inclined, please consider leaving a review of **Death Before Dawn**. I would love to hear your feedback.

Amazon: **https://www.amazon.com/dp/B0CV645LXB**

Goodreads:
https://www.goodreads.com/author/show/18986676.William_Coleman

Website: **https://www.williamcoleman.net**

Facebook: **https://www.facebook.com/williamcolemanauthor/**

Many Thanks,

William Coleman

Jack Mallory Mysteries series:

MURDER REVISITED
DOG WALKERS
FATAL ACCOUNTING
DEATH BEFORE DAWN

S. Hawke Investigations series:

THE CONTRACT
THREE DAYS GONE

Other novels by William Coleman:

THE WIDOW'S HUSBAND
PAYBACK
NICK OF TIME
FIRST FRIDAYS

Made in the USA
Las Vegas, NV
13 May 2024